IN THE Shadow OF Light

Tracy Causley

The Amethyst Press

CHANTILLY, VIRGINIA

The Amethyst Press LLC
15125 Elk Run Rd
Chantilly, Virginia 20151

Publisher's Note: This is a work of fiction. Names, characters, places, and incidents are a product of the author's imagination. Locales and public names are sometimes used for atmospheric purposes. Any resemblance to actual people, living or dead, or to businesses, companies, events, institutions, or locales is completely coincidental.

Book layout by BookDesignTemplates.com
Cover artwork by Catrin Welz-Stein
Cover design by Sean Causley

In the Shadow of Light / Tracy Causley – 1st ed.

Library of Congress Control Number: 2018901004

ISBN-13: 978-0-692-06278-4

To Sean, for your unwavering love and support

CHAPTER 1

Summer 1630

Marcel Barberini stood in the chambers of the Supreme Sacred Congregation of the Roman and Universal Inquisition. He intended to have an audience with the Secretary. While he waited he fidgeted with his brown leather gloves, pulling the floppy fingers between his digits.

He wore his best attire to visit the Holy Office in the Vatican. His fine taupe damask coat was edged with goldenrod silk on the collar and sleeves and embroidered with black flowers. It was accented with a dozen golden buttons. He wore matching breeches, and stiff black leather shoes completed the ensemble.

His chestnut hair was tucked behind his ears, and his attentive blue eyes darted around the enormous room. Even though he was dressed his best it did nothing to make him feel any less insignificant in the presence of such grandeur, for gold embellishment christened everything. Massive biblical murals, huge jewel-encrusted crucifixes, expertly crafted furniture, and holy relics decorated every inch of the space.

Marcel knew that the man he sought out used this sparkling façade to hide the fact he was a capricious, calculating man.

"To what do I owe this unexpected visit, Marcel?" said a familiar perturbed voice.

Marcel turned and the man he was waiting for approached from an adjacent doorway in the same chamber. The furrow between the Cardinal's stark, straight brows was even deeper than he had remembered, for it had been a year since Marcel had seen him in person. His sour expression further dimmed his already dark, hooded eyes, expressing deep displeasure with his unexpected appearance.

Marcel had always done his best to keep his distance from the Cardinal, but he had no choice but to come all the way to Rome to inform his father of the most devastating news.

"It's Mama," he started, his smooth voice breaking as he spoke.

The Cardinal's face remained impassive, not giving away any emotion to the mention of his former mistress.

Marcel shuffled his weight from side-to-side then ran his long fingers through his locks before continuing. "She's taken her own life," he explained.

Marcel stared down at his polished shoes and waited for the angry outburst that was so common when the Cardinal received unsavory news, but nothing happened, and the awkward silence stretched on. He grew frustrated waiting for the response he knew would never come. He gripped his gloves tightly then glanced up at his father.

"Will you help me lay her to rest...in a *consecrated* location?" he asked.

Cardinal Antonio Marcello Barberini guffawed so loud it echoed through the vast chamber. Marcel winced.

"I will not. She has committed the ultimate sin. How do you think that would reflect upon me? I'm the Secretary of the Holy Inquisition!" he exclaimed, slamming his ringed hand down on his desk.

Marcel flinched but stood his ground.

"Father, I beg you. Please, do this for Mama. She stood by you all these years, and you only ever caused her pain and misery. You *owe* her this much," he argued, feeling his powerlessness fade and the urgency of his mission return.

"I owe her nothing of the sort," the Cardinal replied. "You know quite well that clergy is not to consort with women."

"That never seemed to stop you before!" Marcel retorted, raising his voice.

"You will lower your voice right now or, God help me, I will send you from my sight forever."

"You don't have to worry about that, *Father*."

The taste of the word on his tongue nearly made Marcel sick. He steadied himself from shaking with rage, took a step forward, and locked his deep blue eyes on the Cardinal's.

"Mama was the only person holding me here and, now that she's gone, I am leaving. It's my gift to you. Now you won't be burdened by a mistress or a bastard."

"You will stay put, or I will totally cut off your allowance, " the Cardinal threatened. " Besides, I've already made plans for you."

"I'm not interested in hearing or entertaining your plans. I'm leaving and that's final." Marcel turned on his heel and marched away.

"If you walk out that door, Marcel, don't ever think about coming back!" he shouted. The Cardinal narrowed his eyes, and with chest puffed stalked toward his bastard, scarlet cassock and mozzetta trailing in his wake.

Marcel paused and turned, recoiling at the Cardinal's proximity. His breath smelled of cheese and sour wine, and the left side of his mouth was pulled back in a toothy sneer. The same one he so often used to bully his mother into submission. Marcel lifted his chin higher and stood straighter, using his six-foot frame to his advantage. There was nothing in the world that was going to stop him from getting on that ship in Livorno in October. He had saved his money and planned for this exact threat. He was ready.

"What you will do, effectively, is forget this ridiculous whim of yours. Close the villa and dismiss your mother's maid. Then, return to Rome to take up the post that I have secured for you. There have been reports of witchcraft near Florence. You are to learn the ways of the Inquisition."

In the year since his father became Secretary of the Roman Inquisition, a title his brother, Pope Urban VIII, bestowed upon him, Marcel knew he'd been pulling strings to secure a position in the Church for him too. However, he had no interest in becoming a seeker of witches and heretics, or an exterminator of evil.

Marcel feigned defeat by slumping his shoulders, hanging his head, and letting his hair slip into his eyes. It was a tactic he developed as a child to lessen the ferocity of his father's wrath.

"Yes, Father," Marcel replied, conceding in word but not mind. He had every intention of returning to the villa to prepare for his imminent departure and escape to the New World.

"In addition, you will bury your mother in the pauper's cemetery on the outskirts of Rome, on the road to Siena. Under no circumstances does she belong in a holy plot."

The Cardinal pulled out a bulging coin purse and removed a handful of silver scudo, to pay for his mistress' burial, and shoved it into Marcel's chest. He winced but kept quiet. The Cardinal proved yet again that he was a man incapable of love, and in turn, he was not worthy of Marcel's loyalty.

"You will report back here within one month. By then, you should have a clear head. It's time to put aside childish dreams and folly and take on the real responsibilities of a man. I think your mother's nature had everything to do with how you turned out."

You couldn't be righter, Marcel thought. He was thankful for every moment he had with his dear mother.

"As you wish, Your Eminence," Marcel replied. The man who had fathered him was no father at all. Marcel made a small bow to the Cardinal and took his leave, not bothering to look back as he walked back through the vast corridor from which he had entered. He was glad to leave behind the cause of all the strife in his life. He turned the coins over in his palm.

This will be the last time I ever bow to you, he thought. *It's time to see what life is like far away from here.*

The plague doctor's freakish shadow stretched out over the worn cobblestones. Passersby avoided it as if the blackness itself spread plague from house to house. He scoffed, and the sound morphed into a muffled grunt inside the brown leather bird-demon mask he wore. A strong whiff of ambergris and camphor filled his nostrils.

He arrived for the second time on the Merchant Giordano's doorstep. The door was unlocked and left cracked. He pushed it open and called out.

The wool merchant's daughter, Vittoria, bellowed down from above. "Dottore, come up quickly!"

The plague doctor entered and took the stairs two at a time. His heavy waxed leather coat slapped against his knees and a sweat broke out over his body from the exertion. He stopped to catch his breath, but it was impossible to do so through the mask's two tiny breathing holes.

At the top of the stairs, a wide corridor opened before him. Vittoria poked her head out of a doorway at the far end of the hall. Her jet-black tresses were tousled and the delicate skin beneath her eyes was tinged purple. She was tired, yet still beautiful. Even seeing Vittoria through thick hazy glass eyeholes affected the doctor. He fumbled for his words while fiddling with his cane. Mentally, he chastised himself for behaving like a dimwit.

"This way," Vittoria ordered.

He scurried toward the room. Arriving at the threshold he witnessed one of the most pitiful sights he had ever seen, and he had seen many. Just like her husband before her, Orabella Giordano was hot with fever, tossing and moaning in unsettled sleep. She had kicked the linens off the bed in a futile attempt to cool herself down. Her breath was shallow and the chamber pot near the bedside was filled with sick.

"Mama, wake up!" Vittoria urged her mother. Orabella moaned and rolled her head towards Vittoria's voice and coughed. Tiny blood droplets misted the pillow. Vittoria jumped back.

"Do something!" she pleaded with him.

It appeared Vittoria had already tried coaxing her mother to consume an herbal remedy, judging from the scrapings of willow bark and dried valerian on the polished walnut side table.

The young doctor approached the bedside, so as not to alarm the sick woman. There was no reason for him to use his long wooden cane to lift bed covers or clothing, for she was already naked, so he propped it against the headboard.

Orabella's body had an unnatural sheen, appearing gray as if it had been made of polished Carrara marble. All the natural pink coloring becoming a pregnant woman had disappeared. The skin over her belly stretched so taut that the doctor could see veins and arteries crisscrossing beneath. He placed his gloved hand on her abdomen, feeling for life. There was no response from the nearly full-term fetus in her womb. The baby was likely dead. It was for these reasons that Dottore Paolo Salviati was glad to be wearing his hideous mask because it hid the sad truth of the situation written on his face.

Breathing came in fits and starts, for Orabella kept forgetting she needed to do it to live. Buboes, the size of quail eggs, were swollen in her groin and under-arms. Smaller ones were present on the sides of her neck. He inspected them by gently poking the large puffy mounds. He did not suggest draining the bu-boes because it was painful, and the practice didn't seem to benefit his patients.

Paolo had seen plague in all its horrible stages and knew the woman was indeed dying. There was noth-ing he knew of that could deliver one from Death's iron grip once plague infiltrated the body. Though he had heard rumor of survival cases, he had never wit-nessed a recovery himself, so he believed it to be impossible. The woman should have died already, but she was holding on for some reason.

Orabella's eyes flickered open. With great effort, she whispered to her daughter.

"It's too late for me."

Paolo motioned for Vittoria not to get too close. Heeding his warning, she leaned forward ever so slightly, turning her head to listen.

"You must go. Or you will die."

Exhausted, Orabella panted for breath, sinking back into the pillow. Vittoria's brow knit tightly with worry.

"Where am I to go, Mama? I'll stay and take care of you and the baby."

"No!" Orabella burst, hacking violently. Blood oozed from her dried-out mouth. She wiped at the mess with a pale hand, smearing it into the chapped cracks of her lips. Struggling to breathe, she delivered her final instruction.

"Flee to the country. They will find you."

"Who's *they*?" Vittoria asked puzzled. She searched her mother's face for the answer. Eventually, she looked at him for it. All Paolo could offer her was a helpless shrug.

Orabella's breathing slowed until it finally ceased. Paolo pressed his gloved fingers into her neck beside a swollen lump but found no sign of life. He checked again for a pulse on her wrist. Still nothing.

Vittoria fell onto her haunches beside the bed, her eyes glassy and wide. She asked him the question, which he was sure she knew the answer.

"Is she gone?"

"Yes," Paolo murmured.

"She must have prayers said over her body. Otherwise, her soul will not pass to Heaven."

Because he probably couldn't make good on it, Paolo knew it was not a promise he should be making, but he made it anyway.

"The clergy have their fair share of the dying to tend to, but I will make sure your mother is attended to by a priest and her body is laid properly to rest."

Only a tiny bit of relief shown on Vittoria's sad face. This miffed Paolo, since he generously committed himself to an undertaking he had no extra time, or energy, with which to deal.

"Meanwhile, I suggest you heed your mother's directive."

"That's none of your business!" Vittoria snapped. Angry tears glistened in her green and gold eyes.

"But it is," he replied. "Protocol requires I order you into quarantine, within your home or in a pestilent lazaretto. Though you may have already contracted plague, neither of which I wish to do, because both options lead to certain death. However, if you ran off while I was tending to your mother, there would be nothing I could have done to stop you. Do you understand?" he asked, hoping she realized she had no other choice but to leave.

Vittoria did not respond. Instead, she stood and walked slowly from the room.

Vittoria surveyed her bedchamber in the only home she had ever known. Now she had to leave, and she was afraid.

As apt as she was with the herbs and oils, Vittoria found her skills were no match for the plague. It was the first occurrence of her efforts not having the desired healing effects. The plague was evil indeed.

Vittoria cringed and balled her fists. Hot tears of despair ran down her cheeks. There was only one option for her now—to flee.

She wiped the tears from her eyes with her sleeve, straightened out the front of her rumpled dress, and found an oilcloth bag stored inside a heavy cedar trunk to carry items she figured she'd need for her journey.

It might as well be to the end of the earth.

Vittoria rummaged two simple woolen house dresses, one light blue and one pale green, and put on the flattest comfortable shoes she had. She shoved her coin purse in the bag, then glanced around the room to see if there was anything else she required.

A ray of morning light shone through the window on the most important item Vittoria owned. On her fourteenth birthday, her parents presented her with a small wooden diptych carved on the exterior with a flowing flower and vine pattern. Inside were her mother and father's painted likenesses.

Vittoria picked the diptych up and took one last long look before closing it, realizing that it would be all she had left to remember their faces should her memory ever fail. She wrapped the diptych in a piece of yellow cloth and positioned it carefully in the bag. Drawing the bag closed, she left the room, wondering if she would ever come back.

She hurried into the hallway toward the stairs, stopping outside her mother's room for one last farewell. Mama's hair was matted to her clammy forehead and blood-stained pillow. Death was a comfort to her now.

Crouching by the bedside was the plague doctor who, in all his devilish grotesqueness, was mumbling prayers over her mother. Sensing her presence, he turned his head and spoke. The hollow glass eyes of the mask terrified her. Vittoria heard a one-word rumble emerge as if it came up from a deep dark hole.

"Go!"

Long shadows clung to Emilio and his twin Angelo as they followed their stumbling-drunk cousin down the cobblestone lane. Their path wove through the wool district toward the redeeming steps of the Duomo.

Nico carried a near-empty bottle of wine in his firm grip and the contents sloshed within. His short black hair tousled from the scuffle at the Tre Sorella Taverna. He was the best dressed amongst them and always managed to keep his clothes from getting mussed. Emilio scoffed at the sight of him.

"It's getting worse," Angelo whispered to his twin.

"I know. He's like a wild animal and doesn't even try to hide the fact that he's out for a fight anymore."

"Mama overheard the servants again. She's not pleased that our names were mixed up in their gossip," Angelo admitted. "What are we going to do?"

"We should cut our losses. I'm tired of fighting, especially with him," Emilio said.

"It's like he has a death wish," Angelo observed, shaking his head of curls in dismay.

"I agree. Plague may have delayed us from leaving for Bologna, but we don't need Nico getting us killed in the meantime."

"What if that's it?" Angelo observed.

"What?"

"The reason he's been so irritated the last few weeks," Angelo explained to his brother.

"Because we told him we were leaving for university as soon as the plague has run its course?" Emilio asked.

Angelo nodded.

"Perhaps," Emilio agreed. The furrow in this brow grew deeper. "But we aren't his keepers."

Angelo rubbed his round face and pinched the high bridge of his nose. "Should we bring him with us to Bologna?"

"Are you mad?" Emilio snapped. The force of his words carried far enough for Nico to hear. "We'll finish this conversation later," he whispered through clenched teeth. The strain of dealing with his cousin had become unbearable and it was affecting his relationship with his own brother.

They continued walking in silence. Emilio mulled over all the trouble he'd gotten into because of Nico. Just that very night at the Tre Sorella Taverna he nearly had his throat slit.

Giancarlo Pitti tried cheating Nico out of a gold florin in a game of dice. Nico proceeded to punch Pitti square in the mouth, sending the entire lower floor of the Taverna into an uproar. Benches and tables flew in all directions. Emilio stupidly stepped in between Pitti and Nico. Then, one of Pitti's cronies shoved him against the wall and put a knife to his throat.

Nico was too busy wrestling with Pitti to notice Emilio was about to lose his life. Angelo had pushed his way through the melee to rescue him but suffered a hard whack to the back of his head, sending him to the ground.

Emilio struggled with his assailant but met with the unrelenting resistance of the steel blade at his neck. The dirty blade pushed into the soft skin and blood ran over his collar. He was powerless to help his brother and furious with Nico for putting them into this position.

The thug hollered at Nico to release Pitti, and threatened Emilio's life in earnest if Nico did not comply immediately.

Emilio swore that if he walked away from the mess he was in he was going to punch Nico in his pretty little face.

The room suddenly went quiet and everything seemed to slow down. Nerezza, the madam of the Tre Sorella Taverna, appeared in the center of the room. She was taller than Emilio with long ebony hair, half stacked upon her head with the remainder flowing like a cloak over her back and shoulders. The crimson velvet dress she wore was low-cut, revealing her hypnotizing décolletage. Her svelte body moved towards him. No one else seemed to notice her presence. When she locked her piercing eyes on his, he forgot that his life hung in the balance.

Nerezza drew closer to him and he felt he was being drawn out of his body. She twirled a piece of hair, caressing her bosom with it before withdrawing from her bodice a small glittering dagger of her own. The hilt was the shape of a crowing rooster with red ruby eyes.

Not taking her eyes off his Nerezza wrapped her delicate arm around the neck of Pitti's man and slid the blade across his throat as if slicing through a delicate juicy peach. More blood squirted onto Emilio's collar and spilled down the man's neck. His angry eyes drained of all consciousness, and as his life disappeared so did the pressure of the knife upon Emilio's throat. The thug fell in a heap onto the floor bleeding all over Emilio's shoes.

In his place now stood Nerezza, her breasts pushed into his chest forcing him to inhale her intoxicating neroli perfume. She pointed the tip of her bloody dagger underneath his chin forcing him to lift his head, revealing the damage left by his attacker.

Nerezza entwined her leg with Emilio's and pressed even closer to his body, teasing him. She licked his wound like a kitten lapping warm milk. Emilio found himself equally disgusted and aroused all at once. He stood stock still realizing she was even more dangerous than was the man lying dead at their feet. Nerezza inhaled Emilio's scent from the dip behind his ear and ran her long fingers through his curly locks.

"Until we meet again, Emilio" she whispered, licking her swollen lips before letting him step free. "And don't make me wait too long."

Then Nerezza disappeared as quickly as she arrived. Time sped up once again and Emilio regained his senses. He scooped his twin up from the dirty tile floor and yanked Nico, by his ear, off Pitti. He dragged them both through the Taverna out into the cobbled alley. Not forgetting his promise to himself, he took the opportunity to deliver a gift to Nico—an eyeful of his fist.

The black and blue shiner around Nico's right eye was now clearly visible. Emilio smiled as he admired his handiwork, but what fleeting joy there was disappeared when he realized the bruise enhanced Nico's rugged good looks. Emilio flexed his sore right hand, which itched to blacken Nico's other eye.

The Ascerbi sisters lounged in their lavish den hidden in the belly of the Tre Sorella Taverna, a place where bad behavior was given a royal welcome. Power mongering and greed thrived in Florence, and the Ascerbi family had grown powerful from its influence, for it was the fuel that strengthened their magic.

Nerezza, the Taverna's mistress, was tall and slim. Long black hair cascaded over her ample breasts. Her icy green eyes were made more mysterious by the cover of full dark brows. Her plump lips tinted red. Sucking her lower lip, she savored his scent. Emilio's fear sent shivers all the way from her head to her nether regions. He was angry and so hungry for her she could smell it. He would make a fine toy for her to play with.

Nerezza took notice of Emilio months ago. He was knocking around with Angelo and Nico. She would secretly watch him from the brothel on the upper floor or from the glamour glass in her den. She could observe whomever she wanted through the mirror, once she had seen or made physical contact with the person of interest.

Emilio had grown weary of Nico's antics, and he was itching to wrap his fingers around his neck, but Angelo always talked him out of it. Emilio's anger wanted to be validated. She would do that for him. For her own benefit, of course.

Nerezza's magical ability had grown stronger since plague began taking lives in Florence. It had been no easy task for her to summon and wield the power required to unleash death upon the people, let alone merge it with that of a flaccid old man. But she had her reasons for setting pestilence loose over the land. Avenging her mother, whom the Benedanti took from her, and stepping out of the shadow of light long since cast upon her family, had consumed her thoughts for years. However, she knew the spell had garnered the attention of her sworn enemy.

The Pope, on the other hand, desired control over his flock, and illness always brought the sheep back into the Church's fold and money into coffers.

Opportunity knocked years back when Pope Urban VIII, then just a Cardinal, arrived in Florence to procure lodging for his brother's French mistress and child. They visited the Tre Sorella Taverna, and her mother, Vadoma, offered her services to the Cardinal. Eventually, her magic propelled the Cardinal into the highest office in the land. But to remain the most powerful man on the face of the earth, stronger Malandanti magic was required.

Nerezza would continue aiding the Pope, so long as he held up his end of the bargain to help her wipe out the Benedanti entirely. It was her dream to see shadow reign supreme. The plague was going to make it possible. The idea so thrilled Nerezza, she laughed aloud.

"What's so funny?" asked her youngest sister, Medea. She sat in the hammered copper bathtub by the fire, washing her curly amber hair.

"We're so close to having it all. Can't you feel it? This city has come alive with pain and suffering, and the strength of our magic has multiplied," Nerezza replied.

"It's true," Ulyssa agreed. The second of the sisters reclined on a Roman couch picking her fingernails. Her eyes flashed. "Just last night, I gave Giovanni Bianco the fright of his life when I appeared in his dreams as a snake-haired monster, with razor-sharp teeth, ready to eat him." She laughed with unadulterated mirth. "Such fun!"

"Well, I hope you're up for the task tonight because you must infiltrate Emilio's dreams. It's time to make him mine."

Ulyssa flicked her hand nonchalantly. "I could do it in my sleep."

"What do I get to do?" Medea sulked. She stood naked in the tub ready to dry herself.

Nerezza rose from her velvet perch, smooth and even like liquid mercury, and crossed the vaulted stone room. Her delicate feet treading over luxurious Turkish carpets. The rough-hewn walls were covered in magnificent tapestries given as gifts by the Pope.

"My sweet baby sister, don't fret. I'll require your skills soon enough." She picked up a clean sheet smelling of lavender and wrapped it around her sister. She kissed Medea's perky nose and lips. "Don't I always save the best of everything for you?"

Medea smiled, and driblets of water slid down her chin. "Yes, sister, you do."

"Have patience. You will have someone to terrorize soon enough." Nerezza flashed a wicked smile and chuckled. The fun was indeed about to begin.

Vittoria threw open the front door of her home and stepped onto Via del Corso. Death seemed to come at her from every angle. As she rounded the corner, she nearly collided with a gravedigger whose cart was piled high with bodies.

"Watch where you're going, girl!" the man scolded, his rotten teeth showing through a sneer.

Vittoria leaped back and made way. She recognized Signor Batista, an acquaintance of her father's, laying upon the cart. It was hard to tell at first, but a second look confirmed that the swollen, bald, naked man was indeed Signor Batista. The gruesome cargo included his wife and three young sons. No effort was made to dignify the dead. They lay across each other, some nude, some half-clothed.

A low cry reached Vittoria's lips. She steadied herself against the stone wall so as not to fall to the ground. Reclaiming her tenuous composure, Vittoria willed her legs to move into the Piazza della Signoria.

She witnessed a young peasant woman drop dead. Her sun-bleached blond hair was swept back from her pale face revealing black and blue buboes on her neck. Hollow, sunken eyes, of the palest blue, stared blankly into the distance. Her tattered dress was stained with dirt and sweat. A small boy clung to the woman crying and begging for her to wake up.

"Mama! Wake up. Don't go!"

The dirty little boy was about four and had the same pale hair and eyes as his mother. He shook her body as hard as he could, his eyes searching around for help. Vittoria did not move to help him and neither did anyone else. It was too late for them.

Dozens of dead had been laid outside of their homes for collection. People moving about held bundles of odoriferous herbs to their noses to block the putrefying miasma of death that hung over the city of Florence. There was no escaping it.

Exiting the piazza, she was met by a trio of young men who looked worse for wear. As they approached, she noticed the two similar looking men wore the latest fashion of doublets with paned sleeves. The tallest of the three wore a similar outfit except his was beautifully embroidered. Vittoria averted her eyes so as not to invite trouble from the advancing group, but it was too late.

The tall, dark-haired man reached out a finger to touch Vittoria's cheek as he passed.

"Why the long face, young lady?" he said.

"Don't touch me," Vittoria ordered, shoving his hand away.

"Leave her alone, Nico," one of the short men ordered. He drew Nico by the sleeve away from her. "She looks terrified enough as it is."

"Don't be alarmed, we mean you no harm," the same man said, noticing her unease. "I am Emilio. This is my brother Angelo." He motioned over his shoulder at the other brown-haired, baby-faced, young man who had a similar likeness to his own.

Vittoria's torso turned to move away from them, but her feet did not. Something about Angelo's warm smile was a much-needed balm for her soul.

Curious and feeling a little more at ease, she asked, "Why haven't you left the city?"

"There is nowhere to go. So, why not stay in the most wonderful city in the world?" Emilio answered, sweeping his hands out before him.

"He means we don't have a country villa to run off too," Nico retorted.

"Oh, be quiet, Nico!" Emilio snapped. The edge in his voice was saber sharp.

"Neither do I. But for heaven's sake, won't you at least try to escape to cleaner air?"

"There's no point when you have *this*," Nico said, hefting his nearly empty bottle into the air. "It keeps the plague away. We've been drunk for days and we aren't dead yet, so it must be working!"

Vittoria noticed his right eye was blackened. Whoever had given it to Nico clearly knocked the sense out of him.

"Well, I'm taking my chances in the country," she said.

"Outside the gates?" Emilio and Angelo exclaimed, in unison, their eyebrows raised.

"Are you sure about that? Don't you have a companion to travel with?" Angelo queried.

They seemed worried because the city walls protected citizens from brigands. However, it had failed to protect them all from the most vicious of killers.

"It's not the safest, but it is the only plan that I have."

Emilio and Angelo exchanged a long meaningful look. Nico shook his head and rolled his bloodshot eyes.

"What's the matter?" Vittoria asked. The long silence concerned her.

"We don't think that you should go alone," Emilio explained.

"I'll be fine," she argued, mostly trying to convince herself.

"You are a very attractive young lady...," Angelo paused, realizing he did not know her name.

"Vittoria," she offered.

"Yes, Vittoria. That is a pretty name as well," Angelo complimented. "You shouldn't be wandering about by yourself."

"What am I to do then?" she huffed, adjusting the oilcloth bag on her shoulder. She crossed her arms over her chest.

"Let us escort you to the city gate," Angelo offered, a smile lifting his round cheeks.

"That's not necessary."

"Come on, Vittoria. You don't want to run into another group like us, do you? *They* might not be so nice," Nico taunted.

He was right. Under normal circumstances she wouldn't have spoken with a group of strange men on the street, let alone allow them to escort her through town. Her common sense rejected the idea of accepting the help of strangers, but her gut disagreed.

Emilio pleaded the case. "We wouldn't want our little sister, Lucrezia, wandering about alone, so let us do you this favor. If she were still alive, we'd like to think someone would help her if she were in this same situation."

Vittoria gazed hard at Emilio. Though his cheeks were flushed, and blood stained his shirt, his face seemed trustworthy. He did, after all, stop Nico from accosting her.

Emilio did not flinch under her scrutiny. Instead, he gazed back at her with a disarming gentle smile that reached his soft-brown eyes.

Vittoria resituated her bag while considering her answer. She felt certain that with Angelo and Emilio beside her she'd be safe from Nico and those like him.

"Oh, all right."

A lopsided grin appeared on Angelo's face. "If plague should claim our lives, at least we know that one of our final deeds was to aid a young lady in need."

The bells pealed in the clock tower of Palazzo della Signoria. It was nine o'clock in the morning.

"We had better be going," Emilio said. "You'll need as much daylight as possible to get wherever you are going."

"Ponte Vecchio is the closest place to cross the river," Angelo said.

"We can't cross there. You'll ruin your shoes," Nico said, motioning toward her feet. "That's where butchers and tanners ply their filthy trades. It's better to cross Ponte Santa Trinita."

Vittoria gawked at Nico, as did the twins.

"Fine," she said, not wanting to waste time arguing with a drunkard more concerned about her state of fashion than her health.

"Follow me!" Nico commanded, striding away from the group out of the piazza.

Angelo bowed before her and swept his own puffy sleeve after Nico. "After you, my lady," he said, a lock of curly hair falling into his eyes.

Vittoria couldn't help but smile. He had a charming manner. "Thank you," she replied, curtsying.

The twins fell in on either side of her, chatting as they walked.

"Do you know anything about astrology, Vittoria?" Angelo asked.

"Not particularly. Why do you ask?"

"Because a lot can be determined by studying heavenly bodies, even a man's destiny," he explained.

"Truly?"

"Certainly. We were to begin our advanced astrology studies this year, but they've been delayed because of...," Emilio trailed off, nudging his curly head toward a group of men carrying a funeral bier.

Vittoria understood. The plague spoiled everyone's plans.

"There's always next year!" Angelo replied, his attitude optimistic.

"I do hope so. Surely, you are wonderful students."

"In the meantime, will you let us practice on you?" Emilio asked.

"What if you tell me something I don't want to know?"

"Not to worry," Emilio replied. "All we need is the date of your birth. Do you know it?"

"Of course, I do. Don't be silly."

"Well, what is it then? You're stalling," Angelo pressed, rubbing his hands together.

Vittoria pursed her lips before revealing the coveted information. "February 27th, 1611."

The twins engaged in a silent conference that included animated hand gestures and facial expressions before speaking aloud.

"She's nineteen and the same sign as Lucrezia," Emilio whispered over her head to Angelo.

Vittoria's shoulders tensed, bracing for the bad news. "Your sister? Oh, no. What's wrong? Something is going to happen, isn't it?"

"No, no. Nothing like that," Angelo replied, waving his hands emphatically.

"What is it then?"

"You were born when Pisces, the Fish, reigned in the heavens," Angelo informed her. "It's quite a magical sign."

"Mysterious, too," Emilio continued.

"There is nothing magical or mysterious about me. You probably say that to most young ladies you meet, don't you?" she teased, her shoulders relaxing. Amazingly, their presence seemed to buffer her from the unpleasantness of death all around them.

"Absolutely not! What do you take us for?" Angelo scoffed.

"We really are very shy," Emilio admitted. "Besides, we don't meet many nice girls."

"Except when we've had a bit to drink," Angelo blushed. Reaching around behind Vittoria, he playfully punched his brother in the arm.

"Based on our calculations of the heavenly movements on the date of your birth, your nature should reflect a good intellect and a well-developed intuition," Emilio reported.

"And you have a solitary nature with a tendency toward introversion," Angelo continued. "Which may cause difficulty in maintaining relationships." He shook his head at Vittoria.

"And you want me to take you both seriously?"

Their pace slowed as they talked, and Nico was quite far ahead of them now. He was standing— swaying, rather—watching flames shoot up from a massive bonfire which was burning the contaminated bedding of plague victims.

"Forgive my candor, but why aren't you betrothed or married?" Angelo asked, to Emilio's dismay. "You are nineteen."

"If I ever do marry, it will be for love." Her shoulders tensed again upon realizing she may never get the chance.

"Oh yes, we hadn't gotten to the part about your stubbornness," Emilio jested to ease her tension.

"You would risk living life a spinster?" Angelo blurted. "You are too pretty for that. It would be a complete waste."

"Oh, hush! You two know nothing," Vittoria snapped, the heat rising in her cheeks. They arrived at the bonfire and Vittoria was considering pushing the twins into it.

Emilio shot his brother a chastising glare. "I'm sure the true reason you're waiting is that you haven't yet found your equal," he said, a sheepish expression upon his face. "There's nothing wrong with that."

Vittoria took a deep breath and tried to relax. The twins were only trying to lift her spirits. She felt silly for overreacting, and blinked hot tears from her eyes. She resisted marriage for too long, and any plans she had for her future were lost to the wind.

"You are blessed to have the courage to wait for what you desire," Emilio said, patting her shoulder. "In this world, it is so easy to settle. You won't settle, Vittoria, and you *will* be happy. I know this to be true."

"I do not see how you can be so hopeful. Not with the world falling down around us."

"Why would we not in the presence of a lovely lady such as yourself?" Angelo replied, gazing at her.

Vittoria wiped the tears from her eyes, pulled her shoulders back, and lifted her head up. She would never get to the country if she let her emotions get the best of her.

Sorrowful sobbing filled the air. It was Nico. His face was red and wet with tears. Angelo left Vittoria's side to try and console him. She felt vulnerable again.

"What's the matter with him?" Vittoria whispered to Emilio.

"Nico's suffered many misfortunes in life. His mother died in childbirth and his father sent him away to live with his grandmother. Soon after, he ran away, I'm not sure why, and begged for an apprenticeship with the tailor. He's been raising hell all over Florence ever since."

Vittoria sensed bitterness in his voice. "Are you related?" she asked.

"Yes," Emilio responded, stifling scorn. "We're cousins."

Nico smashed his empty wine bottle into the fire. Broken shards of glass flew up into the air and glistened like fiery diamonds.

"I wish I could smash his face," Nico bellowed. "Just like that!"

"Come now, you don't mean it," Angelo reasoned with him.

"I *do* mean it. Maybe I should leave, like Vittoria, and find a way on my own. You two don't want me around anymore either," he shouted.

"That's not true," Angelo argued.

"Not again," Emilio grumbled, rubbing his reddening face with his square hands. Vittoria noticed that the knuckles of his right hand were bruised and the vein in his temple was throbbing. He massaged his forehead and kicked the ground in frustration. It was clear these two were at odds.

Compelled to find out why, Vittoria marched over to Nico's side. Sensing her beside him, Nico whipped his head around and glared down at her. Holding his angry gaze, Vittoria observed him silently. His sad hazel eyes revealed the frightening depths of pain and dejection threatening to drown him. Taking Nico's large trembling hand in her own, she held it. She said nothing at all.

Looking deeper still, diving into his eyes. Words tumbled into her mind. Nico's thoughts of fear and alienation flooded in. He was tired of fighting the tempestuous tides of the raging sea within. As it was, he was barely treading water. Vittoria sensed that he was ready to give up. Death would be a relief. He welcomed it. Her heart swelled. How very sad he was. How lost. Unlovable, even. He'd been crying out for rescue for so long, but it seemed to him the world was deaf. Not even God heard him.

Fresh tears rolled down Nico's stubbly cheeks. Vittoria could feel how raw he was inside. A sob welled up in her own throat. While wiping away his tears, she noticed he had a lean, rectangular face and a strong jaw though a little puffy from drink. Thick fringes of dark lashes and smooth brows framed his watery eyes. His right eye was blackened, yet it added favorably to his rugged looks. And his close-cropped hair was perfectly messy.

Nico placed his free hand on top of hers and held it to his cheek. Eventually, a flicker of a smile came into his deep-set almond eyes and he broke the silence between them.

"I see you, too." His voice was smooth and low like that of a lover's whisper.

She inclined her head toward the fire. "Come now, there's nothing more to see here."

Vittoria turned to walk away but Nico clasped her forearm. She turned back. He hung his head humbly and apologized.

"I am sorry I scared you. I'm a colossal lout."

"It's forgotten. Think nothing of it," she insisted.

Nico nodded and wiped the remnants of tears from his eyes. He then pulled ahead of the group and lead them south toward the river. It was as if nothing had happened minutes before. Neither the twins nor Vittoria made a move to catch up.

"How did you do that?" Angelo asked.

"Do what?" Vittoria replied.

"Settle him down like that," he clarified. "It's nearly impossible to calm him once he gets himself worked up. I've never seen anything like it, Vittoria. That is quite a talent you have."

Emilio remained silent. His face was stone hard. Vittoria tried not to notice.

"It was nothing," she concluded, trying not to make so important a deal about it since it seemed to bother Emilio.

Angelo wouldn't let it go. "It's like he's gotten his spirit back. When he doesn't drink, he's so depressed. So, he practically drinks all the time."

"He needed someone to see him for the child of God that he is."

"Nevertheless, Vittoria, you've worked a wonder with him."

She grew uncomfortable with Angelo's attention and Emilio's sudden agitation.

"Truly, it's nothing. We're getting closer to the river," she said, hastening her pace to avoid further discussion of the matter.

Vittoria and the twins walked in silence until they arrived at the northern bank of the Arno near Ponte Vecchio. Blood and guts from the butcher stalls ran thick over the bridge, and sewage spilled down into the river turning the water a sickening crimson color.

Vittoria understood why Nico had been concerned about her shoes.

"Ugh!" she gagged.

"I know," Nico grimaced.

They walked further west to cross at Ponte Santa Trinita. It was busy on the river's edge. Carts piled high with dead were driven over the bridge one at a time. The work was slow going.

Vittoria sighed with relief when she caught a glimpse of the expansive fields of grain and olive groves off in the distance, knowing shortly she'd be breathing fresh country air.

"Well, here we are, Vittoria," Emilio announced, his face no longer a stern mask.

"Yup," Angelo mumbled, sadness clouded his eyes.

Vittoria's feet felt to be held in place by an unseen force. She didn't want to go one step further. A pang of sorrow filled her heart. Nico and the twins had made an unexpected impression upon her in their short time together.

"It's a pity we met under such dreadful circumstances. It would have been nice to get to know all of you," she muttered, tears pricked her eyes. "If that were proper."

"Regardless of the circumstances, it was our great pleasure to assist you," Angelo said, looking at her. Emilio nodded in agreement.

"I especially hope to see you return to Florence, Vittoria," Nico admitted. "Life would be much different with you around."

"I hope to see you again too, Nico," Vittoria replied.

Nico's muscular arms swallowed her up in a tight hug. She never felt the urge to resist. Instead, she rested her weary head on his chest. It felt so heavy. His heart beat strong and steady. Grudgingly, she pulled herself from his warm embrace realizing there was never anything to fear from him.

Nico flashed her a brilliant smile. It was the most beautiful thing she'd seen in days. The sentiment of optimism fortified Vittoria for her imminent journey into the unknown. She stepped back from Nico and turned to the twins.

They both bowed playfully and, in turn, kissed her hand. "Farewell, my lady," they each said.

"Farewell, my chivalrous knights," she said grinning. Vittoria hoped to see their faces in the future. That alone would be one good reason to return to Florence. However, she knew it was unlikely all of them would survive to see that day come.

Jogging toward the bridge, she turned one last time to wave at her new friends.

The bridge was ricketier than it looked. Its wood had rotted through in many places and groaned beneath Vittoria's feet with each step. Dread prickled her neck. She could not make a run for the other side because a cart blocked her passage. Behind her, a mule had just come onto the bridge pulling a cart stacked too high with shoddily built wooden coffins. The weary gravediggers had taken the opportunity to overload the mule's cargo, so there was one less cart they had to push themselves.

There was a thunderous crash. Coffins tumbled off the back of the mule-cart. Putrefying bodies flew out onto the bridge. The bang frightened the mule and it charged right at Vittoria. The old man guiding the mule was trampled and screamed as the cart crushed his aged body. She was stuck over the nasty river, blocked from exiting the bridge.

The mule bore down on Vittoria, giving her mere seconds to choose her death—trampling or drowning. She sprung over the side of the bridge and landed hard on a wooden beam. She dangled above the polluted water below. Wood splintered and crashed, and men shouted. The mangled mule-cart slammed through the railing, landed in the river, and sank instantly.

Vittoria panicked and flailed. She couldn't swim and feared meeting a similar end. Her right shoe slipped off and plummeted into the river, making a muffled splash. Her tender fingers were losing their grip on the beam. She screamed for help.

"Vittoria! Vittoria!" shouted agitated voices.

"Over here!"

Her fingers burned, and the oilcloth bag weighed on her. She wished she had ditched it before going over. First Nico, then Angelo and Emilio, appeared on the bridge.

"Stop kicking," Nico shouted down. She stilled herself and waited for rescue, but all she heard was nervous pacing from above.

"We need a rope," said Emilio.

"We don't have time to find one," Nico exclaimed.

"But you can't reach her from here," Emilio argued.

"I'll climb down to her."

"It's too dangerous, Nico!" Angelo argued.

"We can't wait. I'm going," Nico decided.

Vittoria closed her eyes and tried steadying her breathing. Her heart beat wildly in her chest. She wouldn't be able to hold on much longer.

Nico lowered himself onto the beam and stood looking down upon Vittoria. His pupils grew big. Fear was taking hold. Vittoria looked pleadingly up at Nico and he regained his focus. He straddled the beam, locking his feet together for leverage, and leaned over to reach toward her. The twins watched from above.

"I'm going to grab and pull you up. Do *not* make any sudden movements," he instructed.

His legs tensed around the beam. Reaching out his arms, Nico's sturdy hands grabbed her upper arms and pulled her up. Sweat dripped from his brow. As he tugged her to safety, Vittoria's remaining shoe slipped from her other foot.

"He's almost got her," Emilio cried out.

"I can't believe it! Come on, Nico, you've got her!" Angelo shouted.

Nico grunted and strained until finally, Vittoria was eye-level with him. She bent her torso over the beam and rested.

"God in Heaven! He did it!" Angelo shouted.

"You did it, Nico!" Vittoria whispered.

Nico smiled and wiped the sweat from his brow with his sleeve. He sat up straight to give Vittoria enough room to swing her leg over to straddle the beam. "Come to me," he coached. "Steady now."

He stood up and climbed up the side of the railing. Vittoria inched toward him. His hand reached for hers. She grabbed it and stood up, her balance precarious.

"You'll need to get your footing on the railing, so Angelo and Emilio can pull you to safety."

Emilio shouted down. "We're ready!"

"Here we go," Nico said, yanking Vittoria upward. Her bare feet flailed before finding a wooden plank to set them upon. Nico wrapped his arm around Vittoria's body, keeping her close.

Emilio and Angelo reached over for her.

"You have to climb now," Emilio instructed.

Vittoria looked to Nico for encouragement. "You'll do just fine," he assured her.

Making sure not to look down into the river that swallowed up the mule and her shoes, she climbed the barrier to safety. The twins pulled her up and over with such enthusiasm she fell atop them when she landed.

Nico popped over the railing next and swept his short dark hair away from his glistening forehead. Vittoria wrangled herself away from the twins and threw her arms around him. "You saved my life. How can I ever repay you?"

Nico's eyes roved over every detail of Vittoria's face. He stroked her flushed cheek with his thumb and tucked a few flyaway locks behind her ear. Looking deep into her eyes he finally answered.

"Find a way back to Florence," he said. "I'll be waiting for you."

Nico stood silently on the south side of the Arno watching the most intriguing woman he ever met shrink into the distance. Vittoria turned back twice to wave at them. He hoped she'd turn once more, but she never did.

Nico's keen eyes had noticed all her natural details—finely arched brows, smooth round forehead, upturned emerald-gold eyes, delicate nose, and sweet mouth. He had taken full stock of Vittoria's petite frame, her fine neck, and the delicate chain with the strange silver charm she wore around it. He wouldn't forget a thing.

His heart sank into his chest when he could no longer see her loose hair dancing in the gentle breeze behind her. It felt like he'd been punched. Usually, Nico welcomed the pain, but this was much different. It was a sadness—worry, even—that he might never see her again. All the excitement and relief he had felt after her rescue had slipped away with her.

Nico never considered serious relationships with young ladies. Since his brother Lorenzo's death, he'd not considered anyone. He'd thought only of himself.

"What a lovely young woman," Angelo remarked.

Nico had never heard truer words spoken. To his right, his two constant companions stood guard watching after Vittoria as well.

"I can't quite put my finger on it, but there is something special about her," Emilio agreed.

And she has no idea, Nico thought.

He could kick himself for approaching her the way he did. He revisited the moment in his mind and found himself repulsed by his actions. He would never have spoken to Vittoria if he hadn't been drunk. He'd have been too chicken.

The soreness in Nico's chest increased and he coughed.

Angelo pulled his watchful gaze away from the horizon. "Are you, all right?"

Nico coughed again.

"I'm a little dried out after all the excitement. I think we should head home."

Angelo raised his eyebrows in surprise.

"What?" Nico asked, his tone defensive, when he got the same look from Emilio.

The twins looked sideways at each other.

"Seriously, are you quite well?"

Nico cleared his throat.

"I should head back to the shop and take care of the things I've been neglecting."

"I am pretty tired, too, and I want to get out of these clothes," Emilio said, pointing at the blood-stains on his shirt.

"What happened to you anyway?" Nico asked.

Angelo replied in lieu of his twin. "One of Pitti's thugs."

"Oh...," was all Nico mumbled. He couldn't remember what had happened. Most of the night was a blur.

"I don't suppose we'll see him again though," Emilio said.

"Why is that?" Nico asked. "Those twits are always at the Tre Sorella Taverna."

Emilio glared at Nico. "Because I took care of him."

"Is that right?" Nico chuckled, trying to imagine little Emilio taking down one of Pitti's men. "I wish I had seen it."

Before he could ask any more questions about the incident, Emilio stalked away. Angelo lagged with Nico.

"What's with him?" Nico asked, wondering why Emilio was so grumpy.

"He'll be fine. He's just tired, is all," Angelo replied, before changing the subject. "It was brave of you to rescue Vittoria. You should be very proud of yourself. She's going to remember that forever, you know?"

"Well, let's pray that forever turns out to be a very long time," Nico replied.

"You never know," Angelo said. "Maybe she'll come back some day."

Nico was already imagining that moment.

The cousins walked together in silence until they came to an ocher stucco building. The bronze scissors, the sign of the tailor, hung above the entryway. Nico ruffled Angelo's curly hair and patted him hard on the back.

"Same time tonight?" Angelo asked.

"Yes, but let's meet at Neptune Fountain. I can't remember what happened last night, but I assume we should avoid the Taverna...at least for a few days," Nico admitted.

"Probably a good idea," Angelo agreed. "I'm sure Emilio will be glad to hear it. To be honest, I can't remember either. But don't tell Emilio," Angelo said, giving a conspiratorial wink.

"See you later, then," Nico said, and headed to the side alley entrance of his quarters.

CHAPTER 3

Aishe poked her head through the deerskin flap of Celestina's tent. She'd been playing hard and her auburn locks were damp and sticking to her cherubic face. The child's smile was, as always, firmly in place upon her face. It was a light in the darkness for Celestina.

"Grandmother?" Aishe called, pushing back the flap to make her bouncy entry.

"Yes, child. Come in."

Celestina blinked her weary green eyes open from deep contemplation. She extended her arms to receive and squeeze the girl's tiny little body. Aishe's sweetness was a salve for her melancholy. The child snuggled into her grandmother's lap before asking her pressing questions.

"Why is everyone so sad? It feels like a weight pressing on my chest when I open up my heart to the zee in the camp."

Celestina stroked Aishe's arm before answering.

"I've felt it too, little one. A scourge of shadow has emerged."

"But how? Nothing seems to have changed for us," she questioned, her fine auburn brows knitting over her honey-colored eyes.

"Oh, but it has, my dear. The Malandanti acquired the means to cast a grand transmutation spell. Its victims already suffer an inner plague of misery and pain which drains away their life force a little every day, and the spell accelerates the process by means of physical illness. The Malandanti grow stronger by the day because of it."

"Can't we do something to stop it?"

Celestina pinched Aishe's round cheek.

"I'm getting older and without an anointed heir to carry on as Benetrix, the Malandanti will get stronger. They had to wield an incredible amount of force to unleash the Scourge."

Celestina suspected her niece, Nerezza, the Malatrix, was responsible for casting the spell. As there was no one powerful enough, other than herself, to have done it.

"How do you know this?"

"A long time ago, priestesses from Egypt created the Scourge Scroll, on behalf of Pharaoh, to punish invaders in their land. Knowledge of the spell spread like wildfire to Strega clans across the sea. It has been cast several times since, for various reasons. The last occurrence happened nearly three hundred years ago, by a clan of rogue Strega. It devastated the land."

"Were those Strega punished?"

"The Strega who stood trial for their crimes claimed their victims were already killing themselves. And that they were not to be held responsible for their murder."

"They didn't get away with that reasoning, did they?"

Celestina was silent.

Aishe gasped in disbelief. "You mean the Lady of Light did nothing?"

"They were reprimanded, but not stripped of their powers."

"They should have been!" Aishe argued.

Celestina agreed but did not say it aloud. She would never verbalize mistrust in the Lady of Light. Instead, she asked the child a question of her own.

"What is one to do when a man seeks to punish himself by acts of hate and self-loathing?"

Aishe shrugged.

"The only thing that can be done is to offer love at every turn. Most people, though, believe they deserve suffering instead. Sadly, there is no magic in the world that can make people accept love, either."

"Then why do we Benedanti even exist?"

"I've asked myself that many times. I suppose it's to bring the light of hope and possibility to all whom we encounter. To speak kind words, do good deeds, and remind people of the goodness and grace within."

"We can do that without magic, can't we?"

Celestina chuckled. When she smiled, her wizened face wrinkled.

"Yes, I suppose we can."

She was so blessed to have this little person in her life, so loving and perceptive.

"Grandmother?" Aishe asked.

"Yes?"

"Papa told me just now his sister, your daughter, has died of the plague. Is it true?"

Celestina was surprised her son would speak of Orabella to the child.

"Yes, it is true."

Celestina bore this great sadness with the hope that one day they would all reconcile. Now, there was no chance. She awoke early that morning, hearing her daughter's sweet voice in her mind. Calling out for her.

Find her. She needs you, she heard.

She rose and went straight into meditation to listen for instruction from the Lady of Light. She'd been in deep contemplation until Aishe arrived.

"I'm sorry, Grandmother," Aishe's face drooped. "Papa is heartbroken, too. I can feel it."

"They were close, so he would feel the loss deep in his heart."

Sadly, her only daughter and heir left the clan twenty years ago for the love of an ordinary. It was one of Celestina's two great sorrows. The other was casting the deciding vote sentencing her sister to death, for she had performed forbidden magic to resurrect her deceased companion.

Even though her purpose was to offer love to all, it was love that drove both her daughter and sister to make decisions resulting in the ultimate consequence—death.

"With no heir to become Benetrix after you, what will happen to us? We can't allow the Malandanti to grow in power and hurt people we love."

"There is always hope, my child. I'm certain that there is a solution. The Lady of Light would never abandon us."

Aishe perked up. "I believe you, Grandmother."

Celestina wanted to believe it, too. She could see no clear path to a solution. Orabella's daughter was the Benedanti's only hope, but she knew nothing of her kin or the Old Ways.

First, the child would have to be found. Then, she must be convinced to take up her claim as Benetrix and receive the blessings of the Lady of Light. She'd have to grasp centuries worth of wisdom by her twentieth birthday, which was mere months away.

Without the Lady of Light's intercession, the task would be impossible. Celestina didn't think she could pray any harder for guidance.

"What can we do about Tsura? She's been gloomy since...," Aishe trailed off, looking away shyly.

"You think she needs to take her mind off Cai?"

"She's been walking around in a blue haze for weeks. I miss my Tsura."

"It would appear she's lost her direction."

Aishe nodded in agreement.

"That boy is no good for her anyway. Do you know where your sister is now?" Celestina asked.

"Yes, in the same place she's been for days. In her tent, sitting in the dark."

"Well then, let's pay her a little visit. Shall we?"

CHAPTER 4

Vittoria's journey was peaceful as she followed the undulating terrain of the Tuscan country-side. Pretending to be a fearless explorer, she discovered the beauty of her native land for the very first time, taking in all its simple majesty with her eyes—the enormity of the shady green groves of olive trees, the orchards heavy with ripe citrus, fig trees laden with fruits, endless fields of golden grain wav-ing in the afternoon breeze, and ancient vineyards stretching toward the horizon. All the land was over-flowing with bounty left unharvested. She took advantage of her good fortune, picking handfuls of figs to nibble as she walked the dusty sun-bleached road towards an unknown destination.

For several hours, Vittoria walked barefoot along the Strada Chiantiaga, passing quaint whitewashed villages situated upon hilltops in the distance. On occasion, she crossed paths with free-roaming goats and pigs and even a pair of oxen, but the countryside was strangely devoid of people.

Vittoria was used to the noise of folks chatting and squabbling in the streets and haggling in the marketplace. But in the country, this eerie silence had to be unusual, even the birds refrained from chirping. She strained her ears, listening for the sound of human voices.

A cold shiver went up Vittoria's spine even as she stood in the warm sunshine. She should have encountered dozens of farmers working the land preparing for the upcoming harvest. She feared she was not as safe from the plague as she had hoped. She wanted to see somebody, even if from a distance. The growing feeling of aloneness scared her.

Vittoria picked up her pace. The friction of the dirt and gravel caused painful blisters to form on the balls and heels of her bare feet. She pushed through the stinging pain coursing up her calves. The journey had exhausted her, and she feared she'd collapse in the middle of the road if she didn't find refuge soon.

Upon the summit of the next hill, she was relieved to find a villa at the end of a long lane. Tall cypress trees stood guard and shaded the property. The setting sun reflected off the sloping terracotta tiled roof of the square building, and the stone façade darkened.

Vittoria watched the villa from the road to see if there was any movement visible in the high dark windows. She walked toward the villa wondering how she'd convince its inhabitants she was not a plague carrier.

As she got closer, Vittoria realized she had misjudged the size of the villa. It was much larger than she'd first thought. The villa's master could staff a dozen servants to run the business there.

All dusty and disheveled from the long journey, Vittoria was sure she looked like a common peasant. Nervous, she smoothed her loose hair away from her face and wiped sweat from her brow. She tried in vain to brush the dust from her dress, but there was nothing she could do about the sad state of her poor, bare feet. Whoever greeted her, she hoped they would take pity.

Vittoria lifted the heavy knocker and dropped it thrice on the villa's thick oak door. When nobody came to greet her, she paced back and forth thinking of what to do next. She knocked once more and again received no response. Desperate shadows stretched across her path and it would not be long before the sun disappeared, allowing the moon dominion in the sky.

Vittoria scurried around the side of the villa calling out to anyone who could hear. She followed the wall further back and found that as it neared the point where the hill descended it opened to beautiful terraced gardens.

Jasmine sweetened the warm evening air. It was delightful the way the bougainvillea vines climbed high over the walls of the enclosed garden and wrapped around the pergola. The hedges had been clipped into neat boxes, and topiaries and rosebushes lined the garden's arcade.

Exotic flowers of every color perfumed the evening, and even the vegetables of the kitchen garden were cultivated in such a way as to add beauty to the garden itself. The view in the valley was stunning. She watched as the sun painted a masterpiece of jewel-toned colors in the sky for her pleasure.

She again observed the villa for signs of life. Nothing. Vittoria found the entry in the arcade. The door was unlocked.

What luck!

She was an unwelcome guest, and it took all her courage to enter. Vittoria crept inside and from what she could tell in the dimming light the interior was just as wonderful as the exterior.

A sequence of open and airy rooms was decorated with magnificent frescoes of religious scenes, done by none other than a master. The furniture was sturdy and of good quality, but not lavish. A heavy wooden table, chairs, and a sideboard filled the room. The floor was laid with handmade tiles that cooled the heat in her feet. Rugs woven of rich colored thread were strewn across the floors here and there.

Vittoria climbed the central staircase and wandered into a room that looked to be a library. The sturdy desk was piled high with leather bound books. Fresh parchment, quills, and ink were ready for use. She had never seen so many expensive books in one place.

In the corner was a music stand and chair. Beside which stood a lute of the best quality. It had a belly made of pine, the sound hole was a carved in the shape of a rose and accented with ivory.

She dared not touch the instrument. If she broke it, she could never afford to replace it. A closer look at the music on the stand revealed a script of crosses, hatch marks, and vertical rows of neat alphabetical letters all printed within several horizontal tables. The lute player's own musical notations.

Continuing her exploration of the villa, Vittoria found several bedchambers whose windows looked out onto the villa's garden and valley vista. One had a canopied bed hung with a striped silken fabric. The bed covers were rumpled as if someone had recently slept there. The room smelled of sandalwood.

A quick sweep of the room revealed two pairs of soft leather slippers and a pair of boots, numerous pairs of colored breeches, and embroidered tunics and doublets in the latest fashion. Judging by the size she guessed they belonged to a young man. They reminded her of the garments worn by Nico and the twins.

Vittoria backed out of the room. This was the closest sign of life she had seen since leaving Florence, and she was fearful of meeting this man even if he could assist her. She returned downstairs. Unlocking the heavy oak door, she pulled it open and looked down the lane toward the road. Nobody was there. She had the villa to herself.

Shoving the door closed Vittoria slid down its length. Sitting on the smooth tile floor, she dropped her bag down beside her. It was the first time she had rested all day. Easing her head back onto the door and she let the cool tiles sooth her tired feet. She closed her eyes and listened. She could hear the foliage rustling outside the front door. Then she brought her attention to her breath and listened to the whooshing sound the air made as it crossed back and forth through her lips. Listening closer, she heard a creaking sound coming from the northern wing of the villa where she had not yet explored.

She stood and followed the sound, passing through a dark hallway and down a short stair. She pushed open a swinging cypress door which led into an expansive kitchen. A large plank table with benches occupied the center of the room. The wood in the hearth still smoldered so she lit a tallow candle from the embers. The candlelight illuminated the darkened areas of the kitchen where large woven baskets of onions, garlic, and artichokes were hidden. Smaller baskets of black peppercorns, cinnamon bark, ginger, nutmeg, and almonds sat up on a shelf above them. On the table was a crock full of honey and a cellar of salt. None of the expensive spices were behind lock and key, as they were in most households.

On the cold flagstone floor of the larder were containers of dried and salted fish. Large wedges of cheese were stacked in the corner. Crocks of pickled fruits and vegetables lined the shelves. Bags of dried beans and chestnuts slouched against the wall and hanging overhead were dry cured pork legs, whose flavor tasted divine with fresh fruit.

Vittoria's mouth watered, and her hungry stomach cramped and growled. She was ravenous. She found a serrated knife appropriate for carving. Wielding it with precision, she sliced a thin piece of the white fat off the surface of the pork leg exposing the bright pink meat within. She inhaled. The scent was so wonderful she groaned aloud. Vittoria hacked slices of the meat quicker than she could chew and swallow them. With a handful of meat still in her hand, she grabbed a crock of pickled pears off the shelf. Bringing the cache out to the table she gorged herself. Out of the corner of her eye she caught glimpse of an open bottle of Chianti. She nearly knocked over the bench she sat upon jumping up to claim the wine.

She drank straight from the bottle, spilling red wine over her face and down her neck.

When she was satisfied, Vittoria plopped herself back down on the bench and rested her head on the table. A warm relaxed feeling came over her as the wine coursed through her veins. She was content and rested, enjoying the full feeling in her belly.

The clock on the mantel in Angelo's room struck eight in the evening. He was still very tired and could have slept through the rest of the night, but he rose and dressed, tugging on his shoes before descending the stairs of his family home.

His mother was sitting nearby the window utilizing the last bit of sunlight to see her embroidery. Without fail she found her place there every evening after supper. She looked up hearing the stair creak.

"Going out again, Angelo?" she asked, without raising her eyes from the delicate work in front of her. "There is a curfew. You shouldn't be out roaming free and causing mischief."

"Have you seen Emilio?" he asked his aging mother rather than address her concern.

Her once dark hair had grayed heavily since Lucrezia died the previous month.

"Yes, he left about two hours ago."

Angelo opened his mouth to speak but his mother answered his question before he asked.

"No, I don't know where he's gone."

Angelo, snapped his mouth shut.

"Not to that sinful Taverna, I hope!" she exclaimed.

Angelo's round cheeks reddened. "Don't worry, Mama. I'm not going there."

"I should hope not!"

"Please tell Emilio I need to speak to him when he returns."

"Only if you promise to stay out of trouble. My heart can't take it," she added.

Angelo knew she was serious.

"Yes, Mama," he agreed, kissing her soft cheek before heading off to meet Nico. Closing the front door behind him, he prayed. "Please let this be an uneventful evening."

Angelo arrived at the fountain close to eight-thirty. He sat down and waited. The piazza was quieter than usual. Only doctors, death carts, and dogs roamed the streets. He didn't like the feeling that crept into his belly. Angelo toyed with a button on the cuff of his sea green coat and whistled an uneasy tune while he waited for Nico.

The weird activity on the street spooked him. He hopped up from his seat and took off east toward the tailor's shop. It was almost dark, but Angelo had been there so many times he could find his way in his sleep. He slipped down the side alley off the main street where Nico made entry to his quarters. A cat jumped out from behind a rain barrel and meowed. Angelo kicked at the cat for scaring him and cursed under his breath.

"Evil creature!"

He tapped on the outside door before opening it. There was no response. Angelo pushed the door open and tiptoed down the tiny corridor to Nico's room and knocked on his door. Again, nothing.

This is stupid. He's probably at the Taverna halfway through his bottle already.

Then he heard a rustling sound, so he pushed the door open. Light from a candle in the corner of the room spilled into the corridor. Nico lay on his too small cot, and Angelo could see there was a strange sheen on his half-naked body. He was sweating. His chest moved very little and his breathing was labored. Then he coughed hard.

No, no, no...no!

Angelo remembered his baby sister, Lucrezia, looked like that before she died from the wretched plague.

"Nico, wake up! Please, Nico! Wake up!"

Angelo dare not get closer. Instead, he placed his nose into the corner of his elbow and banged frantically on the door trying to rouse Nico and get him conscious. He was frightened.

Shit! Shit! Shit!

"Think!" he demanded of himself, as he paced in the cramped area outside Nico's door.

He needs a doctor. There's got to be someone who can help.

"Paolo...Paolo Salviati!"

His friend had become a Dottore della Peste, and he could help.

"I'll be back, Nico!" Angelo shouted at his cousin, hoping that he heard.

He slammed both doors behind him and dashed down the dark alley into the night. The cat howled after him. He raced as fast as he could to the Salviati residence just one block from his own home.

Angelo was out of breath by the time he arrived. He bent over, bracing his knees trying to catch his wind before pounding on the door like a madman.

One of the servants jerked open the door.

"What in heaven's name is going on?" he asked.

"Please, I'm a friend of Paolo's. I need his assistance. Is he home?"

"He just returned and is sitting down for supper. You'll have to come back later."

Angelo was not going to take no for an answer. He pushed himself past the servant.

"I'm sorry but this is urgent, and it cannot wait."

"Paolo!" Angelo bellowed as he jogged down the entry hall toward the dining room.

The servant chased after him. He heard chairs being pushed back in unison, and glassware and silver clinking. Paolo appeared followed by his younger brothers, Aurelio and Crispino.

"What in God's name, Angelo?" Paolo exclaimed. His hooded eyes were shaded, and his plain ruddy face was gaunt. "We just sat down to eat."

"I'm very sorry, but I need you *now*. You know I wouldn't intrude unless it was urgent, and it is."

"What's the matter? You look like you've seen a ghost," Paolo said, while chewing a bite of food.

"I feel like I have," Angelo replied, remembering the wretched sight of his dying sister.

"What is it? Your mother?" Paolo guessed.

"No, but it's family. Bring your gear. I'll wait outside."

Paolo stood gaping after his agitated friend, for he took his leave as quickly as he appeared.

Paolo jogged after Angelo as fast as possible, but he was exhausted. The work of a Dottore della Peste was nonstop. He'd been in the service of the dying for days with very little sleep and almost as little to eat. There was no time for either.

Angelo was kind enough to carry his medical bag but with his waxed leather coat, wide-brimmed hat, and bird-demon mask on, the journey was slow going.

"Hurry, Paolo!" Angelo shouted back over his shoulder.

They had entered the linen district and after a few more twists and turns he saw it, the sign of the bronze scissors above the tailor shop. He knew where they were. Paolo stopped moving and stood still in the street.

"Damn it, Angelo!" The curse echoed through the mask, hurting his ears.

Angelo stopped and turned to look at Paolo, who was standing with his hands perched on his hips.

Paolo then took off his hat and removed the freakish mask. "I'm *not* doing it."

Angelo stretched his arms out petitioning Paolo's help. "I know that Nico has been an obnoxious grandiose ass to you, and everyone else for that matter, for a long time. Honestly, Paolo, he doesn't deserve your time or sympathy."

"Exactly!" Paolo interjected.

"Even so," Angelo continued. "As *your* longtime friend, I'm asking you for this one favor."

"No. I won't see him. You can send for another doctor and when one is available they will come."

"You know that if he has to wait he'll die, just like Lucrezia."

Paolo had long admired the twins' sister. A sadness overcame him. He had often wondered if she would have survived if he'd attended her instead of Dottore Blanco, though it was highly unlikely.

"That was God's will, and no one survives the plague. Even *if* I tended Nico, there's nothing that can be done."

"Then why bother exposing yourself to death, day after day, if it's a hopeless fool's errand after all?"

"I'm not a fool!" Paolo shouted.

"I didn't say you were, but it's a shame that you would decide to quibble over Nico's actions now."

"You know what he's done to me! Always belittling, embarrassing, and harassing me in public. Perhaps Florence would be a better place if he was gone."

Paolo saw the fury explode over Angelo's face.

"You're a petty little shit!" he roared, slapping Paolo. Shocked by the impact, Paolo cradled his stinging and throbbing cheek. "Maybe Nico was right about you. Perhaps he could see what the rest of us could not. That you're a trifling, milk-livered scut!"

Paolo wasn't afraid of Angelo like he was of Nico, who was taller, wider, and wilder than all the rest of them. He and Angelo were matched in size and strength. He was tired of everyone pushing him around all the time and not taking him seriously.

Enough!

Paolo punched Angelo in the stomach, sending him to the ground. Then Angelo launched himself into Paolo, knocking him onto his back. Angelo got in a few good licks before Paolo managed to push him off his chest. They wrestled in the street, ripping at each other's garments, and struggling until Angelo managed to secure Paolo in a tight headlock. The pressure around Paolo's neck scared him into sub-mission. He couldn't breathe, and his face reddened.

Candlelight appeared in once dark windows. Their fighting had alarmed the residents. There was a cur-few in place and it must have looked like Angelo was assaulting a doctor, who was one of the few allowed out after the curfew.

"I can't breathe," Paolo croaked.

"I want you to listen to me. Will you listen?"

A slight nod was the only response Paolo gave.

"If you won't help Nico for personal reasons, do it because you swore an oath to remain free of all inten-tional injustice when tending to the sick and infirm. Do you think you're upholding that oath now?"

Paolo didn't want to admit it because his loathing for Nico was so great, but Angelo was right. He was prejudiced toward Nico.

"I'll attend him," he said, sucking breath. "Let go."

"Sorry," Angelo said, letting go. Sitting back on his haunches, he breathed heavy.

Paolo gasped for air and rubbed at his neck bring-ing back the circulation. "I'm sorry, as well."

"Let's not do this again."

"Agreed."

Angelo stood and straightened himself out. He mumbled under his breath.

"So much for an uneventful night."

The candlelight disappeared from the windows. Since no one was killed, the voyeurs must have deemed it unnecessary to linger.

Offering a hand to Paolo, Angelo pulled him to his feet. He then picked up the leather hat and mask off the ground and handed them over to their owner.

"Shall we?"

Feeling the last vestige of stubbornness rear its ugly head, Paolo shook out his hat and packed the herbs back into the beak of his bird-demon mask before stomping toward the tailor shop. Angelo picked up the medical bag and made haste to catch up.

Before entering the building, Angelo placed a hand on his shoulder. "Thank you for doing this, Paolo."

"You'll make it up to me. I'll be sure of that."

Nico thrashed in the small bed. It was too hot, and the room felt like it was closing in on him. His skin was sensitive to touch and every time he moved it felt like the bed linens burned him.

He coughed and choked on the phlegm in his throat and gasped for air, but he couldn't pull enough into his lungs. Something was the matter, he knew, but he couldn't pull himself from the unconscious state he'd slipped into.

His consciousness was pulling away. Not into a dream, but out of his body. He heard voices— familiar voices—but they were too far away. They wouldn't hear him if he could call out. He reached out toward the sounds, but his arm was very weak, and it flopped back down.

What's happening to me?

As the voices got closer it seemed that he slipped further from them. His heart was pumping entirely too fast.

Why can't I open my eyes?

Nico's body was not responding to his will to wake up. He couldn't breathe. He panted for air.

No, no... this can't be!

On the insides of his eyelids, a spectrum of colors morphed into different shapes and patterns. He focused his attention on the shifting array of sparkling light.

What is that? Why do I see color instead of black?

The colors spun around like they were weaving themselves into a cord of rope. Nico watched with his inner eye as the cord wove itself into his navel and anchored itself there.

He felt buoyant, like something was lifting him up out of the body that he knew lay on the bed. There was pressure as his spirit pushed up through the bone, muscle, and skin that comprised his physical form.

I can't remember feeling this light. My body is so heavy.

Nico floated above his body. Looking at himself, he saw his spirit was made up of radiant white light pulsating with shades of pinks, purples, and blues. He was glowing and so was the cord. He felt connected to everything and he knew who was in the other room— Angelo and Paolo.

Angelo must have had to call in a big favor to convince Paolo to see me.

Both were agitated but he could also sense other emotions as well. Angelo was worried, and Paolo was full of disdain. Without the heaviness of his physical body, Nico could understand why each was feeling the way they were. He had caused them both distress.

Paolo didn't want to be in his presence and it was his own fault. Nico had made a fool out of him too many times to count and was ashamed of his behavior now that he could see how it had affected Paolo. He could also sense how much Angelo cared for him.

More than he should.

The cord pulsated and grew longer, and he floated higher above his body until he was outside the tailor shop, above the rooftops, and up into the sky. He could see the entire city of Florence from his vantage point.

It's so beautiful. I wonder where Vittoria is down there?

A bright light shined from above, blinding Nico. When the light dissipated, and he could see again, he found that he wasn't in the sky at all but in a lush green forest full of wildlife. There were animals of all sorts. Stags, raccoons, wild pigs, owls, hawks, and rabbits all rested in the forest clearing. He could smell the earthy aroma of the moss on the forest floor, and the air was fresh and clean like it just rained.

Nico seemed to be in his own body again. He could see his arm had skin on it once more, and he reached up to feel his head and touch his hair. His feet were bare, and he curled his toes into the thick carpet of moss. None of the animals came near, though Nico could sense that even if they did he would not be harmed. They waited for someone. Then a pack of fine greyhound dogs raced into the clearing harkening the arrival of someone very important.

The animals huffed and squawked with excitement as their mistress stepped from the woods. The delicate sound of singing voices and flutes echoed through the clearing. Nico stood unmoving.

Aside from the white light that moved with the woman, she was a wonder to behold. She walked like rippling water toward him. Long dark hair trailed behind her lithe, naked body. With her proud chin held high she gazed at him with great interest. Her eyes were alternating shades of blue and green. She held a golden bow and wore naught but a quiver full of silver arrows. To Nico she was glorious, and something about her reminded him of Vittoria.

She spoke. Her voice silky and calm. "Come forward, child."

"Am I dead?"

"You are not dead yet. Would you like to be?"

"No, of course not."

"You have persisted in positioning yourself so that you might be killed. I've seen it so."

He had been careless with his life. Picking fights and throwing unkind words at strangers and family alike had gotten him into many tight spots.

"You recognize the truth of my words?"

He nodded but said nothing.

"Come closer. Let me have a look at you."

He stepped forward, keeping his eyes on the mossy ground.

"You mustn't be afraid. Come."

The warmth of her bare body radiated outward and Nico felt the sensation of her on his skin. It enticed him to move closer.

"He hurt you," she said.

Nico understood her meaning. She spoke of his grandmother's husband. The one who took pleasure in touching him in the darkness when he was young. The one who forced him into performing unspeakable acts to satisfy his sinful appetite. The man who destroyed his life.

Tears slipped from his eyes. He wanted to scream and holler and beat his chest to express all the pain and loneliness he had endured at the hands of the man he had escaped as a child. He was also angry with his father for sending him away.

Why did he do it? Couldn't he see?

Reading his mind, she responded.

"Your father believed he was doing the best he could for you," she answered. "He loved you enough to try to find a suitable place for you and your brother Lorenzo."

Nico shrugged, finding it hard to believe that was his father's true intention. The Lady of Light stepped forward leaving little room between them. The light emanating from her skin diminished so not to blind him. He was close enough to look deep into her up-turned eyes.

Green and gold.

She levitated off the ground, leaned forward, and pressed her soft lips to his. Light flashed in Nico's mind's eye, then he was looking back on the day he was born. Specifically, the moment his mother pushed for the final time and he slipped into the hands of the midwife. She popped him hard on the rump and he took his first gasp of air. His mother, a young woman of twenty-three, was tired and sweaty but she reached out to him and smiled. He was placed upon her breast and he felt warm and welcome. She nursed him and played with his tiny little fingers. His eyes were sleepy, and her face appeared blurry to him. She cooed, and he was content.

"You have a son," announced the midwife.

A man appeared at his mother's bedside. It was his father. He kissed his mother on the forehead and then kissed Nico.

"Do you see?" said the Lady of Light.

"Yes, I see," Nico said, acknowledging the love he sensed in his father's first greeting.

Then, he felt like he was being sucked back into a hole made of light to another scene. The two days after his mother had died in childbirth with his baby sister. He was seven years old. His father was devastated at the loss of his beloved wife and new child. He was in the study staring out the window into the piazza below trying not to shed a tear. He was angry, bewildered, and bitter all at once. Nico had hoped to be consoled by his father but found that he was afraid to ask for comfort. Instead, he returned to the room he shared with Lorenzo and they laid upon the bed holding one another.

Sometime later he heard his father speaking with a man and woman. He heard his name and then Lorenzo's. The door opened, and his father stood with his grandmother and her husband.

"Papa, what's happening?"

"You are going to live with Nonna and Signor Basso," he said.

"You don't want us any longer?" Nico questioned his father. Lorenzo started to cry. He was only five and didn't understand what was happening.

"Come now, children. Let's gather your belongings," said Nico's grandmother. She had a shabby look about her and was missing a front tooth. Her new husband smiled revealing several gaps in his own mouth.

"I don't want to leave!" Lorenzo exclaimed, jumping off the bed and clinging to his father's legs.

Disentangling himself, Sansone Apollino turned his back and left the room, leaving Lorenzo screaming and Nico too afraid to say anything. Nico remembered that moment. He watched in disbelief as his father walked away from them both. He never turned back to look. He never said goodbye. He never said he loved them.

Time jumped forward once more, and Nico saw his father in his study looking out the window. Below, Lorenzo and Nico and their scant belongings—a small chest of clothing and a few wooden toys—were being loaded onto a worn-down cart attached to a tired brown mule.

Sansone sobbed as he watched the children he loved so much disappear into the distance. His wife's passing had been a complete shock to him and he couldn't fathom life without her, let alone dealing with children who were so young and needy. He couldn't afford a governess for the children on a clerk's salary and after thinking through his options he deemed it was the most appropriate decision. The children would live with his mother on the outskirts of Florence. They would be provided for and he would send money to take care of their expenses. Once the cart was out of sight Sansone slid to the floor and remained there for hours crying.

"What have I done? What have I done?" he repeated over and over like and incantation.

It was the one question he kept asking himself. His father hardened his heart against the hurt and sadness. It was his only hope for survival in a world without his dear wife and children. He had to push the pain away or it would crush him.

Nico's knees gave way beneath him. The Lady held him up by his elbow. He understood now. He had believed his father had given him away because he wasn't wanted anymore. That he wasn't loved. He had been looking at life through a child's eyes all these years.

"Take me away from here," Nico whispered, then he was whisked back to the forest amongst the animals and the enormous trees.

"Your skewed perspective is ruining your life," said the Lady of Light.

"I know."

"You're attracting many enemies, and those who love you are now at risk."

"What can I do?" he asked, thinking of the twins and Vittoria.

"You must forgive yourself *and* your father. Make amends and change your ways. You *must* change your ways. Vittoria's life depends on it."

"How do you know about Vittoria?" he asked.

"I know you saved her life and you'll need to do it once more."

"You mean, I'll see her again?"

"Yes, but you must *not* seek her out. You have work of your own to do to prepare for that day. You are not ready yet."

"When will I be?

"If you were to die right now, would you be happy with the life you have lived thus far?"

"Of course not."

"Then you must make adjustments so that you may answer differently next time."

"Am I going back to my body?"

"Yes. The balance of shadow and light has been corrupted."

"Balance?"

"Remember this encounter when you are made privy to information that seems implausible, unimaginable even. It is very important. Swear that you'll do your best to remember."

"I swear. If it means I will see Vittoria again, I'll remember.

"Very well, my child."

"Who are you?" Nico finally asked.

"I am Diana, Queen of all Strega, Mother of Witches, Lady of Light," she replied, with a sparkling smile. She leaned forward and kissed Nico on the lips once more. "Until we meet again."

Then she vanished.

After dozing briefly in the kitchen, Vittoria returned to the villa's library, where she found and lit more candles. Once the room was aglow, she sat in a comfortable brocade chair at the desk. She looked over the collection of books stacked upon it. The subject matter was vast and interesting and included Herodotus' *The Histories*, Homer's *Iliad* and *Odyssey*, and *The Travels of Marco Polo*.

On the corner of the desk, obscured by a short stack of papers, was a Book of Hours. The mahogany leather-bound book was embellished with delicate gold filigree, cabochon rubies, emeralds, and sapphires the size of her thumbnail. They were mounted at intervals around the border of the text's cover. A heavy golden latch held the book closed from prying eyes.

Vittoria had never seen such a sumptuous book, not even on display in at church.

It must have cost a fortune to obtain and here it was shoved under a pile of papers. She couldn't resist the temptation to look inside.

The breath caught in her throat as she beheld the embossed vellum pages of a brilliant illuminated book. She admired the craftsmanship and rich use of ultramarine blue, the most expensive of colors that a painter could use. It was filled with heraldic emblems, biblical miniatures illustrating the Passion of Christ and the Life of the Virgin, and flowery decorations in gold leaf decorated the margins.

It was exquisite in design, and she could not help but feel her spirit elevated as she enjoyed the masterpiece dedicated to the glory of God. She marveled at it for hours and fell asleep in the chair caressing its delicate   pages.

CHAPTER 5

G ruff voices outside awakened Vittoria from her slumber. She panicked and scrambled out of the chair knocking the Book of Hours to the floor. It landed with a tremendous thud. The candles had all burned out and she had to feel her way around the room.

She tiptoed with stealth over to the window in the corner. Keeping her body pressed close to the wall, she pulled back the draperies just enough to peek out. Holding her breath Vittoria listened for the voices.

In the predawn darkness, it was hard to see. But, by the remaining light of the bright moon, she saw a man and woman hiding in the shadowy cover of the cypress trees.

The man was of short, stout build with thick arms and squat legs. His stringy hair hung limply at his shoulders and the shine of the moon on his head revealed he was balding.

The full-figured woman wore a tattered tan dress. It was too short and exposed her bare legs. The bodice was tight and strangled her breasts. She had a long angular face, and a tangle of black hair knotted at the nape of her neck.

The suspicious couple scrutinized the window where she stood hidden in the darkness. Vittoria didn't move a muscle.

"Do you see anything?" the man asked.

"There aren't any candles burning now."

"But someone must be in there, Magda" he insisted. "Perhaps, he's returned."

"Impossible! We've been watching the house for over a week, and the maidservant left with her belongings within days of his departure."

"I know."

"I don't plan to wait any longer. You know the riches that lie inside that villa, Ugo. It couldn't be any easier now."

Magda withdrew a large dagger from the sheath on her hip. The blade gleamed as it caught the moonlight's reflection on its shaft. Ugo whipped out his shorter, less impressive, dagger and raised it in solidarity.

Vittoria shuddered. Releasing the curtain from her iron grasp, she inhaled slowly to prevent herself from hyperventilating. She needed to procure a more suitable hiding place. Collecting her belongings, she dashed for the door.

Vittoria moved toward the main staircase but stopped short.

It's too risky. They'll see me from the garden entrance.

Backtracking down the dark hallway, stopping to listen for the intruders. She heard Ugo's gravelly voice and knew they were inside.

"Be quiet! There may still be somebody here, and I don't want them sneaking up on *us*," Magda warned.

Vittoria's breath came faster, and she could hear the blood rushing in her ears. A cold sweat broke out on her upper lip and nose.

"Keep going, keep going," she whispered, coaxing herself forward.

Inch by inch, she searched blindly for a doorway. The friction of the dry skin on her fingers sounded, to her, like a beacon for the intruders' downstairs as they swept over the walls.

"I can't see anything," Ugo complained.

"Open the curtains to let in the moonlight," Magda instructed.

Vittoria waited until she heard them rummaging through a room to open the second door she found. It swung open and she shut it behind her. The only noise, a minuscule click of the locking mechanism.

A large armoire stood against the far wall. It was big enough to climb into. The sky was changing outside. Deep violet and blue light christened the dawn. As she pulled opened its doors, she prayed that the light of day would save her.

Vittoria stepped up into her hiding place and settled atop folded garments, which felt to be made of silk and velvet. Plopping her bag down beside her she heard the jingle of coins. Closing the doors, she sat in the darkness with her racing breath and imagination to keep her company.

"Look what I found! A bejeweled book," Ugo proclaimed.

"Let me see that. It must be worth a fortune. Look at all the jewels and gold." Magda cackled with satisfaction.

Vittoria could hear the opening and closing of sideboards, chests, and drawers throughout the villa. Fear turned Vittoria's stomach in somersaults with every step they came closer to her hiding place.

"What did you find?" Ugo grunted.

"What I knew we would."

"More jewels?" Ugo asked.

"Gold coins, and lots of them."

"Where?"

"In an *unlocked* trunk under the bed," Magda revealed.

Vittoria prayed that they would hurry, take what they want, and leave. Her right leg was cramped from sitting in an awkward position, and her nose was itching. The lavender sachets in the armoire were irritating it.

"Quick, load up the coin," Magda bid Ugo. "I'll check the last of the rooms."

Madga's heavy footsteps echoed in the hallway, coming nearer to her hiding place. Vittoria's eyes watered and she rubbed her nose, hoping to alleviate the urge to sneeze. The dawning light grew brighter and filtered through the crack between the armoire doors. The arrival of the morning gave her hope the ordeal would end soon without any harm to herself.

Vittoria heard Ugo laughing. She held still as a marble statue. She closed her eyes and prayed to God to deliver her.

Magda opened the bedchamber door of her hideout. The sudden opening and closing of the door stirred up the air. The potent aroma of lavender overcame Vittoria. Her reflexes weren't fast enough to suppress the loud barking of the sneeze she'd been trying to quell. It happened so fast.

The armoire doors flew open. The light blinded Vittoria. Then she was yanked out of the armoire and thrown to the floor. She landed hard on her back.

"Ugo!" Magda shouted. "Look what I found."

Ugo barreled down the hallway skidding to a halt in the doorway. "Where did you find her?"

"In there." Magda pointed at the armoire. "I would never have found her if she hadn't sneezed," she explained, shaking her head in disbelief.

"I *knew* somebody was here!"

"Oh, shut up! Make yourself useful and grab her."

Ugo's hulking, sweaty body strode toward Vittoria. He could have just restrained her arms behind her back. Instead, he wrapped his brawny arms around her and groped her breasts. Pressing himself against the back of her, he buried his pock-marked face into her neck and inhaled her scent.

Vittoria struggled against his grasp with all the power she could muster, but it was no use. Ugo's grip grew stronger the more she thrashed about. He moaned in her ear and pressed harder into her back. Vittoria's resistance encouraged his urgency.

"Ugo!" Magda shouted, trying to regain his attention. "We don't have time for this."

"Why not? You promised me treasure and I have it here," he argued, squeezing Vittoria's breast. "You know how I desire you, Magda. And you haven't fulfilled your promise."

"I know what I promised, but you must wait until we are away from here. If she's here, then who else may be?"

"He *will* be back," Vittoria told them, remembering tidbits of the conversation she overheard.

"I don't think so, my sweet," Ugo said.

"Didn't you hear what she said?" Magda hissed.

"It's true, I am a servant here. One of the last remaining."

"You lie!" Ugo shouted, calling her bluff.

"No, my master went into town. He'll return soon."

"Where does he keep the rest of his riches?" Magda demanded.

"I don't know."

"There's no time for games, at least not the kind *I* like to play," Ugo warned, inhaling once more of Vittoria's scent before pushing her down to the floor.

Ugo adjusted his crotch. He strolled over to Magda and grabbed at her breasts.

"You'd better give me what you promised, or I'll take it."

Magda glared at him.

Vittoria wanted to scratch out his bulging eyes. Hate for the vile man boiled within her. She needed to escape.

"I don't know where he keeps his riches. But I do know that he comes through the kitchen for refreshment when he returns home. You can ask him yourself. Afterward, you can kill him."

"You have an attractive imagination," Ugo praised, his pupils widening in excitement.

Though it disgusted Vittoria to suggest murder, she played along. "I can help you."

"You have no choice but to help us," Magda said, wagging her blade in Vittoria's face.

Bright morning rays now poured through the window.

"Quick, gather up *everything*," Magda ordered. "I'll wait here with the girl."

Ugo nodded and dashed toward the door, stopping to drink in the sight of Vittoria once more before disappearing down the hallway. Vittoria realized she feared death from plague less than suffering heinous acts of degradation at Ugo's hands.

Once Ugo was out of hearing range, Magda spoke.

"It is a pity that you happened to be here. You understand the problem I'm dealing with, don't you?"

Vittoria nodded. She understood completely.

Magda paced back and forth mumbling to herself. Vittoria dared not move from her position on the hard floor even to relieve the throbbing pain in her knees. Instead, she focused on her own escape.

"I know of something that will put Ugo to sleep for a *very* long time," she whispered.

"And what would that be?" Magda replied, her interest peaked.

"Well, there's nothing unusual about a small dose of belladonna to cure a headache or women's pains, but a large dose in a cup of ale would be enough to rid your problem," Vittoria explained.

Magda's eyes widened. "Are you sure that is all it would take?"

"I have a thorough knowledge of the plant and the precautions one must take to use it. So, I expect death would occur if we throw all precaution to the wind," she reasoned.

"But what if it doesn't work, and he only takes ill?" She squeezed Vittoria's chin with her long dirty fingers. "It must *kill* him."

Magda's intensity so alarmed Vittoria that she couldn't bring herself to meet her steely gaze.

"It will," she promised.

Ugo reappeared. His stout arms full of their spoils.

"Is the girl giving you trouble?" he asked. "I can rectify her behavior."

"All is well. The girl was explaining her plan, and she's *guaranteed* me it is flawless."

Vittoria shook her head in agreement. "It is, I swear it."

She was relieved Ugo was unable to touch her, but that didn't keep his eyes from roving over her body.

"Let's go," Magda ordered.

Vittoria stood up, her legs ached from kneeling on the hard floor.

"You go first, and if you try *anything* you'll feel this blade in your back," Magda warned, shoving Vittoria toward the door.

Vittoria led them down the main staircase into the large kitchen. It was hard to believe that just hours before she was enjoying the peace and quiet of the villa. But now it had turned into her nightmare. She had no idea if the man they spoke of would return.

She hoped for his sake that he did not. On the other hand, she wanted to live and feared her chances were slim if he didn't.

Ugo unloaded the loot near the larder and stood guard inside the kitchen entrance. Magda and Vittoria sat silently at the table, both lost in their own thoughts. Vittoria fiddled with a lock of her dirty hair. Magda clicked her jagged nails on the cold metal of her dagger.

Vittoria closed her eyes and listened as hard as she could. But all she heard was Ugo's ragged breath as he paced by the door, the clicking of nails, the skittering of a mouse in the pantry, and the maddening thumping of her own terrified heart.

Disheartened by her circumstances she pulled deeper inside herself and prayed, saying every prayer she knew. The familiar words soothed her frayed nerves and she got lost inside herself for an unknown amount of time. Not even Ugo or Magda bothered to interrupt her, for they were probably saying their own twisted prayers to manifest their despicable desires.

The peaceful rhythm of prayer in Vittoria's mind was interrupted by a steady, but faint clipped staccato sound. She strained to hear it at first, but then it burst to the forefront of her mind.

The steady tempo of the cadence quickened. An image of a beautiful white and black horse appeared in Vittoria's mind's eye. It raced along the lane toward the villa. The rider's identity was obscured. But the frantic pace of which he rode the horse indicated it would soon be made clear. Vittoria gasped aloud, shuddering back in the kitchen from her waking dream.

"What's the matter with you?" Magda jumped in surprise. She grabbed her dagger.

"I need some air," Vittoria stammered.

"Are you daft?" Magda exclaimed. "Don't think for one second that I'm letting you out of my sight."

"Look!" Vittoria said, pointing over her shoulder. "The kitchen garden is just outside that door where Ugo is standing. I can give you a signal when my master makes his way to the kitchen. Then you'll have him!" Vittoria explained, hoping she'd impressed logic enough for them to let her go.

"No!" Magda shouted at Vittoria, clenching the dagger tight in her hand.

Vittoria listened for the galloping of hooves again, but she didn't hear anything.

How could that be?

Her gut felt anxious and her body grew tense. She knew the man was coming, and fast.

"The hearth fire has not yet been prepared for today's cooking. I should have done that," Vittoria lamented, pretending she had shirked her duties as the only remaining servant at the villa.

Ugo grumbled under his breath. "Maybe we should let her get the fire going and pick a few greens. She knows she's not going anywhere without us. Besides, I could go for a meal myself. I'm famished," he said, rubbing his fat hand over his protruding belly.

"I'm hungry too, but this is *not* a good idea," Magda argued.

"He'll be here soon, I know it. If we work together we can get both tasks done quickly. You know how to build a cooking fire, don't you?" Vittoria asked Magda.

"Of course, I do, don't be stupid," she snapped.

"Good, because it takes me a while to get it going," Vittoria lied.

"Fine, I'll do it. But Ugo will have his eyes on you, *all over you*," she threatened. "Won't you, Ugo?"

"You don't have to ask twice," he growled, as he licked his cracked lips.

Ugo's eyes bore into Vittoria's back as she strolled through the kitchen garden. She picked lettuce and a variety of herbs, shoving them into the basket she carried. All the while she listened for the pounding of hooves on the road.

It was hard to hear over the cursing that was coming from the kitchen. Magda was having trouble getting the bellows to ignite the coals in the hearth. Vittoria whistled at Ugo, who had been drawn into the business of getting the fire started.

Vittoria walked circles around the kitchen garden, plucking a little of this and that until she heard it—the gallop of an approaching horse and rider. She froze in the warm sunlight. The dreaded moment was upon her. She trembled like an earthquake and dropped the basket spilling its contents over the ground.

"What's the matter?" Ugo shouted at her from the kitchen.

Vittoria didn't answer, her silence said it all.

"He's coming," Ugo warned Magda.

Magda pushed passed Ugo into the garden. "Where is he? I don't see him?" Her dark eyes searched in earnest around the enclosed garden.

Ugo ran out and joined Magda. "You can't see the road from back here."

"You lied to us!" Magda seethed, grabbing at Vittoria's throat with her filthy claws.

"No!" Vittoria exclaimed, dodging her attacker.

"That's hogwash! You knew we'd be at a disadvantage waiting in the kitchen," Magda shouted.

"You're a lying bitch!" cried Ugo.

He slapped Vittoria's face so hard she fell backward into a rosemary bush.

"I'm going to kill that little bitch!" Ugo swore to Magda.

"No, I'm going to do it after we save our own hides," Magda vowed, blocking Ugo from laying hands on Vittoria again. "He's coming."

Before Magda fled from the garden, she kicked Vittoria hard in the back of the thigh. Pain shot down to her toes. Struggling to her feet, Vittoria rose and brushed rosemary needles from her clothes. She had an opportunity to flee and she was going to take it.

First, Vittoria limped toward the kitchen. Then, she took the meat cleaver from the wooden chopping block. The wine bottle she sampled from the previous night was where she had left it. Gulping down several mouthfuls of the red liquid dulled the pain in her face and leg, boosted her courage, and steadied her nerves.

Vittoria trudged toward the steep terraced garden wall. She kept her head low and shimmied her way down the terracing onto the open area of the hill outside the garden enclosure. She couldn't determine where Magda and Ugo had gone. She peeked over the crest of the hill just enough to survey the villa grounds. She hadn't explored them upon her arrival because she was too engrossed in watching the splendid sunset.

Off to the north, she saw a stable large enough to house several horses. It was less than fifty yards away. The rider was moving at the same swift pace and she didn't have much time to get to the stable. If she kept low and crawled along the ground, she would miss her chance to meet him.

Vittoria's throat went dry and her palms sweat, but she heaved herself over the crest of the hill, wincing at the pain in her bruised leg. Gritting her teeth, she hobbled, shuffled, and limped as fast as she could toward the stable.

The rider neared. His horse was white with black markings, just as she had seen in her mind's eye. She pushed her aching body harder towards the stable.

Confusion and surprise appeared on the young man's face when he saw Vittoria. He pulled back hard on the reins. The horse skidded to an abrupt stop and whinnied in alarm. The rider started to dismount his horse.

"Don't stop! You'll be killed!" Vittoria exclaimed, pointing over his shoulder. Behind him ran Ugo and Magda.

With the quickest of reflexes, he centered himself back in the saddle and swung the horse around to charge his attackers. Vittoria saw that he was armed with a short sword. He drew it and kicked the horse into action. Ugo stopped short and brandished his shoddy dagger at the charging beast.

"Disarm yourself!" the gallant young man commanded Ugo. It was no surprise Ugo failed to obey. Instead, he hurtled himself at the horse and rider.

Magda hung back and let Ugo do the work she'd been dragging him around to do. She threw her hands up in the gesture of surrender. By the look of it, Vittoria guessed she was hoping Ugo would lose his head. Vittoria brandished the cleaver for Magda to see she was now armed.

Within moments, the young man clashed with Ugo. He swung his sword and brought it down hard. It swooshed through the air missing its target. Ugo dropped to the ground and with a chopping motion, slashed at the horse's powerful churning legs. Blood spurted over the courser's white underbelly and soiled the rider's breeches.

Ugo had severed the tendons of the horse's front right leg, and it crumpled underneath the weight of the still charging horse, sending the man flying like a rag doll. He hit the ground hard and rolled several times before coming to rest prostrate on the dirt lane. The sword landed out of reach leaving its owner without protection.

The tide had shifted, and Magda's bosom heaved with the excitement of it all. Ugo rolled his grizzled body up from the ground and stalked his prey. His greasy hair stood up in all directions and he panted, readying the bloody dagger to end the young man's life.

Even from several yards away, Vittoria could hear the man groaning in pain. He had curled up into a ball, hugging his left arm tight to his chest. She wrestled her impulse to flee but feared she would carry the guilt of his death forever if she left him to Ugo and Magda.

She decided to strike. Closing the gap between herself and Ugo, she focused on the exposed flesh of his sunburned neck. She hefted the cleaver and brought it down with all her might, jamming it into the vertebrae of his neck. Yanking it back out she struck again in the same place, exposing bloody meat and bone.

Ugo bellowed in agony. The howling morphed into a strangled gurgle as blood pooled in his throat. Ugo's limp body collapsed on top of his would-be prey. The rider squirmed, desperate to get free.

Vittoria kicked and pushed Ugo's dead weight off the young man. He scooted away from Vittoria. His face and clothing were smeared with blood. The black of his pupils overtook the blue of his eyes. His frightened gaze flickered back and forth from Vittoria's face to the bloody cleaver she still held in hand.

His valiant air had vanished, and his smooth bottom lip quivered. His youthful face twisted in fear. His peeked around Vittoria at the remaining danger to them both.

Remembering Magda was still there, Vittoria spun around and wielded the cleaver at her.

"Get out of here, or I'll do to you what I did to your insidious dog!" she hissed, kicking Ugo's limp leg to make her point.

"Don't think for a minute that you've seen the last of me, girl," Magda warned, flaunting her dagger in response. They were at a stalemate.

"Leave now!" Vittoria shouted. "I pray the plague finds you hiding deep in a filthy hole where you belong, you evil wench!"

Magda turned and dashed through the trees from which she first appeared. When she was out of sight Vittoria crumpled to the ground.

"Who are you?" the young man whispered, so soft she barely heard.

"I am Vittoria Giordano. I mean you no harm," she replied, throwing the cleaver away from her.

She was sickened by her actions. Ugo, as terrible as he was, lay dead by her hand. Her stomach twisted and heaved, and she vomited what little there was in her stomach. When she was through, all the feelings of despair, sadness, and loss she'd tried so hard to suppress rushed to the surface and overwhelmed her. She sobbed for her mother and father, for the life she took, and for her own life which she was a hair away from losing. Her mother's dying wish for her to leave Florence had become an ill-fated disaster with little more than a few misty memories of Nico and the twins to offer her comfort.

Vittoria's youth and innocence slipped away with every tear. She cried herself out on the ground beside Ugo's lifeless body. All that was pure and good in her life had been tainted by death. She was angry she'd become the object of such evil and malice. And perhaps, it wouldn't be the last time. Closing her eyes, she succumbed to the darkness and gloom.

Vittoria lingered in a state of purgatory where time had come to a standstill and all was silent. No light, no dreams. She felt but the calm beating of her own heart. The icy grip of fear that had choked her into unconsciousness on the dusty gravel path had released her.

Upon her cheek, she felt good, soft cloth. Nuzzling the cool material, she found that her whole body was enveloped in it. Nothing short of a miracle would have had to have occurred for her to have been moved to the comfort of a bed indoors.

She blinked open her eyes. Except for a single beeswax candle burning in the stand near the bed, she was in a darkened room. The door to the bedchamber stood ajar. Soft footsteps padded in her direction, then the shadow of a male figure filled the doorway and paused.

"I thought I heard you stir," the young man said, his voice soft.

He held a pewter candlestick in his right hand. His injured left arm was tucked against his side. The soft orange flame of the candlelight illuminated the blond highlights in his light brown hair. Long brows arched gently over deep-set blue eyes, and high cheekbones defined the contours of his face. His nose was straight and came to an attractive point. He wore a loose red linen shirt and cream-colored trousers with soft brown leather slippers. Vittoria noticed he hesitated to enter the room, so she motioned for him to approach.

"How did I get here?" she asked, pushing herself up to sit. She felt aches over every inch of her body.

"You were unconscious, and I couldn't wake you. I managed to carry you inside and set you to rest, though it was with great exertion," he explained, indicating that he did it without the full use of his injured arm.

"I am very grateful." She smiled then winced when pain shot through her cheek.

"You're in rough shape, Vittoria," he said, sitting down upon a three-legged stool by the bed. His brows knit together over concerned eyes. "Your face and leg are bruised, and your feet are blistered. And, I believe, you're suffering from exhaustion. You'll need to rest and regain your strength."

Her eyes felt hot and gritty from crying, her throat was parched, and her breath tasted of vomit. When she moved them under the smooth bed linens, her feet stung. Certainly, she looked like she'd climbed out of the gutter. She lay back down again.

"How is your arm?" she asked.

Though a grimace appeared on his face at the effort, he could flex his arm. It did not, after all, seem to be broken—sprained perhaps.

"Thank God! I thought you'd broken it," she replied.

He smiled, and the left corner of his mouth curled up to reveal shiny white teeth.

"What is your name?" Vittoria asked.

"Marcel Barberini," he replied, sitting up straighter on the stool as he presented himself. A lock of silky hair escaped from behind his ear and fell into his eyes. He tucked it back into its proper place.

"Are you the master of this villa?"

His shoulders stiffened, and he squirmed a little before replying.

"Yes, I am. Well, I mean, this is my father's property. He's in the Pope's service. He never cared for living here because it's too far away from Rome. So, I resided here with my mother on and off while attending university in Pisa."

Vittoria didn't push for further information about his living arrangements. It seemed to make him uncomfortable.

"What do you study?" she asked instead.

His face brightened at her interest in his studies. "Until the plague came, I was studying Law and Philosophy." His shoulders relaxed, and he talked about his curriculum.

"My father wants me to work for the Church," he explained, wrinkling his nose at the prospect. "But I have other plans," he declared.

"You do?"

Vittoria was surprised anyone would reject the promise of a secure job in the Holy Mother Church.

"Have you ever heard of Marco Polo?" he asked, his blue eyes widened and twinkled in the candlelight.

"He was Venetian merchant, was he not?"

"Yes, exactly!" he replied. "He traveled to the Orient and lived in the service of Kublai Khan for many years. He had wonderful adventures."

It dawned on her that she had seen a book in the library about Marco Polo.

"So, what does Marco Polo have to do with your plans?"

"Who knows when the university will reopen. Many professors and students have died. So, I'm going to take this opportunity to live what may be the last of my days on a great adventure in the New World," he explained.

"What of your mother?"

Vittoria watched him weigh his answer. They were beyond the pleasantries and the decorum of mere acquaintances. Several moments passed and, it seemed, Marcel arrived at the same conclusion. He sucked in a deep breath through his nose and blew it out before he answered her loaded question.

"My mother was my father's mistress."

All the light that had twinkled in his eyes dimmed and he hung his head in shame. He had probably never admitted this disgraceful secret aloud, although many must know the truth.

"Since his elevation to Cardinal, his presence dwindled. My mother became melancholic, hardly eating or speaking, and she kept herself locked up in her room until she was gone."

"Where did she go?" Vittoria asked, confused. Still fatigued, she settled back on the pillow again.

The muscles of his jaw tightened, the furrow in his brow reappeared, and his good hand clenched into a fist. "She died. My mother took her own life. My father wouldn't allow her to be buried on consecrated ground. So, I had to bury her in a pauper's cemetery."

Vittoria gasped.

"Within the month, he wants me to return to Rome to take up a post he's procured for me in the Church, but I won't do it. There is nothing holding me here any longer, so I'm leaving."

Marcel continued talking. Vittoria listened for a while, but her eyelids grew heavy. His secrets were safe with her. He must have known it as well. Eventually, she fell unconscious, finding herself again in that dark, still place.

The scent of sizzling meat roused Vittoria from the peace of her slumber. Her stomach growled and contracted with crippling force. Now that she was rested, she was ready to eat.

She untucked herself and found she was still wearing her own green dress. There were blood splatters on the bodice. Her hands, feet, and face had been washed and for that she was grateful. However, she desperately desired a bath.

Upon the stool beside the bed was a linen dress the color of amber, and a pair of soft suede slippers. She undressed and slipped into the new clothes, finding they fit well. The fine weave of the cloth would have pleased any Florentine wool merchant, including her father. Her hair was tangled. She jammed her fingers through her locks and smoothed them as best she could.

Descending the main staircase into the foyer she found, piled in a heap by the entry door, all the valuables Magda and Ugo attempted to steal. On top of the pile, was her oilcloth bag. Marcel must have collected all the treasure while she slept.

Vittoria made her way back to the kitchen, for the third time, and to her amazement, she found Marcel elbow deep in a heap of sticky bread dough. His hair and cheeks were dusted with flour. The tattered apron he wore did little to protect his clothing from the mess. He was in deep concentration and didn't notice her slip into the kitchen.

"What are you doing?" she asked, bursting into laughter.

He tossed his mucky hands into the air in exasperation. "I give up! Bread is much harder to make than it looks."

"Apparently," she agreed. She found the water pail in the corner. She dipped a rag it into the cool water and wrung it out. "Let me help you."

She picked her way through the doughy mess on the floor to stand in front of him. Marcel wasn't near as tall as Nico, nor was he as large, but he was still well built. His body was lean and muscled. His rolled-up shirt sleeves revealed toned forearms. The opening of his linen shirt hung away from his neck, exposing a soft down patch of light hair. His face had a couple of days of jaw-defining scruff. On closer inspection, she noticed he even had a slight dimple in his chin. The cleanup job started there.

"You've made quite a mess of yourself," she scolded in jest. "What made you decide to do this? Doesn't your arm still hurt?"

Vittoria wiped the flour from his chin, cheeks, and nose. He looked at her with his striking blue eyes, then shook his head.

"I've been resting my arm for three days. When I dismissed the help, I told them to take the bread with them. I didn't think I'd need any for guests."

"Forgive me, but did you say three days? Did I sleep for three days?"

"You were quite tired."

"I have been no help to you. You should have woken me." She stopped talking, realizing that there was nothing she could have done over the last three days but recuperate and regain her strength after what she had been through. Even so, she still felt guilty for leaving Marcel to fend for himself.

Vittoria felt responsible for bringing doom upon his house. If she were brave enough to stay out in the night, by herself, she could have avoided all contact with Magda and Ugo. Marcel would have come home to a burgled home, but he would not have been injured and his horse would be alive.

"I know you will tell me what happened here when you feel ready. I owe you my very life because without your protection I would have lost it. Please feel free to stay, if you would like. You don't have a pressing need to catch the plague anytime soon, do you?" he joked.

Words escaped her.

"I have been too forward. Where are my manners?" he stammered.

"No, your manners are beyond reproach," she replied, waving away his apology. "I would very much like to stay, but please allow me to pay for my lodging."

"Absolutely not!" he argued. "I won't hear of it. You are my guest."

When he raised his hands in protest the muscles in his chest beneath flexed. The sweet scent of sandalwood wafted into the air.

She nodded and handed him the limp rag to wipe off his hands. He took it and wiped at them before guiding her over to the bench at the trestle table. He set her upon it to warm in front of the fire.

"I think you need something to eat. That is why you came all the way down here, isn't it?"

Bacon sizzled in a pan. With his bare fingers, Marcel picked a few pieces out and tossed them onto a wooden trencher. He sucked the tips of his thumb and forefinger free of hot grease. Vittoria couldn't help but smile. She felt more at ease as she watched Marcel move about like a whirlwind collecting food and drink to make her comfortable. By the time he was done they had cheese, pickled fruits, nuts, hot meat, half-baked bread, water, and wine.

When Marcel plopped down on the bench, Vittoria complimented him on his efforts to pull a meal together. She meant every word of it. Being able to watch his agile body in motion, whirling around the kitchen for her benefit was quite the unexpected pleasure.

"The servants always made the cooking look easy. I watched them make bread many times, and I was certain I could do it too."

"It's a skill, but you made a valiant effort, Marcel," she acknowledged. She liked the way his name rolled over her tongue when she said it.

A boyish grin lit up his face.

Feeling obligated to explain how she came to be at the villa, Vittoria told him everything. To Marcel's credit, he listened attentively, as she described her exodus from Florence, her chance encounter with Nico and the twins, and her harrowing rescue by their hands. He didn't ask questions and appear to be half-interested when she replied, like many young men she knew. He nodded and commented on the stories she told him. There never seemed to be any uncomfortable lulls in the conversation, it was so easy to be with him.

Eventually, Marcel stood up and started clearing away the remainder of their breakfast from the table.

"I don't know about you, but I believe I overdid it," he explained, rubbing his flat abdomen. "Are you feeling up for a walk? It looks like another beautiful day."

Vittoria was content with the idea of staying on at the villa with Marcel. He intrigued her, to say the least. From what she had gleaned about his life, his family, and his aspirations, it was a wonder that he had any interest at all in allowing her to stay. Whatever the reasons, she was glad.

"I would love to," she said, agreeing to his proposal. Vittoria helped him store the leftovers. She felt awkward, not in an embarrassed, awful way, but in an unexplainable tension sort of way. She wanted him to stay very near to her.

Their speedy acclimation to each other was refreshing and exciting. There were no rules to their engagement, so she stepped out into the sunny garden with Marcel.

He took her hand and tucked it in the crook of his elbow, and he kept his own warm, dry hand wrapped over her own as they strolled around the terraced gardens she had admired when she first arrived.

"What made you decide to choose this villa as the one in which you would stop to rest?" he asked.

She pondered the question for a moment, trying to remember what was so appealing to her about its location.

"I suppose it was the beauty of the sunset that evening. I was struck by the wonderful colors in the sky over the villa. I felt drawn to approach and seek accommodation."

Marcel chuckled. "I know what you mean."

"You do?"

"Yes, of course. That's one of the reasons my mother loved it here so much. We would often dine in the garden to watch the last of the sun's light paint the sky," he explained, pointing to an open space in the garden.

"I imagine that was quite lovely, Marcel."

"I would love to show you sometime if that would be agreeable to you," he offered, not quite making eye contact.

"It is very agreeable," she answered.

"Would you like to see the rest of the property?" he asked. "If you are not quite up for it, we can save it for another day."

"No, I'm feeling fine."

Compared to being in the path of the plague or Ugo, it was the truth.

"Very well, then."

Marcel moved back toward the kitchen and on the garden wall—opposite from the side on which she initially entered—he pushed aside a thick bougainvillea revealing a hidden wooden door she didn't realize was there.

"I'll show you the stable and the poppy fields."

"I didn't notice any of those things when I arrived," she admitted.

"They have been hidden a safe distance from the road. We have hundreds of acres here."

"So, your father owns this end of the valley?"

"I suppose you could say that," he said, shrugging. "We even have a chapel and a little grotto just like the ones so prized by the Romans. I'll show you that too."

She was stunned.

How had his father amassed so much wealth?

Again, her feet felt cemented to the ground. Marcel tugged lightly on her hand.

"Vittoria, are you quite well? No, of course, you are not," he said, replying to his own question. "I'm sorry. It was stupid of me to assume you were ready for such exercise so soon after your ordeal."

All she could do was nod her head.

"Let me escort you back to your quarters so you can resume your rest."

"Perhaps we can go tomorrow?" she said, offering a tight smile.

"We'll see how you are feeling," he replied.

She remained silent while Marcel guided her back inside and up to her bedchamber. He settled her onto the bed and slid off her slippers. Her head felt heavy and the knot reappeared in her belly. She lay back on the down pillow and closed her eyes.

"I will bring you some wine," he said, brushing the stray hair out of her eyes.

"You don't need to attend me, Marcel."

A man of his wealth and stature did not need to wait upon a wool merchant's daughter.

"I want to," he replied, smiling at her. He slipped out the door and down to the kitchen to fetch her some refreshment.

Vittoria chastised herself. She couldn't spend the rest of her days hiding in bed, but for now, there was nothing more to do.

Ambient lute music lulled Vittoria from her slumber. It had been a long time since she had heard any music, and none so sweet as that which caressed her ears. She lay still with eyes closed, and for a long time to the complex tunes he plucked from the lute. They were melancholic then sprightly, heartbreaking then upbeat. It was like having a peek into Marcel's private mind and his entire life experience all at once. He perplexed her in that he seemed to have it all but would give it all up in the blink of an eye.

Vittoria rose and marched barefoot toward the sound of music. Marcel sat on a blue damask cushioned bench of oak. A matching wooden music stand in front of him. He strummed the lute, trying out a variety of different combinations of chords before deciding on a set that most pleased his ear. Then, he rested the lute on his knee while jotting notations onto the paper.

"Are you going to come in?" he said, without turning from his work. "Or are you going to stand there and watch me?"

She could tell a smirk was playing on his lips by the tone of his voice.

Vittoria entered the library and sat in the high-backed chair at the desk piled with books. "Well, if you insist."

"I am so glad you didn't make me beg," he replied, winking at her.

It made her squirm in her seat. He was attractive and desirable. Surely, he had a dozen young maidens in Pisa. Attempting to mask her interest in him, she examined the books before her.

"I'll be finished in just a moment," he said, pointing at the paper in the stand with his quill.

"You've been at practice for a while. Doesn't it make your arm ache?" she asked, gauging the rate of his recuperation.

"Quite honestly, I'd forgotten all about it until you mentioned it," he replied, stretching out his arm. "I forget a lot of things while involved in my music," he admitted.

She chuckled. "I know what you mean. When I study my herbals, I become absorbed in them."

"Really?" he asked. "I think women would make the best physicians. They are very insightful."

"That's what my father said," she admitted.

"Then he was an astute, forward-thinking, man."

"I would say so," she agreed.

"I am sure I would have liked him very much," Marcel stated, again meeting her eyes.

She blushed.

"I have portraits of my parents. Would you like to see them?" she offered, hoping for an opportunity to escape to recover her wits.

"Certainly," he said.

Vittoria trounced toward the main staircase to recover her bag from the pile of riches in the foyer and dashed back to the library. She slung the satchel up onto the desk and rummaged in it until her fingers felt the smooth yellow cloth in which she had wrapped the diptych. As she unwrapped it, she admired the craftsmanship of the flower and vine carved frame.

Marcel placed his lute on its stand. He stood, walked up behind Vittoria, and peeked over her shoulder.

"It's exquisite," he complimented.

"It is," she agreed, caressing the smooth dark wood. She opened the attached panels revealing the likenesses of her parents, and the breath caught in her throat seeing them both happy and healthy once more.

"These look to be painted by a master," Marcel marveled. "They are ten times better painted than most of the work in the villa even!" he admitted. "May I have a closer look?"

"Of course," she acquiesced, placing her most prized possession into his hands.

He examined the work by the late afternoon light streaming through the window. "You look like your father, but you have the eyes of your mother. They are a handsome couple. Most people who marry for love favor and complement each other to some degree.

She tilted her head to look again at their faces. She supposed there was truth in his theory.

Marcel continued. "Arranged marriages are easy to identify. It's usually a pretty young woman with an ugly old man."

Vittoria nodded in agreement. She'd noticed the same dynamic.

"Your parents were lucky," he acknowledged. "Few know what true love is."

"Have you ever known true love?" she asked, feeling her cheeks flush again.

He pondered her question for a moment before responding. "No, I haven't."

She had tensed with anticipation and was relieved by his answer.

"Then how do you know that my parents were in love?" she asked.

"Well, it's so rare, that it is hard not to miss," he said, his upper lip stiffened. "You're blessed to have had such loving parents," he said, a sadness came into his eyes.

She remembered what he had revealed to her the very first night they talked. His mother was a kept woman, as it were. There was no real love in her relationship with his father, only distance, and melancholy.

"I am sorry, Marcel," she said, caressing his tense upper arm, which relaxed under her touch.

"Never mind," he said. "It's not worth talking about anyway. Besides, when I am in the New World, it will be the last thing on my mind."

A far-off look glazed his eyes and he fell silent.

Vittoria's heart sank. She didn't know how to respond, so she tended to the business of returning the diptych to its cloth covering.

She would avoid all talk of love or relationships in the future. Her upbringing was very different from others and she had to be mindful of that. She was stopped by his warm hand on her shoulder when she took her leave. She turned back to face Marcel.

"Forgive me," he said. A slip of hair had fallen across his high forehead. "I did not mean to make you feel uncomfortable. Jealousy overcomes me sometimes. I've had to deal with it my entire life. It has nothing to do with you," he admitted, forcing a smile that didn't reach his eyes.

"Please, come over here," Marcel insisted, taking her hand in his and ushering her to sit on his bench. "Let me play you a song."

Vittoria's mood brightened. He picked up his lute and strummed it a few times, listening for any discordant sounds. Then he pushed aside a pile of expensive books from the edge of the desk, perching himself on the cleared space. He strummed the strings once more, letting the notes hang in the air.

Vittoria held her breath until he smiled at her, showing all his white teeth. He tucked hair behind his ear before beginning. She exhaled in hopes of steadying her pounding heart.

Marcel's sang a song of his own composition and his voice was exquisite. It was a story of a distant place filled with mystery, magic, and love. She could not say how long the performance lasted for she was enchanted by the tenor of his voice. Marcel strummed the strings as he crooned, the words painting a picture of paradise in her imagination of the mighty and savage King of the Mongols, Kublai Khan, a fierce warrior, and the master of a great harem full of beautiful dark-skinned beauties who smelled of jasmine and neroli and could make a man fall to his knees just by the seductive bat of a lash.

Marcel told of the great ceremonial halls in which Khan held court and a great many subjects and foreigners who paid him homage. He frightened her with lyrics of Khan's wicked temper and ruthless justice, and the men who served him for decades of their lives. He intrigued her with tales of the Silk Road, a long and arduous road through the lands of Arabia and China, where traders sold their exotic goods.

It was clear as day to see that Marcel was in love with the idea of the adventure. Vittoria felt a pang of jealousy all her own. She wanted his affections for herself.

As the days passed Vittoria settled into life at the villa. She took a proper bath and tended to her wounds. Her face was healing, as were her feet. The angry purple bruise on her thigh was fading, too. With her improved appearance, she found herself more comfortable in Marcel's presence.

He had even given her leave to wear any of the clothing and shoes she found in the wardrobes. One of her favorite garments was a dark blue velvet dress. It was fashionable, low cut at the neck, and accented with a golden cord around the waist. Vittoria made a point to wear it when Marcel determined she was well enough to tour the grounds of the estate.

Marcel waited for her in the foyer. His blue eyes beamed at her as she descended the stairs. "You are a vision, Vittoria," he gushed.

"Thank you," she replied, happy that she made such a strong impression. "I think this is your mother's dress."

"I thought I recognized it. It looks better on you," he decided.

She had taken the time the night before to wash her hair and brush the tangles out. That was a terrible chore to undertake, but she found a set of ivory combs to hold the hair away from her face and allow the remainder to flow down her back.

As she reached the bottom stair, Marcel stepped forward and grasped her hand, then twirled her in a circle to get a thorough look at her ensemble.

"I am very lucky to have such a radiant young lady to escort me today. The color of the dress enhances your eyes."

Moving her toward the heavy oak door holding her hand in his own. "Shall we?" he asked.

Stepping out into the September morning, Vittoria inhaled a breath of fresh air for the first time in nearly a week. Marcel had kept very close watch over her, insisting she continue to rest and build up her strength. At last, she persuaded him she was ready to leave the confines of the villa.

They strolled down the long drive leading up to the villa from the Strada Chiantianga. Cedar trees loomed over them and cast soft westward shadows along their path. A dirt path led off the main lane.

Marcel tucked her right hand into the crook of his left elbow, drawing her closer. Vittoria leaned into him for support while they made their way down the dusty path.

A vast field of red poppies appeared before them. It went on for acres. They stood in silence observing the flowers sway in unison. Then Marcel told her about how, as a child, he used to run and play in the poppy field with the servants' children.

He picked a few poppies and placed them in Vittoria's hair. She held very still as his hands worked the stems through her tresses and tried not to stare at his handsome face, even though it was just inches from her own. She breathed in his sultry sandalwood scent.

"Perfect!" Marcel exclaimed, stepping back to admire his handiwork.

Vittoria reached a hand up to feel the flowers on her head.

"No. Don't touch. You will ruin my masterpiece," he jested. "You look quite like a living goddess," he added.

Color flushed Vittoria's face and neck. "I doubt that," she scoffed. "Thank you, nonetheless."

"My pleasure," he said, again reclaiming her hand. They continued their walk. She was content with the handsome young man escorting her through his countryside acreage.

They arrived at the stable. A natural spring ran behind it and served as the main water source for the animals that resided within.

The smell of hay and manure permeated Vittoria's nostrils, but it wasn't altogether off-putting. It quite reminded her of the odor in the street back home, and that was a somewhat comforting memory. It smelled of life, not death.

Something rustled in the back of the stable and Vittoria followed the sound to find a young white horse.

"This is Bellance, the offspring of my horse Lunetta," he explained.

"Oh," she said, looking around for the other horse she knew she would not find there.

"Lunetta died, as you know," he said. "She could never have survived her injuries. The vultures came for her while you were recuperating."

Tears pricked Vittoria's eyes. "I am very sorry, Marcel."

"As am I, but that brute got what he deserved. You made sure of that," he acknowledged, squeezing her hand, and gazing at her with admiration.

She caressed the pony. Bellance nuzzled her hand with her muzzle. Marcel stroked her snowy mane and patted her shoulder.

"Have you ever ridden a horse?" he asked.

"No."

"Bellance is the perfect size on which to learn, and she is ready to stretch her legs."

Bellance whinnied in agreement. She was overdue for exercise. Marcel sauntered over to where the tack was stored, grabbed a saddle, and fit it to the horse.

"Up you go," Marcel commanded of Vittoria, bending low with hands laced together for her to mount Bellance. She hitched her dress up to swing her leg up and over. She settled into the saddle without falling off the other side. Marcel walked Bellance outside into the tall grass.

"Relax," Marcel said. Vittoria thought he spoke to the horse. Until he put his hand on top of hers. "You're holding on for dear life," he chuckled. "Relax. Bellance can sense your tenseness. Trust her and she will trust you."

Vittoria made a conscious effort to loosen her grip on the reins, relax her legs, and sway with the horse's motion.

"That's it, you've got it now," Marcel said, with an approving smile. "See! Bellance is relaxing too. Now hold the reins taut, but not too tight, and talk to her. Tell her what you want her to do."

"Hup!" Vittoria commanded because it was always something she heard men shout to their steeds. Bellance kicked into a swift canter, and it jolted Vittoria in her seat. Marcel ran beside them for a while until he felt certain Vittoria had control, then fell back, and shouted out commands and instructions for her to give the horse.

Soon Bellance was galloping zigzag through the field, and Vittoria was smiling and enjoying the feeling of her poppy-adorned hair billowing in the breeze behind her. She laughed aloud for the first time in what seemed a lifetime. The freedom of riding was exhilarating. Vittoria felt alive.

Marcel stopped calling commands after a while and lounged in the grass. Vittoria let the horse gallop around the field to work out her pent-up energy. The entire time she felt Marcel's eyes following her. Eventually, she guided the pony back toward the stable. As they approached, Marcel stood and brushed the grass and dirt from his breeches.

"You're a natural, Vittoria," he proclaimed. "Are you quite sure you haven't ridden before?" he asked, cocking his smooth eyebrow.

"I swear it," she said, handing him the reins to guide Bellance back into the stable.

"I think you have made a friend for life," he said, patting the horse's neck.

"I believe you are right. We'll have to do this again tomorrow."

"If you'd like," he agreed. The dimple in his chin appeared.

His smile set her heart aflutter and tied her stomach in knots. A prickle of sweat appeared on her brow and her hands became clammy.

Marcel directed her to swing one leg over so they both dangled over on his side of the horse. He reached up and lifted Vittoria down by the waist. She stood in from of him and did not make any move to widen the space between them, nor did he. His firm hands remained in place on her body, and she could feel his thumb stroke the velvet of her dress. They gazed at each other. As far as she knew they were the last two people on the earth and, if that were the case, she would be glad of it.

She laid her head on his shoulder. Marcel's scent encouraged her to press further into him. Sliding his arms up along her back, he wrapped them around her and ran his fingers over her hair. She stroked the small of his back enjoying the connection.

Marcel broke the silence. "You miss your parents, don't you?"

Vittoria nodded acknowledging the statement, but it was not the reason she had enveloped herself in Marcel's arms. She was smitten.

"I know it is hard, but I am here for you," he explained, lifting her chin with his forefinger, forcing her to look him in the eyes. "Anything you need, you let me know."

"I will," she whispered, hanging her head before her own eyes gave everything away. The horse was getting restless, and reluctantly Vittoria pulled away.

Marcel whispered some sweet words to coax Bellance back into her stall. Vittoria leaned against the stable wall, picking at invisible lint on her sleeve, waiting for Marcel to rejoin her.

Marcel jogged up and put his arm around her shoulders. "Come on, let's head back. I'm hungry," he said, a lopsided grin on his face.

"I'll race you?" he said, more a question than a challenge.

Vittoria kicked off her shoes, scooped them up, and shot out of the stable shouting behind her. "Catch me if you can!"

Hitching up her dress above the knee with her free hand, she ran as fast as she could with her still sore leg. She squealed with delight at the silliness of it all.

Marcel roared with laughter behind her as he closed the distance between them. Vittoria pressed harder toward the villa, pushing her feet hard into the dirt, trying to get the most distance out of every stride. She was fast, but Marcel was faster. About twenty yards from the villa he overtook her, laughing as he passed by.

Vittoria huffed and puffed as she stumbled over the invisible finish line after him. Dropping her shoes, she fell onto a patch of grass to catch her breath. Marcel jogged back and forth in front of her with his arms raised in the air.

"I'm the champion!" he shouted.

"I'll beat you next time," she promised.

"I don't know. It's a shallow victory to beat a cheater. I won't race again unless it's fair."

She frowned at him.

"I'm joking," he said, helping her to her feet.

The sun had risen higher and hotter in the sky and, after the race, Vittoria was boiling in her dress. She was desperate to change into something lighter.

"Come on, let's go inside," he said, leading her by the hand toward the big oak door. Vittoria followed. Even though she lost the race she felt like she had won his affections, a prize even more valuable.

Days became weeks, and Vittoria's dominant thoughts were of Marcel—the confident way he walked, the flirtatious way he smiled, his boisterous laugh, the tender way he held her hand, the mischievous glint in his deep blue eyes, the animated manner he told stories, and the way he held her gaze as they conversed.

One rainy evening, Vittoria found her way to the library by candlelight. She slid into the desk chair and read the *Travels of Marco Polo*. From what she gathered, Marco Polo, who was a member of a prominent merchant family, traveled deep into the Orient, met, and became a favorite of Kublai Khan who ruled a place called Mongolia for close to twenty years. Before Polo's return to Venice, he also visited a place called Persia. The entire journey took twenty-four years!

A cold unsettling feeling froze her gut. What if Marcel went away and she never saw him again? Her fingers trembled. It was difficult to keep hold of Marcel's most prized possession. She dropped the book into her lap.

Though they had known each other for a short while, she was not only attracted to Marcel but cared for him deeply. He was a kind and interesting person and had all the traits she could have wished for in a husband. With all the pestilence had taken from her, it chilled her to think he might disappear as well. Perhaps she could go to the New World with him.

To shake her now somber mood, she tidied papers and books on the desk. In so doing, she rediscovered the Book of Hours. Marcel must have found and returned it to the library. The light from the candle set the sapphires and rubies alight and they sparkled on the leather-bound tome. She cradled it in the crook of her arm and opened it to have another look at the beautiful works inside.

"It is a thing of beauty," Marcel whispered from the doorway.

Startled by his presence, she stood and slammed the book shut. "I'm sorry. I shouldn't have."

"Never mind," he replied, strolling into the library to stand by her side. "May I?" he asked, reaching out for the book.

He thumbed his fingers over the vellum pages and turned to the frontispiece of the manuscript. It was the image of Pope Urban VIII. He was seated in a regal pose. Around his shoulders was draped an elbow-length red velvet mozetta trimmed with ermine. His fingers were decorated with precious jewels. There was an inscription on the image.

For a most loyal and trusted Cardinal of the Holy See on his confirmation of the irreproachable title and responsibility to God the Father as High Inquisitor.

May you do justice in His name,
Urban VIII

Vittoria's jaw dropped open in disbelief.

"This was a gift from His Eminence, the Pope. It should be kept in a place of honor, a safe place."

Marcel shrugged.

"No one realizes its value except for you and me. My father had no use for it, so he gave it to my mother."

"How could he not find a use for this?"

"Imagine the wealth you would have to have at your disposal to not find this manuscript of much value?"

"My goodness," she whispered. "Your father keeps some very important company."

"I guess he does," he replied, disinterested in continuing the conversation. "Would you like to keep it?" he asked.

"Absolutely not. It is yours."

"And it's mine to give to whom I wish, and that is you, Vittoria."

She balked.

"Oh, come now, Vittoria. It's just a book," he explained. "Besides I have something much more valuable than that."

"You do?"

"Vittoria," he said, placing both hands upon her shoulders. "Do you think this, of all things, has more appeal and value than the beautiful young woman I have standing in front of me?"

Did he feel the same as her?

"I have wanted to do this since the day you found me making a mess of the kitchen."

Taking her face in his hands he leaned in and placed a tender kiss on her lips.

She had always worried that this moment would be awkward and messy, yet it came quite naturally. By following Marcel's lead, she opened her mouth wider to give way for his tongue to meet hers. The sensation of their connection set her skin aflame. Her heart pounded with excitement.

Marcel raked his fingers through her hair. Vittoria's hands explored his muscled chest and shoulders. He pulled her even tighter to him to deliver kisses down the length of her neck. If he hadn't been holding her, she could have floated straight up to Heaven. He was magical.

Judging by Marcel's urgency, he was willing to go further. She pulled away and lifted his face, considering his smoldering eyes.

"We have plenty of time," she whispered shyly.

"You're right," he chuckled, taking a deep breath. "My attraction to you has taken me by surprise. I haven't been this happy in a very long time, Vittoria."

"I am happy too," she admitted, pulling herself together. This moment with Marcel was better even than she could have imagined because it was real.

He hugged her, and she nestled her head on his chest. He kissed her on the nose and forehead. He sat down in the desk chair and positioned her to lounge across his lap. With fingers entwined, they shared intermittent kisses until the candles burned down and they were forced to abandon the comfortable nearness of each other to attend to the mundane need of feeding themselves.

The fires of passion threatened to incinerate Vittoria from within whenever Marcel was near. His presence both comforted and aroused her, and she found any reason she could to be close to him. He never seemed to mind.

"I was thinking of bringing my lute out to the garden. Would you like to join me?" Marcel asked when he found her out grooming Bellance.

"That would be wonderful. I'll finish with Bellance."

"All right."

Marcel marched back up the path to the villa.

"I'm sorry, Bellance. We'll have to cut our time short today."

She gave the pony a good scratch behind the ear and her mane a few more quick brushes before following Marcel.

Excitement welled up inside her and she had to remind herself not to skip like a child. Marcel, she realized, tried to give her space and time to herself as a courtesy. But she waited all day, every day, for him to ask for her company. She still felt nervous asking for his. She didn't want to appear needy or give him any reason to believe she had worn out her welcome.

Vittoria forced herself to walk at a normal pace to the bougainvillea covered entrance of the garden. She rinsed her hands at the well before heading inside to put together their snack.

With basket in hand, she gathered a bottle of Chianti and two cups, a large chunk of cheese, sliced prosciutto, and a few handfuls of almonds.

Marcel sat upon a sprawling old tapestry in the grass. He played a charming melody she had never heard before. It so captivated her, she misjudged her step on the terrace and tripped. Their snack went flying out onto the ground. Vittoria scrambled around picking morsels of food off the rug and surrounding grass. She was mortified. Marcel laughed and tugged her down to a clean spot on the tapestry.

"I don't care a fig for this old thing. It's you I care about," he said, pulling her close. He stroked her cheek with his finger. "And you could never do anything so unattractive that I wouldn't still find you utterly ravishing."

Blood pumped loud in Vittoria's ears. She leaned in to kiss him. Gentle at first, then wrapping her arms around his neck, passionately. He responded in kind pulling her tighter. She straddled him, his body closer than ever before. Marcel's lips traced her own, and she felt his warm touch through her linen dress, and she yearned for them to be on her skin. Marcel moaned in agreement as her own hands were raking through his silken locks.

Marcel's strong musician's hands explored the curves of her body and made their way underneath her dress. The sensation of his fingertips on her legs and thighs sent her into a frenzy. If her mouth could have pressed any harder upon his she would have swallowed him up. He pulled his lips away to pay attention to her neck and bosom. Every inch of her skin was singing for him. He played her body like his lute, with passionate love.

The pleasure Marcel gave Vittoria was beyond expectation. Now she understood all the fuss. They laid naked on the grass. She allowed her fingers to wander over his body, exploring every little crease, scar, and freckle. She would marry him. He just need ask.

Vittoria lost herself in a daydream about Marcel while wandering once again to the kitchen. She was brought out of her reverie when she found Marcel leaning against the heavy wooden table bracing himself with one arm, his head bowed as if in pain.

"Marcel, what's the matter?" she asked, rushing to him.

Caught off guard, he stood straight again, brushing at his face before answering.

"Nothing."

"Are you unwell?"

"No, I just," he paused. "I just needed a moment," he said, rubbing again at his eyes with his fingertips. They glistened with wetness when he pulled them away.

"Do you need to lie down?" Vittoria asked.

She had never seen Marcel upset and wasn't sure what to do for him. She tried to hug him, but he pulled away. He darted outside. She followed but he was already across the garden. There was no way she was going to be able to question him now. It would have to wait until later. She was left with an odd worried feeling inside.

Marcel slipped away during the night. He left behind a letter which Vittoria held in her hand. It and the rumpled sheets were the only signs he had ever been there at all, for he'd taken his belongings. She read the words on the page a dozen times and yet, she could find no satisfactory explanation for his hasty departure.

Dearest Vittoria,

Please forgive me. I haven't the heart to bid you farewell in person nor bear to see your face when you read these words. I cannot stay. My father is a very powerful man and he is a threat to you and all that we could build together. For your safety, I must go. Please try and forget me. I will keep your love locked in my heart forever.

In disgrace,
Marcel

"No! This cannot be!" Vittoria howled.

She stormed naked about the room. Her body still remembering the love they shared that very night.

It was like he knew it was the last time.

Tears spilled down her cheeks. Everyone she loved had left her. The fire in the hearth burned low. She tossed Marcel's letter onto the embers. The flames leaped up at her ice-cold body. All feeling drained from her fingers and toes, her heart dropped deep into her gut, and her knees buckled. Vittoria fell to the cold tile floor and wept.

The villa was eerie quiet like a tomb and Vittoria was sealed inside. She had nothing left to do but to waste away for eternity.

The days blurred together but it felt to Vittoria like one perpetual night. She never felt hungry, but her thirst was insatiable. She uncorked bottle after bottle of wine and poured herself cup after cup until she either passed out or got sick.

She couldn't stop thinking about how she came all this way to be left with even less than she started with. She had even killed a man. Her heart didn't ache anymore because it was dead.

Nico had it right all along. I knew nothing of pain.

Nico's face appeared in her mind's eye, so different from Marcel's. He was so real and raw. He didn't hide who he was. That put a lot of people on edge, but underneath all that he was tender and caring, or so it seemed.

Marcel seduced her.

No. I allowed myself to be seduced.

Vittoria stared into the flames of the fire and hovered between sleep and awareness. Images of Marcel, Mama, Papa, Nico, the twins, the plague doctor, the countryside, the villa turned over and over in her mind. None of the images ever crystallized before another appeared in its place. Everything was gone. There was no point to any of it. She drank until blackness set in.

CHAPTER 7

Autumn 1630

It had been two days since Marcel left Vittoria sleeping alone in the bed they shared together. Like a thief in the night, he absconded with the dreams and aspirations for their future. He tried not to think about her reaction to finding his letter explaining his sudden disappearance. It was too harsh to bear. He had caused the woman he loved pain and he felt sick about it, but he was desperate to put a vast ocean between him and his father.

When Marcel arrived in Livorno he paid a wiry young boy to tend to Bellance, so he could seek out the ship's captain. The *Ave Maria* was a stout little boat heading to Lisbon. It was moored in the harbor being loaded up with trade goods. He carried very little with him, a small trunk of clothes and his savings. He dressed in plain clothes to blend in with the other passengers.

However, Marcel stood out from the swarthy Italians down at the dock. He favored his mother with his fair French complexion and coloring. His light brown hair was swept back revealing a fine composed face, cleft chin, and light blue eyes. He was slimmer and leaner of build than most, holding steady and strong in his above average frame. Women and men noticed him alike, and it didn't take long for the Cardinal's men to identify the Barberini bastard the minute he stepped foot on the dock.

Marcel was approached and surrounded by a gang of men whom he suspected were also passengers aboard the same vessel. The moment they flashed their weapons, he knew he was mistaken. He should have known that his dastardly father would track him down when he didn't return to the papal offices within four weeks, as expected.

One of the men dug around the inside of his cloak and pulled from it a folded letter marked with the red seal of the High Inquisitor, Cardinal Antonio Marcello Barberini. Marcel's heart felt like it fell into his guts. He knew exactly what the letter would say, he didn't even have to open it. Sliding his thumb under the paper, he popped the elaborate seal holding the letter closed. He unfolded the paper, revealing the frenetic handwriting of a domineering man.

In short order, the letter instructed Marcel to desist from carrying out his trifling escape and travel with the men, of his own free will or under duress if necessary, to Civitavecchia to enter the service of the Church as planned. The Cardinal made it clear to his bastard that there was no other option to be considered in the matter. Period.

Marcel let out a defeated breath. He folded the letter and placed it in his cloak pocket. "So, gentleman," he said. "I suppose we're heading to Rome."

"We hoped you would suggest that," the letter deliverer responded. "My men will handle your baggage and horse from here."

Marcel pointed at the boy patting and talking to his white horse. "Bellance, my horse, is over there. My luggage is on the dock to be loaded."

"We'll inform the captain that you've changed your plans. We've secured another vessel to sail to Civitavecchia. We'll travel overland from there to Rome. The journey should take about three days."

"Right, then," Marcel said. There was nothing more he could offer.

Celestina sat alone and still in her deerskin tent. Only she had permission to use the hide of Diana's sacred stags for her dwelling. Though the material kept the tent warm and comfortable, her aging body was cold.

She had grown tired and sadness saturated her soul. The yoke of responsibility as Benetrix, the anointed mother luminary of the Benedanti Strega, had its trials and challenges. At fifty-eight years of age, the time was nearing to return to the Lady of Light's side.

With no heir, the mystery wisdom of the Benetrix, bestowed by the Queen of Strega, would die with her. As Benetrix, succession passed from mothers to daughters, not through the line of sons.

In over a thousand years, a direct descendant, of either the Benetrix or Malatrix, had never abandoned their clan. Yet, her own daughter, Orabella, did so for the love of an ordinary. She gave up everything to live as a merchant's wife. Orabella's defection had weakened the strength of the Benedanti, and their efforts to uphold the balance of light and shadow.

The best hope for Benedanti survival was her granddaughter, and she had no idea of the powerful light she was destined to wield. For those who abandoned their people were forbidden to speak of the clan or use magic for any reason, ever. By law, Orabella could never have taught her daughter of her rich heritage and rights as a Strega.

Vittoria would not know how to harness the power of the elements and the moon, to communicate with the kingdom of animals, or even how to propel her zee through the ethers.

Celestina feared the extinction of the Benedanti. But if Vittoria didn't lay her claim as the Benetrix by her twentieth birthday, which was less than four months hence in February, a great shadow would forever poison the lives of the people of Italy and beyond.

She had witnessed many miracles in her life, but the most miraculous of all would need to manifest for the Benedanti, Bringers of Light, to continue serving humanity. She still could see no clear path for that to happen. So, she brought her heavy heart to the goddess Diana, as she had so many times before, to petition for guidance and a way to save her people.

Magda needed money and a place to hide out for a while. As she lay awake one evening, on the ground in an abandoned barn, she remembered a fellow prostitute once told her of a busy brothel on the west side of Florence run by three sisters. She was practiced in the business of whoredom. It was all she knew.

For years, she tried to leave that life thinking there had to be something better, but maybe there wasn't. When the plague ravaged her town, she took a chance at changing her fortune. Perhaps her lot in life was to use her body for personal gain. That was better than roaming around the countryside with a madman.

Thank God, that girl took care of Ugo, she thought.

Magda arrived in Florence in the morning. The few gravediggers were already busy in the field. No one in their right mind would enter a plague-ridden city, but Magda found it was no better in the country than in the city. Either way, she had to play her hand. The Porta Romana had been left open and Magda slipped through unnoticed.

Magda washed upstream in the river Arno and used what little coin she had to buy a secondhand dress. She tidied her haggard appearance, as best she could, and asked directions to the Tre Sorella Taverna. She made her way to an old two-story brick building built into the western wall of the city. A painted wooden sign of a huntress shooting three arrows at a stag hung above the entrance.

Magda pushed open the door and smelled the familiar scent of sweat and blood in the dark open room. A couple of drunkards slept in chairs and one on the floor. There was no one else there.

"Hello!" Magda called out and waited.

Then, on the landing above, appeared a fierce beauty. She looked down her nose upon Magda. She was clothed in the finest red cloth and was very clean. Even though she had on a new dress, Magda felt like she should have kept on the rags she was wearing. The woman's steely gaze seemed to burn her skin and drill into her heart, seeking out her purpose for appearing. Magda started to think she had made a terrible mistake.

"Are you lost?" the woman asked, her manner haughty.

"I am looking for work."

"Only courtesans of the highest caliber work here. You do not appear to be that."

Magda hadn't come all this way to be turned away.

"I was told that you seek loyalty and information. I can give you both."

The woman's dark brows shot up. "And where did you hear that?"

"From one of the girls at the brothel in San Gimignano."

"Is that so?"

"Is that what you seek?" Magda queried back. "I excel in providing pleasures of the flesh and I have a talent for procuring information."

"You're too old. Men desire the company of young ladies."

"I'm just a little tired from the long journey. I clean up very well," Magda insisted, sweeping her hands over flyaway tendrils. "I'm not asking for anything grand, work and a place to sleep. I'll do whatever you ask. Please."

"Ulyssa! Medea! Come," the woman ordered, without breaking eye contact with Magda. Two younger women appeared at the balustrade, one with shoulder-length black hair and green eyes, the other with blue eyes and amber curls.

"Who is she, Nerezza?" one asked.

"I can find out," the other offered.

"Yes, Medea, why don't you," Nerezza said.

The amber-haired girl placed her hands on her temples and gazed hard at Magda. There was a bone-crushing sensation and Magda clutched her head. Memories of her entire life flashed before her eyes before slowing to when she met Ugo and schemed and plotted with him to steal and get rich. Visions of Vittoria and the man on the horse moved through her mind and then Ugo's death. Then, the focus of a memory sharpened on something Vittoria was wearing around her neck, a silver charm of some sort. The vision was held in her mind's eye even though she tried to change it.

"She's seen the Benedanti!" the Medea exclaimed, her eyes gleaming. "The girl was in the countryside. She wore the Cimaruta around her neck, and even killed a man!"

"Perhaps she could be of use to us, though she's not much to look at," Ulyssa said.

Nerezza's eyes grew wider with excitement. "Perhaps we can find a different kind of work for our new friend. She's new and nobody knows her. We know the Benedanti will come. Tell me your name," Nerezza demanded.

"Magda."

"Magda can be the eyes and ears on the street for us."

Ulyssa and Medea nodded in agreement. Magda nodded, too.

"Anything you wish, I'll do it."

"Oh yes, I know you will," Nerezza said.

One of her sisters giggled. The other sniveled.

"Darlings, have the girls clean Magda up. Give her some proper clothes and shoes to wear. We have a reputation to uphold here at Tre Sorella Taverna."

Magda curtsied clumsily and thanked Nerezza.

"Silence!" Nerezza commanded. "Don't think for one moment that we will forgive disloyalty. You have seen what power Medea wields, and I don't think you want to find out what the rest of us can do."

Magda nodded.

"Very well. Lucky for you we have a free bedchamber, the last tenant discovered my powers, and now she's gone. Poof!" Nerezza flicked her fingers up in the air to exaggerate the expression.

"First, remove that hideous dress and throw it in the fire," Ulyssa demanded. "Then you may come up and get cleaned and settled," she said, pointing to the bottom of a hidden staircase.

Magda stripped off her garments and stood naked in the center of the cold room. She trembled with fear. These sisters held great power over her, but if she served them well perhaps she would be given power as well, and that excited her.

She dashed over to the roaring fire, chucked the dress into the flames, and climbed the stairs to her new life in service to the three sisters.

Angelo stayed with Nico throughout his illness. Nico had a high fever which caused him to sweat profusely, then suffer bouts of teeth-chattering chills. His nose bled, and he vomited what little he had in his stomach.

There was a strange period, at the beginning of the illness, when Nico's body went dead still, his breathing slowed, his pulse dropped, and he and Paolo thought he might have died. A spooky feeling filled the small quarters as if something was there watching them, but they could not see it. It fell quiet for about fifteen minutes. Then Nico took a huge gasp of breath as if he hadn't breathed in days and coughed until he passed out again where he remained unconscious for a week.

By God's good grace, Nico regained consciousness, but he was very weak and remained in bed for three more weeks. Angelo fed him broth, and little bits of bread, to soothe his stomach and build his strength. It was no less than a miracle that Nico still lived.

Emilio sat slumped in a chair in the dark. The dimming fire cast light upon the mantle clock. Three o'clock in the morning and still he could not sleep. For weeks on end, insomnia tortured him. His brown eyes were bloodshot and burned at the touch. His body was sore and tense, unable to find comfort and peace in his goose down bed. Whenever he dared close his eyes visions of monsters, beasts, and ghouls attacked from all angles. Never in his life had he experienced such night terrors. They were petrifying. So real.

The last time his eyes closed he found himself outside the city walls by the plague burial grounds at dusk. The ground rumbled and moved, and all the dead arose from their graves, skin hanging from faces, eyeballs dangling from sockets, sores oozing foul liquid, and he couldn't run away. His feet were lashed to the ground. The dead converged on him, eager to eat him alive. He woke up screaming, so scared he almost threw up. His heart raced, cold, clammy sweat iced his brow, and he couldn't breathe. He heard a woman laughing. Stumbling out of bed he paced round and round the room until he could calm himself to some small degree.

Emilio was unnerved. That dream happened days ago, and he hadn't slept since. Hallucinations were occurring during his waking hours and he was irritable. Every sound was louder, smell stronger, light brighter. His senses were overwhelmed. He couldn't concentrate on anything, which led to further frustration.

He thought often of the Tre Sorella Taverna and Nerezza. Her angular features, full bosom pressing into him, her mouth and tongue on his neck, and then the strange laughing would fill his ears. Shaking his head to clear the eerie sound, he sank deeper into the chair.

I must be going mad.

The thought made him even angrier at Nico, who should have died after contracting plague. But he still lived. What's more, his own brother risked his life to care for him. Angelo told him that Paolo said his recovery was nothing but miraculous.

Emilio believed he'd be free of Nico, but now he had succumbed to his own mind-numbing illness.

"That bastard always gets what he wants. Damn him!"

The anger he harbored toward Nico tightened his chest and throbbed at his temples. He got up and threw on the same clothes he'd worn the last several days and made his way through his family home. He stepped out into the cool autumn night. A compelling urge sent him walking in the direction of the Tre Sorella Taverna.

Emilio arrived at his destination and found the entry door ajar. He paused, listening before entering. It was oddly quiet. Pushing open the heavy door he tip-toed inside. Alone in the middle of the cavernous room stood Nerezza, considering the firelight. She was as stunning as the last time he had seen her. A scarlet gown adorned her statuesque body. The low bodice highlighted her breasts. Nerezza said nothing as he appraised her, though a sly smirk raised the corner of her mouth.

While entranced by Nerezza's beauty, Medea and Ulyssa appeared beside him. Medea upon the left and Ulyssa on the right. Slipping their arms through his, they escorted him forward to their elder sister, Emil-io still in the daze they perpetuated. The closer they moved to Nerezza the more dangerous she appeared to Emilio. So appealing and terrifying at once, yet she captivated him. Her green eyes beckoned him closer and her neroli perfume intoxicated him. He moaned aloud.

"You are exquisite," he said, bewildered by her beauty.

Nerezza stepped forward. Reaching out her fore-finger she caressed his lower lip. Emilio panted. He closed his eyes, his skin tingled. She drew her fingers down the length of his neck along his nearly healed knife injury. She kissed him on the mouth. He reeled from the taste of her.

"I need your help. Will you help me with something very important, Emilio?" she asked.

Emilio blinked himself back from the brink of ecstasy. "Help?"

"I need you to help me destroy the evil that brought plague to Florence."

"Evil?"

It seemed he was incapable of speaking in multisyllable sentences.

"You can help me to find these people."

Nerezza nodded once at Medea.

Medea turned and projected into Emilio's head the images she'd seen in Magda's mind of the girl wearing the Cimaruta.

"This girl is Strega, a very dangerous witch. The charm she wears about her neck is a tell-tale symbol of her intention to harm and murder. She must be found, as well as those with whom she collaborates."

Emilio recognized Vittoria. He could not believe what he was seeing in his mind's eye. His body recoiled when he saw Vittoria jam a meat cleaver into a man's neck. His knees buckled beneath him.

"This cannot be," he murmured. "I know that girl. There must be some mistake," he explained, his face pained from the sight of sweet Vittoria killing a man.

"There is no mistake. The girl must be found and put on trial for her crime," Nerezza stated, her voice clear and strong. "You will locate her."

Emilio shook his head again in disbelief. The vision was so real. It must have happened.

Ulyssa giggled again and Emilio recognized the familiar sound.

"It was you! You've been in my dreams."

"Pleasant dreams you've been having, Emilio," she taunted.

"But how?" he pressed.

"Because we too are Strega, the most powerful of all. We've been called upon by the Church to eradicate witches who work against it," she explained. "You don't intend to work against the Holy Father and the will of the Church now, do you, Emilio?"

"No, of course not," he sputtered. "I don't understand."

"Do you understand this?" Medea asked.

Emilio's head felt like it had been pressed into a vice. Distant memories from his life flipped before his eyes, slowing down as more current memories appeared, stopping on the day he met Vittoria. He experienced again, in slow motion, every observation and feeling he had about her. The panicked look in her eyes when Nico approached her, her nervous fidgeting, and her smile. How smitten they had all become in the hour they spent with Vittoria. He recalled the fear and intensity of her rescue on the bridge, and how she gazed at Nico after he saved her life. In all those visions, he did not notice the strange charm hanging from her neck. He saw a cross on a silver chain.

Medea let go of his mind and informed Nerezza of her findings.

"The girl is quite cunning. She had them all fooled. They even rescued her from an accident on the bridge."

"Just our luck," Nerezza retorted.

"She was wearing a cross around her neck, not that *thing*," Emilio argued.

"That *thing* is a Cimaruta. It's a witch's talisman. It appears as a cross to ordinary folk but reveals its true form to another Strega. She cannot hide from us," Nerezza explained.

"The girl has some power in her. She tamed Nico's raging tempest with just a look. She has great potential to do us harm. That power cannot be allowed to blossom," Medea said.

Emilio tried to make sense of everything happening.

"Are you going to hurt me?"

"Would you like me to hurt you?" said Nerezza, her voice silky and warm.

"No."

"You had better acquiesce to my request then, or else I'll allow my sisters to have their way with you. You've already had a taste of the beautiful night terrors Ulyssa can dream up and Medea would not mind keeping your mind clamped in a vice. Would you like that?"

Emilio shook his head in opposition to the threat.

"Very well then. You may join me in my quarters," she said, kissing him again on the mouth. This time Emilio felt Nerezza's tongue. His body slacked as her magic took hold of him again. She pulled back from Emilio, drawing her finger down his chest.

His eyes had glazed, and blood rushed into his ears. He stumbled forward into Nerezza's arms. She embraced and pulled him to her swelling bosom.

"You'll be safe with me," she cooed. "I won't let her hurt you."

Medea and Ulyssa closed in on Emilio and caressed his hair, neck, and face.

"You'll be safe with us," they concurred.

To Nerezza's surprise, Emilio turned out to be a very good lover. Relaxed and satisfied, she lay naked in her fur-lined bed. While Emilio slept beside her, she projected her zee three hundred miles away into Pope Urban VIII's bedchamber.

The Pope lay tucked into his large carved and gilded bed, adorned with red velvet covers and pillows. His white beard trimmed in the style of a long goatee and mustache. He wore a linen bed shirt open at the neck and a cap covered his close-cropped salt and pepper hair.

Upon her arrival in his chambers, he shifted in his sleep, becoming aware of her presence. Nerezza called out to him in her mind and the mouth of her zee image opened and spoke to the Holy Father.

"Your Eminence, arise."

Urban VIII blinked open his brown eyes. Startled by her specter's presence, he shot straight up in bed.

"I hate it when you do that!" he sputtered.

Nerezza ignored the comment, though she wanted to laugh aloud.

"I have news. Very exciting news."

"Go on then," he replied, wiping the sleep from his watery eyes.

"We've identified a Benedanti Strega who will take the fall for witchcraft in Florence."

"How do you know she's a witch?"

"Medea retrieved visions of her from two reliable sources. She is dangerous and cunning, and she's killed a man!" Nerezza exclaimed.

"We must be very careful then. Is she in Florence now?"

"We've determined that she is a citizen, though she left the city during the plague's crescendo, to seek out her own kind. It won't be long until she returns, and we can move to identify her location. I'm putting spies in place and will report when I have news."

"We'll not move in until you are certain that the Benedanti are there. We cannot risk civil unrest following the plague. People are building back their trust in the Church. Money and power are at stake."

Nerezza pouted. She wanted to move forward as fast as possible. Pillage and burn, as it were. The Benedanti were going to pay for what they did to her mother.

"The Inquisition must have irrefutable proof of these Benedanti, and a trial is essential to condemn them to burn. The witch trials in France and Germany have been effective in eliminating diabolical witches in the area. The laity finds great pleasure seeing evil punished."

"You will have your trial," Nerezza promised. A sour look twisted her face. The Pope noticed.

"This is a long game we're playing, Nerezza. Let the Scourge do its work. People are begging mercy across the land. Many chapels have been built, and money and alms are filling the Church's empty coffers."

"So, you are pleased?" Nerezza asked.

"I'll be more so when we can take back my homeland. My brother is awaiting the arrival of his bastard who is going to join the ranks of the Church. He's to learn the way of the Inquisition and will be my representative in Florence. Once you are positive of a glorious victory for the Inquisition, only then will I give the order for him to descend upon the city."

"It may be many months."

"As I said, I'm playing the long game. The trials must go off without a hitch."

Nerezza didn't like it, but she acquiesced.

"Very well."

The Holy Father laid back into his pillow signaling to Nerezza their conversation had come to its end. She drew her zee back into her own room and was met with the feeling of Emilio's warm naked skin upon her own.

She couldn't control the pace at which the Pope was willing to move, but she could control Emilio. Rolling out from underneath him, he roused from his slumber. She needed to find Vittoria fast, so she could have her revenge and Emilio was the key to her success. He'd remain under her enchantment until she had Vittoria and all the other Benedanti kneeling before her. Kissing his mouth, he heeded her unspoken call.

The first night he had the energy to sit up in bed, Nico asked for paper, pen, and ink. By candlelight, he wrote a very long list of names in a neat column. Beside each, he wrote the nature of his error. He vowed to apologize and seek forgiveness from every person he had wronged—if they were still alive. The person Nico most wished to apologize to was Angelo, his silent shadow for the last month.

When Angelo arrived the next morning, his face was drawn and his under-eyes dark. He needed rest, that much was clear. But he smiled at Nico and took his usual seat upon the stool at the bedside.

"It's good to see you up this morning," Angelo said. "You gave us quite a scare, you know."

"I do."

Angelo shook his head of dark curls, leaned back against the peeling plaster wall, and exhaled.

"I'm sorry, Angelo," Nico said, holding his hazel gaze steady upon Angelo while speaking. "I'm sorry for all the grief I've caused you and Emilio over the years. I've been a surly earth-vexing lout and I don't deserve your love or friendship. I know my words aren't much, but I intend to demonstrate with my actions that I appreciate you and that I wish to atone for my mistakes. I hope you can forgive me."

"I forgive you, brother," Angelo said, leaning forward to pat Nico on the leg.

"Brother?"

"Yeah, you big dolt. *Brother.* I love you. Why the hell do you think I've been here this whole time?"

Nico smiled. He placed his own hand over Angelo's and squeezed.

"Because you're absolutely mad!" he answered.

"I supposed I've been hanging around with you too long," Angelo shot back, before pulling his hand away.

"Where's Emilio? I need to apologize to him as well. He was angry with me the last time I saw him. I want to make things right."

Angelo didn't respond right away.

"What's the matter? Is Emilio all right?"

"He's fine, it's just that..."

"It's what?"

"The night we were supposed to meet after helping Vittoria, Emilio left the house without me. He's been at the Tre Sorella Taverna for the last few days. Something has changed in him. It's like he's *you* now. I mean, the *old* you."

"What?"

"He's really angry, I mean."

"What does that have to do with anything?"

"When I confronted him, he told me that he didn't want to see me anymore, and that he didn't want to see you either. He was hanging around with Nerezza, the scary beautiful one of the three sisters. She seemed to have him in a trance or something. I couldn't figure it out. He hasn't been home since. Mama is beside herself."

"She blames me, doesn't she?"

Angelo nodded.

"I'm going to fix this, Angelo."

"Sure, I know," he said, half-hearted. "Well, I'm going to go home and get some rest. Paolo will be by soon to check on you."

"Paolo? Seriously?"

"Yes and, believe me when I say, you owe me."

"I bet I do."

Marcel sat in a tiny damp cell. The small window to the outside world was barred shut. He was under constant surveillance by the men who had captured him. After three days at sea, they had finally delivered him to the Vatican to be instructed in the ways of the Inquisition.

It was an hour still before sunrise, but Marcel could tell that it would be another dreary, overcast, rainy day in Rome. The weather did not suit him, and he felt on the verge of body-racking shivers. The monk's habit he'd been given to wear was made of rough scratchy sack cloth. His leather boots were taken from him and he was given, in exchange, a pair of flimsy leather sandals. His clothes and money were being held, on orders from his father, for he could not be trusted to stay put.

He hadn't been able to sleep. The rigorous practice of getting up at all hours of the night for prayer was taxing and he felt out of balance within his body. The stress of the situation in which he found himself, the guilt he felt for leaving Vittoria, and the powerlessness he perceived over his future was nightmare-inducing. He sat on the edge of the lumpy cot, elbows upon knees, hands over the fine features of his face. He rubbed his sunken eyes.

His hair had been shaved and when he massaged his head, as he was accustomed to doing when deep in thought, he was always shocked to find rough spikes where his silky locks once were. The hair that Vittoria had taken pleasure in caressing as they lay together at night. The prickly hairs beneath his fingers set him even more on edge instead, so he stood and paced around the infinitesimal room he was locked inside.

Until Cardinal Barberini gave the order to set him free, he was a prisoner of the Church. He was being punished—plain and simple. He wasn't a flight risk, and they knew he couldn't go anywhere, he had nothing. They'd stripped him of his clothes, his hair, his money, and his horse. All he had left was his wit, a worn-out copy of the Bible, a jug of mildewed water for washing up, and a chipped pot to piss in. Other than that, he was at the Church's, rather, his father's mercy.

He hadn't said a word to anyone since his arrival in Rome. Though he attended masses, he didn't sing or say the prayers. He sat in silent protest. Marcel expected when he was put in front of Cardinal he would be expected to speak of his own volition or by force. Either way, he had been beaten by his father.

He would bide his time until the opportunity arose for him to escape. It could be a few months or even years, but he would do it, and disappear forever. He now knew for certain the type of man he was dealing with. He underestimated his father before, but never again.

Marcel stood at the window looking up and out in the direction the sun was to rise and vowed to be patient. He'd be the best inquisitor the Church had ever seen. He would plan his deliverance to freedom in the New World, all the while playing the part to precision. And when the time is perfect he will make his move. He couldn't make another mistake. That's how he ended up in captivity in the first place.

Gripping the cold metal bars over the window Marcel hardened his resolve to make his father pay in the process. He'd take great pleasure in observing his father disgraced and in pain—the type of pain his mother suffered before taking her own life.

Marcel took in a deep breath, solidifying the vow within every muscle in his body. Every fiber of his being buzzed with the resonance of his solemn vow. His father had ruined his future with Vittoria, a happy life filled with love and children, and that was unforgivable.

CHAPTER 8

In the distance was the groan of keys in a stiff metal lock. Marcel pulled himself together and sat down on the edge of his cot. Today his captors were taking him to have an audience with Cardinal Moreau, the man who would train him to hunt witches for the Inquisition. He had kept Marcel waiting, under arrest, for two weeks.

Marcel was escorted through the streets of the Vatican on foot by the same group of men who'd been with him since Livorno. Though they hadn't said so, he was sure the men in black were reporting everything he did or didn't do to his father. He decided it was time to start acting like a normal human being rather than a beaten animal.

"I hope your quarters are better than mine. My cot is quite lumpy, and it's been difficult to sleep," he said, directing the comment to no one. But the man who delivered his father's letter to him looked surprised he had spoken. Marcel hadn't said a word since they boarded the ship.

"They're suitable," he replied.

"I figure we're going to be together, the lot of us, for a while. So, what should I call you?" Marcel asked, looking sideways at the lead man.

The others kept quiet waiting for their leader to respond.

"My name is Claudio," he replied, not turning to look at Marcel, keeping his distance.

Marcel glanced over his shoulder acknowledging the other two men.

"Pay them no mind. Think of them as your shadows. Address me alone, I'm responsible for your welfare. Best case scenario, you are clothed, fed, and take up your post without any violence. Be advised that I have been given liberal reign to correct behavior if I deem it necessary. Understood?"

Claudio had established a clear boundary with Marcel. They were not going to be friends or even acquaintances.

"Yes, I understand," Marcel replied, peeking out of the corner of his eye at the middle-aged man with receding salt and pepper hair and soft jaw. Claudio was taking extra care to keep his eyes forward, navigating the winding path toward the Cardinal's offices, instead of looking at Marcel.

Young monks, and aloof cardinals in their red hats, headed in their respective directions. The short walk in the dismal morning drizzle seemed to Marcel to last forever and he was chilled to the bone. Rubbing his icy hands together for warmth did nothing to ease his discomfort.

Claudio noticed. "You'll have new clothes, warmer ones, soon enough. Just humble yourself to Cardinal Moreau and they will arrive sooner rather than later."

Marcel acknowledged the insight. As much as he would prefer to remove his own left eye than to humble himself before anyone, he had to play the part of the prodigal son—one who was beaten, humiliated, and incapacitated by sin.

Resistance tightened in his core at the thought of begging forgiveness for wanting to live a normal life. Then he had an idea. He would pretend to act out the role of a downtrodden character in a performance, pushing his own personality into the background for a while and just like every drama, eventually, it had to end. Then he could resume his life where it had left off.

The idea brought a crinkle of pleasure to the corner of his eyes which he was quick to blink away. Marcel Barberini, he decided, would assume a mask, don a fictitious cloak of shame, and humbly meet the man whom he needed to convince of his subservience.

Cardinal Moreau's quarters were well lit. Ensconced wax candles burned brightly all around the spacious room. The corpulent man, swathed in crimson robes, sat in an ornately carved chair by the fireplace. He poured over the piles of correspondence that lay before him on a makeshift table. Seals of wax and ribbon adorned the letters from officials in the land petitioning his time or resources for some matter or another.

His pudgy face was pinched in concentration and his eyes narrowed as he read the document in hand. The hair upon his round head was still dark but thinning, yet it seemed to be in high supply upon the backs of his hands and ringed fingers.

Though Marcel, Claudio, and the shadows entered minutes before, no one spoke to the Cardinal until he set aside his object of concentration and looked up to acknowledge their presence in his chamber.

"Your Eminence, I present to you Marcel Barberini, relative to Grand Inquisitor Barberini of the Supreme Sacred Congregation of the Roman and Universal Inquisition. He has been sent to learn the proper way of administering justice, in the name of the Church, from a great man such as yourself."

Claudio held out a letter of his own with a red wax seal upon it, which Cardinal Moreau opened his hand to receive. Claudio deposited the letter within his meaty grip, then stepped back into position amongst the other men.

Without saying a word, the Cardinal opened and read the letter, folded it again, and placed it with the others on the table. Turning his inquiring gaze to Marcel, he observed the young man in detail.

Fit, handsome, terribly outfitted in that dreadful brown habit. He looks a prince in paupers clothing. Clearly, he's in trouble of some kind.

The Cardinal had developed a keen eye for discerning these things over the course of his twenty years of service to the Church. It was his job to root out the truth. He hadn't gained his post by being ignorant to the emotional state of men. If anything, it was his greatest gift—seeing straight into the crux of the matter and using that knowledge to his benefit. That's what made him the Church's most effective Inquisitor.

It was common for nephews and bastard sons to be sent to him to learn the inquisitorial arts. From the tone of Cardinal Barberini's letter of instruction, and the steely defiant look in the young man's eyes, it must be the latter.

The youth didn't have any distinctive Italianate features or coloring that would point to kinship to the Cardinal. However, the emotions simmering under the surface were that of a strained father-son relationship.

I'll have to be careful of this one. He's intelligent and focused. He'll tell me everything I want to hear and behave impeccably.

At last, the Cardinal spoke.

"From this letter, I am to presume that you are indeed Marcel Barberini who is related to the Holy Father himself and are here to be under my tutelage for the coming months to learn the ways of the Roman Inquisition, after which you will be dispatched to your post in Florence under direct command of Cardinal Barberini. Is that correct?"

Marcel moved forward two paces from his captors and in his most poised and penitent manner, blue eyes cast downward and humble in presentation, spoke.

"Yes, Your Eminence. I am Marcel Barberini. I am here to learn from you as your pupil so that I may take up my post, as you say."

Moreau pointed to the letter.

"It also says that you are to make your vows to the church and remain under my watchful eye until you are called to report. And why, pray tell, am I to keep such close tabs on you?"

"It is believed that I may flee."

"Is that true?"

"No, Your Eminence. It is not true, not anymore. I've accepted my responsibility to my family and the Church, and I will not flee."

The Cardinal eyed him again and Marcel held his gaze this time. Just as he suspected. The boy was saying the words he wished to hear.

"I shall give you the benefit of the doubt once. Should you break my trust in any way, large or small, there will be consequences. You will arrive in my quarters every day after Matins and we will begin your intensive training. You have much to learn. A report will be sent to your patron weekly."

Marcel nodded his understanding.

"Also, you will be given new robes and decent shoes. One must feel the part of Inquisitor if he is going to play the part."

The Cardinal looked to Claudio.

"See to it that the young man has the proper attire when he arrives in the chapel to take his vows and swear loyalty to God and the Church at Compline tonight."

Marcel's eyes went wide for an instant before he willed his face back into submission.

This charade just became very real to him, the Cardinal thought.

"Yes, Your Eminence," Claudio replied.

"One more thing. See to it that his quarters are upgraded as well. We cannot, after all, have him sleeping in monk's chambers. He's going to be an Inquisitor, for God's sake!"

The Cardinal rustled some of the papers on the table and pulled from underneath a thick book with gold script upon the front cover.

Sacro Arsenale

"You seem to be a learned man, young Barberini. You may have access to the library and inquisitorial records to read up on past cases and church law. And for all intents and purposes, *this* will be your manual. Read it, keep it with you always, memorize it from cover to cover. Every practical aspect you'll need to know about your work is inside this book."

The heft of the book felt like a weighty brick in the Cardinal's hands as he transferred it to Marcel.

"Thank you, Your Eminence," Marcel said then waited for further instruction.

"You are excused. Please wash and prepare yourself in fresh robes for the taking of your vows into the Jesuit order this evening."

All the men nodded and bowed before the Cardinal. His word was law. They all backed out from his quarters and Cardinal Moreau returned to his reading.

Within the hour, Marcel was settling into his new quarters. His room wasn't as large as the Cardinal's, but it was room enough. A much better, lump-free, bed was situated in the corner, away from a drafty window. A wooden cross hung on the stone wall above his bed and another above the entry.

He had a fireplace by which a simple desk and chair were positioned where he could both eat and read. The view from the window looked out upon the central courtyard and gardens which were no longer in bloom in late October. Marcel imagined they were quite grand in the spring and summer, though he did not expect to be around to see them in their fullness.

Marcel suspected this veiled act of kindness was a measure to soften his resolve, but he was committed to keeping up the façade. Besides, he desired a better bed and some books to read to pass the time.

He bathed and cleaned under his nails and received, from a dower old monk, two new sets of robes to wear while in training with the Cardinal. There was a meal of bread, meat, and potatoes set upon his desk, along with a jug of decent wine and water. The scent of the food made his famished stomach growl. He hadn't had a good meal in weeks. His stomach was looking concave as of late. Careful not to wolf down the food, he took his time so as not to cause a stomachache. He was able to consume half of the rich food on the plate. Pushing the rest aside, he picked up the *Sacro Arsenale* and thumbed through the pages of the book to see what it was all about.

It was exactly as the Cardinal had said—a precise manual outlining the entire inquisitorial process from start to finish. Marcel placed a few extra logs on the fire before settling back into the chair to read, from the beginning, the book that was to be his Bible for his toughest role yet.

Paolo hurried back to his small office from his rounds in the wool district. He still attended occasional plague cases that cropped up in the wake of the wave of death that crested in Florence. Winding his way through the dim interior passages of the old building, he arrived at a pine door marked with an engraved plaque.

Paolo Salviati, Dottore della Peste

The title once gave Paolo cause for pride, but now it made him cringe. He didn't have a clue then what it meant to serve the city as a doctor of death, which is what the living called him. Nor did he ever have the means to heal those who fell ill. His title was worthless.

When folks saw him coming, in his freakish getup, they believed him the Angel of Death. He'd seen more slow, repugnant, anguishing death that one person should ever care to know. All told, there were no redeeming qualities about the work at all, except one, Vittoria Giordano.

He saw to it that her mother was removed from the home and laid to rest in her church's cemetery. He had to dig deep into his own pocket to bribe a couple of overworked gravediggers to bury Orabella Giordano. He marked the grave with a wooden cross that he inscribed himself. It was no easy feat to accomplish. It cost him time and money. And the most precious commodity, his energy, was in very short supply. He lived in his leather mask and duster sixteen hours a day, for the last three months, tending the dying.

Paolo planned to take up a new line of work, perhaps as a doctor who delivers babies and cares for children. It would be a delightful change of pace and respite from the harrowing suffering and pain of the end of life, and instead, he could help support life and the living. There was bound to be a boom of births in the coming years. He got that familiar chill up the back of his arms and neck, so he knew he was on to something big.

He pushed open the door to his office and found Angelo snoozing in his extra chair. They had planned to meet and discuss Emilio. He shut the door behind him moving silently as possible, but the leather duster swished around his legs. He crept toward Angelo, placed his bird-demon mask back over his curly head, and in his deepest most sinister voice he boomed.

"Angelo! I command you to wake!"

Angelo's relaxed body shot to attention, eyes wide in surprise. The shock of the horrifying creature in his presence sent him tumbling backward out of his chair in fright.

Paolo whipped off his mask and laughed at Angelo, taking a deep bow for his performance. Angelo cursed amply, drawing ragged breaths to calm his racing heart.

"Dammit, Paolo! Why did you do that?"

"I told you that you'd owe me big time, for tending Nico, and now I have claimed my reward," he explained, still smiling. His ruddy face shining with cheer. Paolo could feel the strain of the previous months draining from his body. He hadn't had a hearty laugh like that in recent memory.

Angelo was bent over, hand on his knees, reclaiming his composure.

"My God, you're an ugly scut. That mask does absolutely nothing for you, Paolo."

"Good to see you too, Angelo," he replied to his oldest friend, still chuckling, removing the remainder of his getup to hang it up on the large hook on the wall. He'd taken to the habit of wiping down the duster, mask, and cane with a concoction of vinegar, clove, and orange oil to freshen up the gear after each use. It seemed to have worked to keep plague miasma from affecting him thus far.

"So how is Nico doing?" Paolo asked Angelo. "I saw him heading over to the Linen Drapers' Guild building yesterday."

Righting his chair, Angelo sat back down. Kicking his long legs out, crossing them at the ankles, he folded his arms behind his head before answering.

"He's well! I mean, he's different—better—in many respects. He's stuck to his word about making amends with those he's offended, and he's committed to taking his place among the Linen Drapers as a proper guild member. He plans on succeeding Signor Amore as the maestro in the tailor shop."

"Sounds like he's a changed man. Do you think it'll last?" Paolo asked, settling down into his own chair behind his shabby desk.

"I can't be certain, but I do know that he's taking great strides to make positive adjustments in his life. He hasn't put a sip of wine to his lips since before he was ill."

Paolo's short brows jumped up into his hairline in surprise. "Is that so?"

"It is," Angelo declared, proud of his cousin's progress. "He's finalizing his application for master tailor status at the Guild. That's why you saw him heading there. Nico discussed his future with Signor Amore. Both his wife and daughter died, too."

"God rest their souls," Paolo responded by rote.

"Nico is going to take over the business for him so he can retire. You know, try to enjoy what little life he has left to live."

"That's kind of Nico."

Speaking those words of Nico was foreign to his tongue, and they felt strange as they crossed his lips.

"I know you still have your doubts about him, and who could blame you? He was always a horse's ass to you. It's just that you, your family, your education, your life in general, made Nico jealous. It's what he should have had and still wants, so he punished you for representing what he believed was taken from him. Please try not to take his actions to heart. He's made amends to you, hasn't he?"

"Well, yes. He came here within days of his recovery."

Paolo still couldn't believe of all the people in the world who could have been given a second chance at life it would have been Nico Apollino. God certainly worked in mysterious ways.

"He told me he had a vision of a lady and that he knew he'd been given another chance to help someone, though he didn't say whom, and he intended on being the best possible version of himself when the time came to do so."

"Is that right?" Angelo thought for a moment. "Well, I suppose he's got a purpose now, and just be thankful that purpose is no longer to destroy your life."

"I'll agree to that," Paolo replied, leaning further back in his creaky chair so he could prop his feet on the edge of the book-laden desk. "So, what did you want to talk to me about?"

Angelo grew tense and his brows knit together. He drew his square hand down over his face before speaking.

"It's Emilio. Something has happened to him, but I don't know what. It all started the night before we met Vittoria. Nico started a fight at the Tre Sorella Taverna. Somehow, we all managed to get out of there alive though one of Pitti's guys ended up dead. Then Emilio punched Nico in the eye. I'd never seen him so angry. I didn't see him much for about three weeks after that, then finally he just disappeared. Mama has been beside herself with worry. I know you gamble there when you're able, so I need to ask you a very important favor."

"What do you need me to do?"

Though Angelo was Paolo's true friend, he liked Emilio well enough to help.

"Please ask around about Emilio the next time you're at the Taverna and see what you can find out. I feel he's in trouble, something is wrong."

"I'll see what I can do. I haven't been over there in a while, but perhaps I'm due for a little rest and relaxation."

"Thank you, Paolo. You're a good friend." Relief emerged upon Angelo's amiable face. "I just hate seeing Mama so upset."

"I understand. I'll head over there tonight."

"I appreciate this very much." Angelo stood, shook his friend's hand, and left.

Dusk settled upon the tired city of Florence. The clamor and hum of activity was just a whisper of what it once was. The curfew had since been lifted and people were free to walk about as they pleased, yet Paolo met few out on the street as he made his way through the wool district. The area suffered a tremendous amount of death. Many leading merchant's and their families were some of the earliest to contract pestilence and the disease rippled outward from that epicenter.

He noticed many doors of once splendid homes were boarded shut and sagged with sadness and grief. Homeless dogs and cats had found solace in the neighborhood as there were fewer people to shoo them all away.

When he approached the familiar yellow stucco home of the Merchant Giordano, he slowed his pace and peered up at the topmost windows looking for any signs of life.

He remembered when, after Vittoria fled and her mother's corpse had been removed for burial, he sneaked into her room for a look around. Even through the thick glass lenses of his mask he could see that Vittoria was a learned young lady. Several herbal texts had been stacked on one shelf, Greek and Roman mythology on another. For some reason, the selection of books didn't surprise him. He noted to himself that books could be a good point of conversation if, *when*, he saw her again.

Upon the writing table, space was left bare as if something of great importance had once stood there but had since been carried off. Her cassone had been rifled through and several embroidered brocade and silk dresses were left rumpled within. Pairs of fashionable shoes were strewn about, and the bed was left unmade.

If he had been braver he would have removed his mask to breathe in Vittoria's essence before leaving her room, but he wasn't.

One day he hoped to see lights again in those windows. A sure sign that Vittoria had returned home. He'd check back in a few days. Besides, Angelo's coins were burning a hole in his purse and he had some gambling, and spying, to do at the Tre Sorella Taverna.

A chill set in once the sun dipped behind the ancient Tuscan hills. Paolo stamped his feet and rubbed his itchy gambling fingers together as the heavy door slammed behind him. It had been quite a while since he'd been to the Tre Sorella Taverna. Nonetheless, it was still full and frisky. Paolo thought it was strange to see all the same faces inside, curious that the plague seemed to have left the population of scoundrels, thieves, and gamblers intact. It was like things never skipped a beat there. A few familiar faces peeked up from their cups and nodded to the recently absent company.

Paolo strode toward the roaring fireplace and took his favorite seat at the card table. The three men already there had just finished a hand and the dealer was reshuffling the cards. Paolo withdrew coins from his purse and declared his bid to the table.

"It's been a while," old man Aldo grunted at Paolo. His bushy white eyebrows lowered over his watery blue eyes while he analyzed the quality of the cards in his hand.

"Yeah, you too good for us now, Paolo?" asked Santiago, a wily card shark from down Siena way, looking him up and down. He jutted out his stubbled chin to point out Paolo's flashy new doublet.

"Gentlemen," Paolo replied. "I'm a doctor and as you might have guessed I've had my hands very full the past few months. Plague is a tireless taskmaster."

The men drew back at the mention of the word. Paolo noticed.

"My dear friends, if the plague was going to take me, it would have done so already. It would seem plague only has the taste for the pure and innocent, so you have nothing to fear."

Santiago chuckled and relaxed. "Seems so. Nothing much has changed here since you've been away."

"Except that degenerate Nico doesn't come around here anymore. Come to think of it, neither does one of those twins," Aldo added.

"Which twin?" Paolo asked, being careful to act casual.

"How the hell am I supposed to know? Who can tell the difference between them?" Aldo chuffed, throwing down his cards. He was out.

"Darling, don't you fret," said a sweet female voice. The serving girl, Constanza, cozied up behind Aldo and massaged his slumped shoulders. "I'll bring you another ale. It'll make you feel better."

A twinkle returned to Aldo's eyes and he pinched her pert rear end. She giggled.

"Hello Paolo, it's good to have you back," Constanza said, rumpling his head of tight curls, then pulled her hand back feeling something slick on her fingers.

"What's that? You got oil in your hair?" she asked, wiping her fingers off on her apron.

"It's so he can be even more slippery than usual," Santiago teased.

Everyone, including Constanza, laughed.

Paolo blushed and smoothed back his rumpled hair. "Very funny."

Constanza leaned over and kissed Paolo's cheek. Aldo's grim expression returned.

"You look handsome, even so. You want a drink?" she asked Paolo.

He nodded, sitting straighter in his chair to re-claim his composure. He didn't want to lose his chance to get information about Emilio. Constanza sidled away to get their drinks.

"You were saying that one of the twins is still around. Is he here tonight?" Paolo asked, pretending to look over his cards. He had a pretty good hand.

Santiago gestured toward the staircase heading to the brothel upstairs.

"Up there?" Paolo asked, finding it hard to believe one of the twins could afford to spend time up top. The women of the Tre Sorella Taverna could not be bought cheap. Only men of power and means could afford to climb those steps.

"Yep, always in the company of the two younger sisters, Medea and Ulyssa," Santiago replied.

Aldo whistled through the space where his two front teeth once were and wiggled his bushy brows. "I'm sure he's having the time of his life with those two."

"I'm sure," Paolo replied wryly. His heart skipped a beat. The sisters were beautiful, that much was clear to every man who saw them, but he always felt uneasy in their presence. They scared him. He much preferred girls with sweeter temperaments, like Constanza.

Santiago continued. "I think he even lives up there now. We haven't seen him leave the place and he's always here when we arrive."

Paolo knew that Santiago and old Aldo were fixtures in the place, so that implied that Emilio was probably now a resident. His eyes darted around the upper level seeking any sign of Emilio, but instead, they met the kohled green eyes of Nerezza, the eldest of the sisters. She gazed down at him. Her face severe in expression. He couldn't pull his eyes from hers though he tried. The left corner of her lips pulled up into a sneer revealing white, dare he say pointy, teeth. His heart palpitated and sweat broke out on his brow. She turned and disappeared into the dark shadows.

Santiago noticed. "You all right, mate?"

"He just realized his hand is as shit as mine," Aldo joked.

Paolo gulped. A large lump had developed in his throat and he couldn't swallow it down. Providentially, his drink arrived but was served not by Constanza but by another, older, woman.

"Hello boys!" she said, her voice, unlike Constanza's. She plunked down Aldo's ale and set down Paolo's cup of wine in front of him. Leaning far enough over to reveal her abundant cleavage. "And who might you be? We haven't met before."

"Where's Constanza?" Aldo grumbled.

"Busy!" the woman snapped.

"Paolo Salviati," he replied, before pounding the liquid down his parched throat.

"He's a *doctor*," Santiago teased.

"A doctor, eh?" she replied.

Paolo cleared his throat, but the lump of fear remained. "And who might you be?" he asked, avoiding the impulse to look at her breasts.

"My name is Magda. I'm new."

"That explains why I haven't seen you here before."

"I took Maria's place," Magda explained. "You seem like a sweet man. I look forward to getting to know you," she cooed, placing her long thin fingers over his card-holding hand.

Paolo flinched at her touch. "Certainly, Magda. As do I," he bumbled.

"Certainly, Magda. As do I," Aldo mocked.

Without turning her gaze from Paolo's, Magda whacked the back of Aldo's balding head.

Santiago burst out laughing. "Thanks, Magda. He needed a brain jangling."

Paolo couldn't help but smile also.

"Handsome too," Magda added. The velvet of her dress sleeve rubbed over his hand and then his face as she caressed his clean-shaven cheek. She smelled of sweat and musk.

Paolo coughed and excused himself, leaving his coins and cards on the table. He fumbled with his cloak arranging it around his shoulders.

"Hey! Where are you going?" Aldo shouted.

"He can't take all the female attention," Santiago teased.

"No, I just forgot something at home," Paolo lied.

"*Sure,* you did."

"Come back and see me soon, Paolo," Magda said, grasping his hand tight in hers.

"I will," he lied again. Pulling away he took off and stumbled into the cold evening eager to get away, far away from Nerezza's penetrating gaze and Magda's grip, into the safety of his own home. He felt sorry that Emilio couldn't do the same.

Paolo's office chamber was dim like his thoughts. He had held up his end of the bargain with Angelo and determined with fair certainty that Emilio was indeed still alive but holed up with the three sisters in the upper level of the Tre Sorella Taverna. Though he hadn't laid eyes upon Emilio, to be positive, he supposed there was no real need for concern. Emilio is probably just sowing his wild oats with the sisters.

The pine door to his office burst open and in stumbled both Angelo and Nico. Paolo shot up from his slump and swung his legs down from the worn-out desk, knocking papers off the edge as he did so.

"I wasn't expecting the both of you," he sputtered, bending down to shuffle up the papers from the floor.

Nico crouched his tall frame down to help clean up the mess. Paolo still had cause to be wary of him. After all, he used to beat the living shit out of him as often as possible.

"I saw Angelo heading in this direction as I was going back to the shop from a guild meeting," Nico said. "I thought it would be nice to join him and see how you were doing."

"That's very kind, Nico. I'm doing well, thank you," he replied smoothing his oiled hair.

Nico arranged the papers and placed them back on the desk. The top paper was a roughly sketched map on which Paolo had written in bold script *Vittoria Giordano* above a big black X.

"You know Vittoria?"

Paolo stuttered his reply. "Well, I don't know her exactly. But I attended her parents when they were ill and saw to her mother's burial after she fled the city."

Nico was silent. He held onto the map and took in a slow deep breath. "You knew about this too?" he asked, turning to his cousin.

"When you were sick I shared with Paolo our experience with Vittoria. It was one of the few happy times I could think to talk about when everything was looking so grim. I mean, you were on your death bed, and Emilio had disappeared. It was all too much."

Angelo couldn't look Nico in the eye as he spoke.

Paolo knew by previous experience that Nico would become angry and lash out, but no physical violence came. Instead, Nico took another deep breath before speaking.

"I'm sorry you felt you needed to keep this secret from me. I suppose I deserve it. I haven't always been the most levelheaded or trustworthy person."

His hazel eyes gazed back and forth between the two of them.

"I put you both in danger and didn't care about your feelings, or anything, except myself. I'm very sorry for that. I've been given a second chance and I'm going to do it differently this time. It's important for me to earn your respect, Paolo, and yours, Angelo. I'm not the man I was before the plague, and I don't intend on ever being that person again. I hope you'll both come to see that someday."

He laid the map down upon the other pile of papers then moved toward the door to exit. Paolo and Angelo shared a meaningful glance, acknowledging that Nico's shame was palpable to them and that the apology was indeed real.

"I forgive you, Nico," Paolo blurted out.

"As do I," Angelo agreed. "We shouldn't have kept this from you. I know how much you care for Vittoria. She changed you that day. Emilio and I both saw it."

Nico's fingers released their hold on door.

"And it was cowardice of me not to want to do my sworn duty as a doctor to help you. Angelo beat sense into me. You shouldn't have lived, but by some miracle you did, Nico. God must have plans for you. Will you forgive me as well?" Paolo asked.

"There's nothing to forgive," he replied, the angst disappearing from his handsome chiseled face. The puffiness that used to play around his eyes and chin was long gone since he'd done away with drinking.

"I'm sorry too, Brother."

"There's nothing to be sorry for, Angelo. You were there when everyone else would have liked to have seen me dead." Nico chuckled and shook his dark head of short wavy hair. "Believe me when I say that was the entire city."

Angelo laughed. "True!"

"Why don't we start over again?" Paolo offered.

"I'd like that very much."

"Me too," Paolo agreed, extending his hand to shake Nico's.

Angelo clasped them both by the shoulder in encouragement and support. He too seemed happy to wipe the slate clean of past grievances. "So why don't you tell us in on what you found out about Vittoria and Emilio, Paolo."

CHAPTER 9

Bracelets jangled, and the sultry smell of musk filled the air. A husky female voice spoke. "Girl, what are you doing here?"

Vittoria blinked open her bleary eyes. Before her was a woman wearing a loose-fitting white blouse under a blue velvet bodice. Her long brown skirt skimmed the grass. Her dark silken hair was pulled away from her face with a colorful kerchief, exposing her long graceful neck. Her feet were bare, but they did not have the wear and tear of a peasant. Words did not find Vittoria's lips.

"Where did you come from?" the gypsy asked.

Vittoria's brain was slow to comprehend the questions she had been asked.

Where am I? Confusion set in.

"Please don't hurt me," she said, fighting the urge to curl herself up into a ball.

"Don't be silly, girl. I am trying to help you. You could get hurt if you stay here," she said, gazing up toward the evening sky.

Vittoria followed her gaze. The light hurt her eyes. It was indeed quite late.

"I don't have anywhere to go," she admitted.

"Why is that?"

"Plague."

The gypsy stepped away afraid she carried the death sentence with her.

"Show me your body," she demanded. Vittoria tightened her arms around herself for protection. She didn't want to be helped, she didn't deserve it.

"You *will* show me, or I'll leave you here to fend for yourself," the gypsy threatened, her light-brown eyes narrowed.

Vittoria hung her head.

"Don't be ashamed. I need to be sure you do not carry plague before I bring you to my camp," she explained. "We have avoided pestilence by keeping to ourselves and if you have markings I must leave you."

Vittoria felt sick. Her stomach was sour from drink. She needed food and she had none. Unsteady, Vittoria stood and unlaced her dress letting it fall just below her shoulders.

"That is not far enough."

She let the dress slip down to her waist revealing her breasts.

"Lift up your arms so I can check for buboes," the gypsy commanded.

Vittoria lifted both arms. If she weren't still half drunk, she'd feel more embarrassed than ever. Heat rushed up and flushed her neck and face and burned her ears. She could not look the gypsy in the eye during her inspection.

"Turn around."

It seemed like an eternity before the gypsy determined she was not at risk.

"Pull up your dress and come with me."

Vittoria yanked up the front of her dress, still too shy to look at her inquisitor.

"What is your name, girl?" the gypsy asked in a much gentler tone, knowing she had violated Vittoria for her own protection.

"Vittoria."

"I am Tsura. It means light of dawn," she explained. "And I will help you."

"How did you find me?" she asked, still wondering how she came to be where she was.

"I came to gather chestnuts and here you were asleep under this tree," Tsura replied, holding up a full basket of spiky chestnuts.

"Oh."

"My people are camped about a half mile away."

Vittoria nodded and started walking away from the tree.

"I assume that is yours," Tsura said, pointing to the oilcloth satchel on the ground.

Vittoria was both surprised and relieved the bag was there. She didn't remember leaving the villa but, somehow, she had the wherewithal to bring her few belongings with her. Picking up the bag she slung it over her shoulder.

"You don't say much, do you?" Tsura asked.

Vittoria shrugged again.

"Well, maybe after a little food and drink you'll feel like talking. Come on."

Vittoria followed her deeper into the woods.

The sun completed its descent just as Tsura and Vittoria entered a grove of ancient oak trees. The massive branches provided an expansive canopy of natural cover for the transient community below. Colorful open-air tents were scattered a comfortable distance from the next throughout the peaceful grove, providing a degree of privacy for their tenants. A bonfire burned at the center of the camp illuminating the surrounding area. Silhouettes of men and women were visible around the fire and children's laughter filled the air. As they approached a man stepped away from the fire toward them.

"Who goes there?" he demanded from the shadows.

"It's me, Tsura."

"Who is this?" he asked, his voice grave. "You know that we do not bring strangers to our camp."

"I know, Papa" Tsura replied. "I was out gathering chestnuts, where Grandmother told me to, and I found her sleeping under a tree. She has nowhere to go."

"Why?"

"Plague."

Tsura's father backed away from them.

"I have looked at her body. She is not infected with pestilence. I am sure of it."

"She cannot stay. She does not belong here," he argued.

"Papa, *please*, just for one night. She may have been hurt or killed if I had left her behind," Tsura pleaded.

Vittoria remained silent. She wasn't sure herself if she wanted to stay.

Tsura continued her negotiations. "One night, and she will stay with me in my tent."

Her father looked hard at Vittoria's face, then the cross around her neck. He shook his head as if he couldn't believe the words that were about to come out of his mouth.

"One night."

Vittoria realized she'd been holding her breath during the exchange and sighed with relief when she was given permission to pass.

"Thank you, Papa!" Tsura gushed, leaning forward to kiss him on his weathered cheek.

Grabbing Vittoria by the elbow she tugged her away before he could change his mind.

Tsura led her to a small colorful tent pitched near a covered horse cart. She poked at the smoldering embers in her tiny campfire and rolled out a couple of worn rugs for them to sit on. From a large bladder, she poured water into a pot and set it to boil. Then she stepped inside the tent and lit a candle. Vittoria waited by the entry.

Tsura rummaged cups from a decorated chest, painted in bright hues of orange and blue, and she pulled out a pouch. When she opened it the sensuous scent of a rose garden escaped. Tsura crumbled dried rose hips into each cup. Stepping back outside, she then ladled boiling water over the petals and swirled them around the cups with great care.

"Please, sit," Tsura instructed, motioning to the rugs by the fire. Vittoria lowered herself to the rug. "Here, drink this," she insisted, shoving a cup toward Vittoria.

"It smells beautiful," Vittoria said, inhaling the warm vapors.

"It's my sister's favorite," Tsura said.

"Sister?"

"She was one of the children playing as we entered the camp." Tsura bellowed over her shoulder toward the group of children dancing around the bonfire. "Aishe, come here!"

A jubilant little girl skipped towards them. Her hair was undone, and her locks bounced behind as she made her way over.

"Watch me, Tsura. I can do a somersault," Aishe exclaimed and sprang head over heels.

She tripped over her feet. As she tried to right herself, she got caught up in the hem of her oversized dress and lunged headfirst toward the blistering flames. Aishe's auburn locks blended with the red-orange blaze of the fire.

Tsura grabbed for the girl. "Aishe!" she cried, as the material from the back of the little one's dress slipped through her fingers.

Vittoria dropped her cup and leaped from her seat to save the child. By the grace of God, Vittoria's fingers found her tiny tanned arm and wrenched her away from the blaze. Aishe's hair tumbled into her eyes as she fell into her savior's lap. Vittoria wrapped her arms around the girl's small body.

Aishe whimpered into Vittoria's shoulder.

"Hush now, you are safe," she whispered, cradling the child in her arms. She held the girl close and stroked her silky hair.

"Aishe, you must be more careful!" Tsura scolded.

"It's all right now," Vittoria said.

Aishe pulled away to look up into her face, the little one's golden eyes searching hers.

"Are you an angel?" Aishe asked, her eyes opened wide in awe.

Vittoria chuckled. "No, though I should be asking your sister the same thing. She saved me today, as well."

"Oh, you exaggerate," Tsura said.

Aishe settled back into Vittoria's lap. "What's your name? Where do you come from then?" she asked.

"I am Vittoria. I lived in Florence, but plague came, and I was sent away."

"Will you stay with us?"

"No. I can stay but for one night, then I must go."

Tsura picked up Vittoria's cup from the ground. She examined it like the meaning of life had appeared within.

"Oh no, did I break it?" Vittoria asked worried.

"She's reading the tea leaves, silly," Aishe explained as if everyone should know that.

"What do you mean?" Vittoria replied. Astrology was one thing, but divining leaves in a cup was something else entirely.

Aishe perked up. "Tsura is very good at it."

Tsura came and kneeled beside Vittoria and pointed into the cup.

"Look here. See the butterfly. You're going through a period of transition and transformation. There too, the sacred chalice. This is the great symbol of the

Goddess. It is a container in which the divine can enter and be held."

Vittoria considered the empty cup. "I don't see anything," she said.

"There's one last symbol, the cross. You are protected though a sacrifice must be made," Tsura concluded.

"I have nothing left to give but my life," Vittoria responded, irritated.

"I don't think that's it," Tsura assured her, putting the cup down.

"Me either. Your zee is very strong, Vittoria," Aishe said.

"My what?"

"Your life-force. I can feel it," Aishe explained.

Vittoria gave Tsura a puzzled look. "One should beware to claim such a power. People might think you speak of magic."

"She speaks of the ways of the Strega. It is knowledge passed from mother to daughter," Tsura clarified. "Surely, you know this." She moved to the other side of the fire and sat beside the basket of chestnuts. She shucked the spiky shells off and set them to roast while they talked.

"Why would I? I'm a Catholic."

Tsura gave her a patronizing grin and pointed at her neck. "Oh, come now Vittoria. You must be joking. You're wearing a Cimaruta, a Strega's talisman, blessed by the Lady of Light."

Vittoria grabbed the cross that hung at her neck. "I'm wearing no such thing. It was a gift from my mother."

Tsura frowned. Vittoria's behavior confused her.

"You didn't hit your head on that tree before you fell asleep, did you?" she joked uneasily.

"Why would I joke about either?" Vittoria responded, looking down.

Tsura shared a suspicious look with Aishe, who shrugged in response.

"No matter. Anyway, it has nothing to do with the Church," she pointed out. "These ways have been known since the mighty Etruscans ruled this land two thousand years ago and before the Holy Church was even a thought."

"What proof do you have?" Vittoria questioned.

"These are the legends told when we gather around our campfires during the winter solstice," Tsura explained, considering the fire. It warmed her brown eyes.

Aishe piped in. "We stay up all through the night listening to the old women tell us tales of our people."

"We meet kin from other clans, share a meal, and talk about customs and traditions. Because we roam, it is important that we uphold this tradition. All would be lost for us if we didn't pass on the Old Ways to the little ones," Tsura explained, winking at Aishe.

Aishe rearranged herself in Vittoria's lap so she could place her tiny hands over Vittoria's cheeks, and considered her teary eyes.

"Your heart aches. I can feel it," she reported. "It makes me feel so sad that I want to cry."

A single tear slipped down Vittoria's cheek. Whatever Aishe could see or feel, Vittoria knew the child was right about the way she was feeling.

"It seems you have quite a talent, little one," Vittoria acknowledged, forcing a weak smile.

"It's her gift. She was born with this ability," Tsura clarified.

"You have it too," Aishe stated and kissed Vittoria's wet cheek. She slid her smooth little arms around Vittoria's neck hugging her.

"Vittoria, do you know why I decided to help you today?" Tsura queried.

"No, and I can't figure out why you did."

Tsura turned the skewers in the fire.

"Though your familiar looks drew me to you, I decided to help you when I saw your eyes."

"My eyes?" she asked. "What about them?"

"It's the green with the gold ring in the center. Do you know anybody else with eyes like yours?"

"My mother," she answered.

"I have only ever seen your eye coloring among my own people." She paused for dramatic effect. "Strega."

"I'm not Strega!" Vittoria exclaimed.

"Are you sure about that?"

"No. I'm not sure of anything," she admitted. "Mama once mentioned that her people were descendants of this land. I thought she meant that they were Roman."

"I can see how you would assume such a thing. There aren't many of us left and it is rare that we reveal our heritage to strangers."

"Why not?"

"Because the Church would accuse us of being witches."

"Witches?"

Vittoria toyed again with her necklace.

"We are Benedanti. By the blessing of Diana, the Lady of Light and mother of all Strega, we can harness the elemental powers of the natural world to help and heal. We would never do you harm, Vittoria," she explained, sensing her growing unease.

"Is that why you hide out here?" Vittoria whispered, sweeping her hands out toward the dark old woods. "So, you won't be persecuted?"

"Yes and no," Tsura smiled. "You see, we are not in hiding. We enjoy living in nature. Here we feel closest to the Goddess, though some Strega have settled in the cities."

"Goddess? There is no such thing!" Vittoria retorted.

"That is your belief. I understand."

"Tsura speaks the truth," Aishe claimed, supporting her sister.

Tsura observed the Cimaruta around Vittoria's neck again. "Was your necklace a gift?"

"It was my mother's. She gave it to me when I was confirmed in the Church."

"It is beautiful. What was your mother's name?"

"Orabella."

Aishe's golden eyes widened in recognition.

"Vittoria, you may believe me or not. I think you have much to gain if you choose to. My instinct tells me you are kin. I believe that is why I found you today."

Vittoria steadied her head between her hands, and tears slipped from her tired eyes. "They will find you. Those were my mother's parting words to me."

Tsura smiled. "You have heard that God works in mysterious ways, have you not?"

"Yes," Vittoria answered, lifting her head.

"Well, we say the Goddess reveals all."

Vittoria, Tsura, and Aishe stayed up late into the night enjoying roasted chestnuts and talking.

Though the company was pleasant, Vittoria needed to close her eyes. She hadn't slept without the influence of drink in many days. Tsura gave her a blanket and she lay back on the rug letting her stiff limbs relax. Her bare feet rested in the cool grass and the crisp autumn breeze caressed her face. Vittoria looked up through the giant old oak trees in the grove toward the night sky. The stars twinkled brightly in the heavens, and the waxing moon illuminated the camp. The leaves of the trees rustled, and the crickets chirped.

"Tsura?"

"Hmm?"

"I don't want to close my eyes. I'm afraid of what I'll see," she admitted, worried that images of her past would come rushing back again.

"There's no need to worry, Vittoria. You're safe here," Tsura promised.

Aishe nestled herself under the blanket with Vittoria. The child was warm and smelled of honey and smoke. Her presence quelled Vittoria's worries.

"Rest now," Tsura urged.

"I'll try."

"That is all you need to do. I'll take care of the rest," Tsura assured her.

Vittoria let her eyes flutter closed and fell asleep.

Quick footsteps rustled the grass. Before she could lift her head to see who was coming, Aishe sprang upon Vittoria.

"Good morning, sleepyhead," Aishe giggled.

Vittoria freed herself from Aishe's grasp and rolled the little sprite onto her back. With Tsura's help, they tickled her until she squealed for them to show mercy. Her sweet contagious laughter infected them both with mirth. They doubled over laughing until their sides ached from the effort. Vittoria fell back onto the grass to catch her breath.

Once they regained their composure Aishe took up her seat in Vittoria's lap and Tsura handed them both a bit of bread with honey. Tsura munched on her breakfast, while Aishe and Vittoria made faces at each other.

"Do you want to see how fast I am, Vittoria?" Aishe asked.

"Yes, and I bet you are so quick I won't be able to see you when you run."

"Why don't you run over to Papa's camp and back," Tsura encouraged. "Ready? Go!"

Aishe was off and running. Not as quick as she imagined she was, but she was precious just the same. Tsura watched her little sister as she sped toward a tent on the far side of the grove.

"Vittoria, I spoke to my father about you this morning. I asked him if you could stay with us."

"Oh, Tsura, you did not have to do that. You've already gone out of your way for me."

"Vittoria, my suspicions about you are strong, and we always help our kind," she said, looking back over her shoulder at Aishe, who had just turned back toward them.

"But I don't belong here," Vittoria argued.

Tsura waved off Vittoria's comment. Aishe returned to the camp winded and tumbled to the ground next to Vittoria.

"It's time to go," Tsura announced.

"Where?" Vittoria asked.

"Papa wants to meet you."

Tsura's father was a weathered-beaten man. Deep lines meandered all over his leathery face. His once thick black hair had thinned and was streaked through with silver. His heavy brow shaded his astute eyes. He sat on a tree stump and leaned on a carved oak staff decorated with colored stones and strange symbols. His eyes were serious as he watched Vittoria approaching with his daughters. His face revealed nothing.

Aishe ran ahead and greeted her father. "Good morning, Papa!" she said, wrapping her arms around his neck.

"Good morning, Aishe," he replied, with a booming chuckle. His eyes crinkled at the edges as he smiled at her.

"Papa, this is Vittoria. Vittoria this is my father, Lucio LaGuardia."

Lucio looked at Vittoria's face for a long time searching for clues. Vittoria noticed several amulets draped around his neck. Vittoria grabbed the small cross that dangled from her own neck and fiddled with it to quell her uneasiness.

"Good morning, Signore. Thank you for your hospitality. Tsura has shown me great kindness and I am very grateful."

A smile appeared on Lucio's face. "You are most welcome, Vittoria," his dark eyes flickered toward Tsura with an approving look. "Please sit down. Would you like something to eat or drink, perhaps?"

Tsura nodded her head encouragingly, so Vittoria accepted the invitation. They sat down side by side on a rug outside the entrance to his tent.

Lucio passed Vittoria a piece of bread and poured a cup of herbal brew for her to drink. Aishe recanted to her father how Vittoria saved her from tumbling into the fire.

"She's like an angel, Papa," Aishe avowed.

"I am sure that she is," Lucio said, patting Aishe's little leg. "Thank the Goddess you are safe. What would I ever do without you, my love?"

Vittoria drank the herbal concoction. It was much stronger than what Tsura had served her. She choked and sputtered on the first sip. Wiping at the dribble on her chin, Vittoria recovered from the surprise.

"Forgive me, Vittoria." Lucio apologized as she coughed. "I tend to prefer my drink on the bitter side," he explained, offering a small shrug. He sent Aishe to fetch the honey.

Tsura laughed and patted Vittoria on the back.

"I'm fine," she said, struggling to clear her throat.

"Did you sleep well?" Lucio asked.

"Yes, I did. But I am still tired. I haven't been sleeping well recently."

"Sleeping under trees is generally not very comfortable," Tsura joked.

"How did you come to be under a tree that far away from Florence? That is where you're from, isn't it?" Lucio asked, his heavy dark brows raised in question.

Vittoria wasn't sure how she came to be under that tree. She didn't remember very much after finding Marcel's letter. So, she avoided answering the first portion of his question.

"I am from Florence. My parents died, and I left home the end of August to seek refuge in the countryside."

"You've been wandering *alone* for two months?" Lucio asked.

"I'd be terribly bored if I were by myself for that long," Tsura stated.

"Well, no. I, uh, I was only alone for a few days," Vittoria replied. "I found shelter for a while in a country villa south of Florence, but it didn't feel right to stay on, so I went wandering."

"It's not safe for a girl to wander about alone," Lucio chided.

Vittoria knew all too well the truth in that statement. "Yes, but I don't know if it is yet safe to return home."

Lucio nodded, understanding her point. "From what I have heard, there was a mandatory quarantine for those exposed to plague in Florence. How did you come to escape confinement?"

"That is true. It was my mother's dying wish for me to flee the city, and the plague doctor encouraged me to go."

"Perhaps he knew he'd be sending you to certain death," Lucio reasoned.

"He was sweet on Vittoria, that's why he let her go," joked Tsura, again.

"Nevertheless. There is a reason for everything. You can be sure of that," Lucio concluded.

Vittoria begged to differ. There was no reason for her parents to be taken from her, or for Marcel to leave with no good explanation. None of it made

TRACY CAUSLEY

sense to her at all. And not knowing the reason for either made her angry.

"It seems to me that God is angry with us."

"Is that what you truly think?" Lucio inquired.

"What other reason could there be for so many people to suffer and die?" Vittoria reasoned.

"What if it has nothing to do with God?" Lucio challenged.

"That's impossible!" Vittoria exclaimed.

"What if it weren't?"

Vittoria looked to Tsura for clarification.

"You know what I told you last night about our people, the Benedanti?"

Vittoria nodded.

"There is another group of Strega, the Malandanti. They are our kin, yet they draw their power from perpetrating pain and suffering, rather than from the inexhaustible source of nature. They live in cities where the population is greater, and the energy of adversity, power, and control is in great abundance. They must generate chaos to thrive."

"I don't understand."

"Tsura means that the plague is not God's doing, it's that of the Malandanti," said Lucio.

"You cannot be serious!" Vittoria cried. "You mean that there are witches strong enough to kill thousands of people at once?"

"With help from a powerful source, they are," Tsura added.

"But who would do such a thing?"

"You'd be surprised the lengths some would go to achieve their ends, for better or worse."

"What are you going to do about this?" Vittoria demanded. "You can't allow *your* kin to take lives. They killed my parents."

"Your parents were already dying," Aishe said. She'd been quiet the entire time until then.

Vittoria was stunned. "Why would you say such a thing, Aishe?" she asked, appalled she would make such a claim.

"Grandmother told me so."

"Your grandmother is *wrong*," Vittoria retorted.

"She would never lie to me," Aishe replied, matter-of-fact.

"We would not lie to you either," Tsura concurred. "We speak the truth about our kin. We speak the truth to you."

"We are *not* kin."

"Was your mother's name Orabella Giordano?" Lucio asked.

"How do you know that?"

"Was it?"

"Yes."

He sighed, setting down his cup. "Then you are my niece."

The memory of her mother dying came rushing back to her. It didn't make sense.

"But, how?"

"Your mother is my younger sister."

Vittoria gasped.

"And we are your cousins," Tsura added, pointing to herself and then Aishe.

"I don't understand. How could I not know about you? What did the Malandanti have to do with her death?"

"Your mother left this clan twenty years ago. She fell in love with your father and gave up her life here. By law, she was never to cast another spell or speak about her life as Benedanti. That is why. Imagine leaving your entire family behind and never speaking of them to a soul. Imagine knowing that your departure weakened the strength of your clan, leaving it vulnerable to the shadow cast by the Malandanti. The guilt and regret your mother harbored must have eaten at her like a disease for years. The spell cast by the Malandanti transmuted her great pain and suffering into a plague," Lucio explained.

"But what about my father?"

"Your father knew our customs but was unwilling to join our clan as ordinaries do when they marry one of our own. Instead, he sought success as a merchant in the city. Your mother sacrificed her life, and relinquished her powers, for him. Perhaps he felt guilty for demanding this of her, though we cannot know for certain the reason."

Vittoria shook her head in denial. She didn't want to believe any of it. Tears filled and spilled from her sad eyes. Her life as she knew it was a lie. She had no idea who she was or what purpose her life held.

"It's much to take in, Vittoria. But you must know that you are among family now," Tsura said, making the effort to comfort her cousin.

Aishe hugged her father for her own comfort. It seemed to pain her to see anyone upset.

"You are my sister's child and you have a place here with us, Vittoria, if you wish it."

Finding her voice through the tears, Vittoria responded. "I need time to think."

"Take as much time as you need," Lucio encouraged, hugging Aishe tighter to him.

Vittoria stood and walked away. She needed to be alone.

Vittoria rambled around the boundary of the camp. She didn't want to meet anyone new, so she kept to the tree line in the shade of the old oaks.

A few horses grazed in the meadow nearby and she stopped to watch them. They were clean and strong and seemed very content. Pieces of bright colored cloth had been woven into their manes and tails and when they moved she heard tiny chimes tinkling.

Looking closer she saw bells had been attached to the cloth. The horses were so beautiful that she was compelled to approach them.

She remembered that brushing Marcel's horse, Bellance, always relaxed her, so she tiptoed closer. Just as she put out her hand to stroke a large black mare something brushed her shoulder. Spinning around she found herself face-to-face with an old woman.

"You scared me!" Vittoria exclaimed.

"I have been here the entire time. You should be more conscious of your surroundings, Vittoria," the woman said.

"How do you know my name?"

"I know about everything and everyone in this camp," she replied, a placid expression upon her wizened face.

The woman looked like a witch. Vittoria stared at her wide-eyed. Her long hair was silver and pulled into a loose braid that ran the length of her back. Her eyes were keen and perceptive. They looked like they belonged to a much younger person. She was small in stature but stood straight as an arrow. Her voice was clear and unhurried.

The woman wore a dark green dress with strange symbols embroidered along the sleeves. Around her neck hung charms like Lucio's, and on her fingers, were several bejeweled rings. She allowed Vittoria the time to appraise her before she spoke again.

"Pretty creatures, are they not?" Her wrinkled hand stroked the mane of the black horse.

"Yes, they are," Vittoria replied, eying the strange woman beside her. "Are you Strega, too?" she blurted.

"My name is Celestina. I am Tsura's grandmother and the matriarch of this clan of Benedanti. And so, I think you know the answer to that question, my dear," she replied.

Vittoria dropped her gaze.

"You are still doubtful of all that you have been told," she sensed of Vittoria. "That will change." The dark horse whinnied as if to agree with her. "Why don't you accompany an old woman on her walk," Celestina said, wrapping her arm through Vittoria's and leading her away from the horses.

Vittoria knew she did not need her assistance but followed without protest.

"You do have the look," Celestina said more to herself than to Vittoria. "It is fortunate that Tsura found you, isn't it?"

Vittoria shrugged. She wasn't so sure after all.

"It was no coincidence she found you."

"Of course, it was. She did not know I was going to be there," Vittoria disagreed.

"Is that so?" Celestina queried.

"There's no way she could have known."

Celestina took a different tact. "That may be true, but why do you believe she brought you here?"

"I don't know *why*," Vittoria replied, her tone petulant.

"It's quite simple," Celestina pointed out. "It is not yet your time to die. You have undiscovered talents that will be of great benefit to others in the future."

"How do you know that?"

"I know a lot of things, my dear. That is why you have come to us. This is the first step in the rest of your life's journey," she explained. "What do you think the years ahead will hold for you?"

Vittoria pondered the questions. "I hope there is some happiness ahead. Well, as much happiness as possible without my parents."

"That is a good start, but I think you'll find you have more family than you ever expected. What about a husband and children?"

"I don't need a man to care for me," she answered. Throwing herself into the torrent of love had almost drowned her.

Celestina chuckled. She looked at Vittoria with her penetrating gaze. "You have been hurt by love," she said, more a statement than a question.

Vittoria shook her head in agreement but remained silent.

"Don't worry, I think you might be surprised by your luck," she smiled and patted her hand. "I would not worry about the dowry either."

"You can't get married without a dowry!" Vittoria exclaimed. "Every girl needs a dowry to give to her husband."

"But you aren't an ordinary girl," she retorted.

"What other kind of girl would I be?" Vittoria scoffed.

"You tell me."

They wandered in silence for a while. Vittoria's mind worked hard to figure out what this woman was trying to say without directly saying it. They passed a few men and women who were busy outside of their tents. They looked up from their work to greet Celestina and offer her a smile and a wave. None of them seemed at all surprised to see her strolling with the old witch.

"Why don't they seem alarmed by my presence?"

"Should they be?" Celestina's constant questioning was beginning to chafe her.

"Well, I don't belong here. I'm an outsider," she said, explaining what she believed was so obvious.

"That is untrue."

"No, it isn't!" Vittoria cried out, tired of all the banter. She came here to be alone. Celestina remained quiet.

"Forgive me," Vittoria said, embarrassed by her childish outburst. "I'm very tired."

"My child, I understand you feel lost. Your old life was ripped away from you, and though I am sure it was comfortable, it was not the one you were meant to lead."

"How do you know that? You don't know anything about me," she argued, folding her arms in defense.

"What do you know about yourself?" Celestina countered, her dark eyebrow raised, emphasizing her question.

"I know enough," she retorted.

"Now, don't be cross," Celestina said, patting Vittoria's forearm. "You are very fortunate. The wheels have already been set into motion and your journey will take you far," she said, reaching her aged arms out to her sides to express the vastness of the world of which she spoke.

"What do you mean?" Vittoria murmured, still not meeting the old woman's eyes with her own. Celestina didn't notice. She had a faraway look in her eyes like she was envisioning the journey in her mind. Her strong clear voice became a whisper and Vittoria had to strain to hear what she said next.

"Your fate is tied to many others. If you fail to live authentically, you will bring danger and pain to those whom you love and who love you."

"You are joking," she chuckled, not believing a word of what the old woman prophesied.

Celestina's sharp eyes snapped back into focus on Vittoria's face. "I never joke, when it comes to life and death, and neither should you. You are still very immature, but that is not of your own doing. Life will unravel quite quickly for you from here on. You will be required to gain much experience in a short period. I trust your cousins will help you along with your education."

"My cousins? Did Tsura tell you?"

Celestina did not respond. Walking in silence for several paces they reentered the main camp where a cluster of tents was set together. From out of the silence, a trill of youthful laughter filled the air. Aishe popped out from behind the tents with another little dark-haired girl about her own age of seven.

"There she is!" Aishe laughed, pointing Vittoria out to her companion. "That is my angel," she declared, waving to her.

Vittoria waved back, surprised, and happy to see Aishe's smiling face. It came as an unexpected relief to her.

"Tsura told us to come and find you," Aishe explained, her auburn hair was wild around her heart-shaped face.

Vittoria now had an excuse to relieve herself from Celestina's company.

"It was a pleasure," Vittoria said flatly.

"A truer statement has never been spoken," the witch replied, sticking her tongue out at the children before walking away toward the horses.

"I had the delightful pleasure of meeting your grandmother," Vittoria said, before recounting the details of her time with the terrifying woman.

"She is sweet, isn't she," Tsura replied, batting her thick dark lashes.

"Tsura, tell me something. Had you ever been to collect chestnuts in the location where you found me?"

"Why do you ask?"

"I'm only wondering why you wandered to that particular place all alone."

"Grandmother told me where to go to find the chestnuts," she admitted.

"Isn't that a coincidence?" Vittoria mumbled under her breath.

"What?"

"Nothing," Vittoria mumbled again, realizing there was more to the story. None of it made sense. Yet, she could not argue with the fact that she was grateful she had been found regardless of the mystery behind her recovery. Vittoria was going to have to wait patiently to uncover the reason for all these coincidental occurrences. Unfortunately, patience was not one of her greatest virtues.

"Tsura, may Jina come with us to wash up?" Aishe asked, motioning to her friend.

Jina smiled. Two of her front teeth were missing. The wide dark gap gave her a curious mischievous look when she grinned.

"Of course," Tsura agreed. "We were just getting ready to go."

"Where are we going?" Vittoria asked.

"We are going to a little stream on the other side of the grove. Do you have something clean to wear once you've washed? You'll want to change out of that," Tsura pointed towards Vittoria's dingy dress. "It needs a good cleaning."

"I don't think so." Vittoria wasn't sure if she did or not. She didn't remember packing her bag before leaving the villa. There could be anything in there. She did hope she remembered the diptych. It would be a devastating blow if she hadn't. It was all she had to remember her parents.

"I'm sure I can find something for you. Go on ahead."

"Come on, Aishe," Jina lisped, in her squeaky little voice. "Let's race!"

And off went the two of them, their auburn and black manes whipping in the breeze behind them.

Neither of them had a care in the world. Vittoria was envious.

"I'll bring the soap," Tsura called after them.

Aishe and Jina had already rid themselves of their clothes and were splashing in the clear cool stream. The sun glistened off their wet skin and their long hair bobbed back and forth in the current. Mouthfuls of water muffled their constant laughter. They challenged each other to see who could hold their breath longest, and as hard as Aishe tried she always popped up for breath before Jina.

"Vittoria, count for us," Aishe shouted when she reached the edge of the stream. "We want to know who can stay under the water longest. I think Jina is cheating."

"I am not!" Jina argued.

"Don't argue, you two," Tsura warned. "We'll judge your contest to see who the best is. Won't we, Vittoria?"

"You'd better get in the water, so you can watch Jina," Aishe insisted.

They undressed on the large smooth rocks by the edge of the stream. Vittoria felt less nervous undressing because she was not under inspection this time around. However, she noticed Tsura was so much rounder and developed in her hips and breasts than she was. Tsura was a woman in every physical way.

She looked like Aphrodite worshiping the warmth of the afternoon sun as she floated on her back in the water. Free and uninhibited, she was so comfortable in her own skin.

"Are you getting in Vittoria or are you just going to stand there?" Tsura inquired as she floated by.

"We're waiting," Jina whined.

"I'm coming," she said, sliding into the babbling stream, and submerging herself. She heard Tsura snicker before going under.

When Vittoria resurfaced Tsura made lots of light-hearted chatter while they washed up. Tsura managed to get the girls clean between rounds of contest. Vittoria relaxed into the moment with the girls. Tsura perplexed her in that she could make her uncomfortable one moment, then the very next she'll have made her forget why she had felt that way.

They swam, splashed, and played in the water until their fingers and toes shriveled up and goosebumps covered their bodies. They were having such an enjoyable time that Vittoria didn't notice Tsura had disappeared from the fun and games.

Tsura had docked herself on one of the flat rocks and was lounging languidly. She had not dressed yet but lay on her side with her long smooth legs stretching toward the water's edge. Her head was propped up on her toned tan arm and her heavy wet hair draped over her shoulders. She looked at something upstream. Following her gaze Vittoria saw a young man slight of build with shoulder-length brown hair tied back at the nape of his neck. He stood in the shadows of a willow tree swaying over the stream. He watched Tsura, and she watched him. Vittoria saw the corner of his modest mouth curve with delight and his light eyes flashed lustfully.

Tsura hadn't even noticed that the noise in the stream had died down and that she was being watched by more pairs of eyes than just those of the stranger in the shadows.

"What are you doing? That man is watching you."

Tsura's head snapped toward Vittoria, the fires of seduction burning in her brown eyes.

"Don't you see him there?" Vittoria asked, pointing back toward the willow. But the man had disappeared.

Tsura never responded to any of Vittoria's questions, nor did she acknowledge that she had let that man observe her nakedness. She remained mum about the incident. Even after they dressed and made the walk back to camp. Tsura was quiet. Her mind was elsewhere, somewhere in the clouds. A strange wistful smile played on her full lips. It was as if she knew her admirer was going to be there, and she was contenting herself with memory of the encounter.

"Do you do that often? I mean, that isn't very proper, is it?" Vittoria fumbled with her question.

"The way things are and the way they should be are two different things, Vittoria. When you fall in love you'll understand. Your body will make decisions that your mind cannot overrule and there is nothing that can be done about that," she said, an edge of finality in her usually smooth voice. The topic was closed to further discussion.

Vittoria nodded her head because there was nothing else to say. She felt a sour pang of regret thud in the pit of her stomach. She misplaced all common sense when she was lost in her romance with Marcel.

Vittoria observed the people and activity in the Benedanti camp. Every passerby inclined their head in greeting to her as they swept by, never giving her the impression she was an unwelcome guest among them.

Most of the women were tall and their skin was bronze and smooth. They strolled barefoot in the grass, their toned bodies graceful. And their hair was either wrapped up in a kerchief or trailed loosely behind them. The men, for the most part, were as handsome as the women were beautiful. They were broad-chested and strong in the arms. Most of them wore their linen shirts unlaced revealing soft pelts of hair.

Over the course of the week, Vittoria had lots of time to think about the turn of events that had brought her to this place. She had yet to wrap her mind around the idea that her mother was Benedanti and that despicable witches were responsible for her death.

Nothing seemed real. It felt like it was all part of a dream, including the people she encountered along the way—Nico, Marcel, Magda, and Ugo. Tsura sensed her discomfiture for she and Aishe did everything possible to make her feel welcome and comfortable. They introduced her to other people in the camp, ate meals with her, and gave her plenty of time to be alone.

Vittoria listened to the people speak to one another. Their voices silky and melodic. Their accents were different than the Florentino dialect spoken at home, even some of the words sounded foreign to her. Whatever it was, Vittoria could not quite place it. It was like nothing she had heard before. She closed her eyes and listened. The lull of the smooth inflection and rounded vowels was relaxing.

The people in the camp could have been from another time and place in antiquity. She tried to envisage an Etruscan city full of glistening temples with statues of pagan gods and goddesses. The women just as lovely, except wearing more gold and jewels. The men, strong powerful warriors, glorious to look upon in their shining armor. The daydream brought a smile to her face and she pondered.

Could I be descended from these people?

Vittoria hoped that Lucio and Tsura were both right, there was a reason for everything and that the Goddess revealed all. She had nothing left to do but wait and see.

"Vittoria?" Tsura called from inside her tent. "What are you doing out there?" she asked, popping her head outside the tent to see what she was up to.

"Nothing. Watching," Vittoria explained, pulling herself out of her daydream.

"Well, since you're doing nothing, why don't you come in here. I have something for you," she ordered.

Vittoria hopped up from her place on the ground and winced at the painful sensation in her legs and rear that comes after sitting still for too long. The sun was almost down, and candles had been lit inside the tent. When she entered she was that Tsura was wearing a sheer gown of a silken material. The curves of her body lurked in the shadows of the dress and when she moved closer toward the candlelight they were nearly exposed.

"What are you wearing?" Vittoria inquired, dazzled by the sight of her.

"This is my robe for tonight's ritual. I have one for you as well," she replied. She held a similar garment up in front of Vittoria's body to evaluate the fit.

"I think this will work," she said, satisfied with her estimation.

"You want me to wear this?" Vittoria balked. "You can see right through it!" she exclaimed.

"Would you rather go naked? I can arrange that," Tsura threatened, yanking the garment out of Vittoria's grasp.

"No!" It would mortify her to stand naked next to all the beautiful women in the camp. "You are all so beautiful. I feel like I shouldn't even stand next to you."

"Oh, come now," Tsura chided. "You are a very becoming woman. You need to embrace your beauty. In a couple of years, you'll complain that you have too much of what you hope for today," she explained, motioning toward her barely-there breasts.

Vittoria sighed. "I suppose you are right."

"See there, now you'll have something to look forward to!" Tsura said, pinching her reddening cheek.

The gown was not so terrible after all. The material felt cool to the touch as it slid over her flushed skin and clung to her body around her shoulders and waist. It fell loosely around the neck and legs. Her arms and back were bare. To her surprise, the embarrassment and feeling of inadequacy dissipated. She twirled once for Tsura.

"If I didn't know any better, I'd think you like the way you look," she said.

Tsura was right. Vittoria tried to hide her smile as she spun around again.

"If you could stand still for one moment I would like to fix your hair."

She brushed out Vittoria's snarled locks and then braided the front of her hair so that it looked like an elaborate crown upon her head. The remainder she let flow down her back so that it covered the skin that was exposed. Before Tsura let her gaze into a polished looking glass, she decorated Vittoria's green eyes with kohl. When she was able to glimpse herself in the mirror, Vittoria almost didn't recognize the person looking back.

She looked like one of the Etruscan beauties she had imagined moments before. Vittoria's chest swelled with gratitude towards Tsura, and her eyes brimmed with tears.

"Don't cry, silly girl! You'll ruin my handiwork," she warned, although tears welled in her eyes, too.

"Thank you so much," Vittoria gushed. She hugged Tsura tightly.

As Tsura pried herself out of Vittoria's clutches, she replied jokingly, as always. "I'll have to do my best to keep you out of Cai's line of sight tonight, or I may have my work cut out for me."

"Yes, you may want to do that. I might get burned by his smoldering gaze," Vittoria retorted, finally getting the last word.

The full moon hung high overhead flooding the meadow with its luminous light. Butterflies swarmed in Vittoria's stomach. It was time for the Benedanti to begin their ritual. Her heart fluttered from the anticipation.

The meadow was no longer the horse's grazing place. It had been transformed into a place betwixt and between, neither heaven nor earth, but a place of wondrous magic.

More strangers emerged from the trees smiling pleasantly. Their eyes twinkled in the moonlight as they walked two by two, man and woman, boy and girl, into their respective places within the circle.

Tsura took Vittoria by the hand and guided her to a place on the eastern edge of the meadow. The circle grew full and round with people. Each held their head high, proud to be Strega. Tsura grinned at Vittoria and she reciprocated with a gleaming smile of her own.

Greetings of good cheer were uttered around the circle. All the women were dressed the same as she, in their diaphanous gowns and braided crowns of hair stacked upon their heads. The men wore shin-length breeches with their hair loose and free. They exuded such masculinity. She was reminded of Nico.

The ritual circle became silent and Vittoria watched with interest as Celestina and Lucio entered the circle together. Celestina wore a white velvet robe with strange symbols embroidered in black and gold thread. The images Vittoria recognized were commonplace items such as the head of a rooster, a snake, a dagger, and a spring of rue. She carried herself regally as she took her place at the center of the circle.

She never needed my assistance, Vittoria observed.

Celestina's eyes roved over the circle of people allowing her gaze to linger on Vittoria. A flash of hot fear blazed over her skin. It was cooled by the inkling of a smile Celestina let flicker from her eyes. It seemed to Vittoria, a hint of approval.

Tsura received a nod from Celestina about something known only to the two of them. As she continued her inventory of all in attendance, Lucio stepped forward in a black robe. Like Celestina's it was embroidered in white and gold thread. They represented day and night, light and dark, young and old, male and female.

Lucio spoke first.

"We gather here in love and trust, to honor the living and the dead. We have witnessed the loss and destruction of life, more than any person should have to bear in a lifetime. It is incomprehensible that so much has been taken from the world in so little time. Yet we must be thankful for all that we still have— the love of our families and the strength of our clan— without which, we would have perished long ago."

Everyone nodded in agreement and Lucio continued.

"Tonight, we welcome into our fold new life, one that has yet to bloom. Each one of you has taken notice of her presence and understands why she is here with us tonight."

All the eyes that had been watching Lucio flickered in unison at Vittoria and then right back to him. He carried on.

"May the light of Diana shine on you and all who gather here this night," he said, with a knowing glance and nod in Vittoria's direction.

Celestina stepped forward toward a rather large stump of a long ago felled tree and retrieved a short, deadly sharp, dagger. She held it up in front of her. Closing her eyes, she whispered some words over the knife. Its blade glinted in the bright moonlight. Then she raised the dagger high above her head and cried out several words, foreign to Vittoria's ears. As she did so, the air around her crackled. Her arms tingled, and the hair stood on end.

Celestina extended her arm and pointed the dagger out in front of her. She twirled in place thrice. Each time she spun her white robe whirled around her body and the pressure in the air rose. During Celestina's ancient chanting, Vittoria caught a word she recognized from the late-night conversations with Tsura.

Diana

The intensity of the atmosphere grew, and Vittoria's common sense told her to run away as fast as her legs could carry her. Synchronously, she was pulled closer to Celestina, to the dagger, and to the one called by many names.

The Strega in the circle closed ranks as if an invisible rope had been cast about, compelling them to move ever closer to the source of its power.

Lucio turned to face eastward, and with his arms outstretched in front of him, in a gesture of welcome, said with a booming voice.

"Guardians of the Watchtower of the East, and the Element of Air, we bid you welcome! Guard and protect this circle."

Winged creatures of all sorts flew into the meadow and alighted in the trees including birds, bats, butterflies, and flying insects. Celestina lit a censer full of frankincense and myrrh as an offering to them, and a plume of sensuous smoke spiraled heavenward reminding Vittoria of the hundreds of masses she'd attended in her lifetime.

Next, Lucio faced south.

"Guardians of the Watchtower of the South, and the Element of Fire, we bid you welcome! Guard and protect this circle."

Snakes and lizards slithered, and bees flew into the southern corner of the meadow. Celestina lit a red candle upon the altar to welcome them.

Facing west, Lucio called out.

"Guardians of the Watchtower of the West, and the Element of Water, we bid you welcome! Guard and protect this circle."

Turtles sidled, and frogs hopped, into the western edge of the meadow. Celestina lifted a bowl full of water from the natural altar, dipped her fingers into it and then sprinkled the surrounding space with the water as a blessing.

Finally, Lucio faced toward the North.

"Guardians of the Watchtower of the North, and the Element of Earth, we bid you welcome! Guard and protect this circle."

Horses and greyhound dogs pranced, and gophers burrowed up from the ground, into the northern end of the meadow. As blessing for their presence, Celestina raised a bowl of salt and then sprinkled a handful around the altar.

Lucio returned to his place next to Celestina at the altar and together they invoked the Goddess.

"Diana, Lady of Light, Mother of All Strega, we bid you welcome. Bless us with your love and light."

The greyhounds howled, the birds flapped their wings, the horses whinnied, and the frogs croaked. The light of the moon grew brighter and a diffuse sparkly haze appeared in the circle. Together Lucio and Celestina lit a great chalice at the center of the altar and from it blazed a blue flame. The Goddess was present.

Vittoria wished to know more about this being of light and, as if her mind had been read, Celestina told the legend of Diana, Queen Mother of the Strega.

"It was upon these rolling hills many thousands of years ago, that Diana, the Mother of All Strega, anointed a peasant girl called Aradia as her mortal daughter and heir. She was blessed with two gifts—the light magic of clarity and shadow magic of contrast—each of which benefited humankind. Aradia bore twin daughters, one the moment the moon was fullest and the other as it fell into shadow once more. The children were marked with eyes of green and gold, the embodiment of light within Diana's sacred circle grove."

Vittoria gasped. She had gold and green eyes.

"It is from the twins that the lineages of the Benedanti, the light bringers, and the Malandanti, the shadow casters, sprung. Our purpose is to preserve balance in the land forevermore, so humanity can flourish, it is not to seek dominion. This tenuous balance has tipped and shadow reigns. It is with great urgency that we petition the Lady of Light to rebalance the scales. During this great period of contrast, we trust clarity will spring forth. So, we come together this night to offer our thanks and prayers."

Celestina bowed and the Benedanti followed suit. Vittoria heard a muffled cacophony of prayers and thanks mumbled by Tsura and the others.

Celestina continued.

"We honor Diana's light by protecting this land from darkness. The Malandanti have harnessed a power stronger than we've ever seen. Should they succeed in overturning the balance they will claim dominion over the entire known world, casting a long shadow of malevolence and cruelty upon it."

The entire circle gasped.

"From my visions, I have seen that my own niece, the Malatrix Nerezza, has conspired with the Church at the highest level. She obtained the Scourge Scroll, and with the help of the Holy Father, drew down power strong enough to desecrate the land and its people with plague."

Celestina's proclamation shocked Vittoria. She couldn't believe her ears.

Has the Church been infiltrated? Was that even possible?

The idea of it made her feel sick.

"This malice has incited fear and anger amongst ordinaries and we Strega are at risk. Though we serve the people of this land we are perceived as outsiders and, as such, a threat. Fearful people looking to blame something for this terrible pestilence will look to us. It has become a dangerous time for Benedanti."

People murmured to one another. Vittoria was scared. Lucio spoke, his voice ringing loud and clear.

"Tonight, we will be not afraid. We will dance, and we will sing, and we do it all for the glory of our beloved Lady Diana, from whom all life springs. We live on in her service and will do so until she sees fit to snuff out our light. Until then we will celebrate life and goodness, for there is still plenty of it."

"We will raise power within our circle by stating, in turn, what we wish to seek out and celebrate. Then we will commence our act of worship," Celestina informed them.

It became hard for Vittoria to concentrate. She was nervous and afraid. Tsura squeezed her hand, pulling her away from the precipice of fear before she jumped off the cliff. Words of hope poured into the darkness from the Benedanti, connected to her through the power of the circle. Vittoria focused her attention on all the simple, yet poignant answers given by the Strega.

"Love."

"Joy."

"Peace."

"Wisdom."

The list went on and on. While the queue shortened, Vittoria tried to sum up her experiences from the last two months. What was the one thing she felt she was missing? What was the one thing she would go to the end of the world to obtain? The heat of Celestina's gaze fell upon her and she blurted her wish into the circle.

"Truth."

Sheer satisfaction crossed Celestina's wizened face. Up until that point, she had responded to no one else.

"You might find it yet."

Vittoria's mind swam with memories of the ritual. Under a blanket of stars and a moon so full and bright, in the center of the Benedanti circle, she was made privy to thousands of years of secret knowledge.

The rite under the full moon was a profound and majestic experience and she felt a deep shift had occurred within her. It was like a secret door had been unlocked in her heart and from it spilled forth hope. Her body buzzed with clarity. She knew for certain the realms of magic and make-believe existed.

All the elements of the ceremony were simple and collective. The free-spirited dancing, melodic chanting, and primeval drumming stirred up an atmosphere conducive to receiving and understanding the mysteries of the world, those seen and unseen.

Vittoria found herself participating in the ritual, enjoying herself, and when it came to its conclusion she yearned to continue. She wanted to know more, and she realized that she never had anything to fear. She had become aware of her connectedness to these strangers, her people.

As she lay on her bedroll staring up at the sky, she toyed with her necklace. It felt different between her fingers. She unhooked the clasp and took it off. Holding it up to her eyes, she saw it. The cross had disappeared. Hanging from the delicate chain was something else entirely.

"It's a Cimaruta," Tsura said. She lay beside Vittoria.

Vittoria speculated on the meaning of the strange word. "Sprig of rue?"

"Yes!" Tsura's face was bright with delight at her accurate guess. "Rue is the sacred herb of the goddess Diana, and because she is the Goddess of all Strega we hold the herb in high regard and use it often in our magic. The Etruscans, our ancestors, also used this herb as an amulet for protection," she explained.

"Will it protect me too?"

"Of course, it will protect you. It brought you here, didn't it?"

Aishe and Celestina surprised Tsura with their unexpected visit. They caught her crying again.

"What are you doing here," she sputtered, wiping the evidence of tears from her face though she could do nothing about the red splotches.

Aishe went to Tsura and threw her arms around her neck. "I'm worried about you," she told her big sister.

"So am I," Celestina concurred, sitting herself down upon a stack of cushions.

"You didn't seem to care about my feelings when you and Papa told Cai to keep his distance from me."

"Don't you understand? He's not good for you. It was my hope to match you with one of the young fellows from another clan, but it's clear you're not open to that now."

Tsura shook her head. She didn't want to be matched with anyone else.

"Perhaps some time away will benefit you."

"Time away?" Tsura was puzzled.

"Yes."

"Where?"

"Vittoria has told me that she wishes to return home to Florence," Celestina said, her face drooped with disappointment.

"Do you think it's safe?"

"Even more reason to make sure Vittoria has company, don't you think?"

Celestina winked at Aishe, who tried winking back though hadn't quite gotten the concept of only closing one eye. Instead, she opened her mouth wide and shut both eyes hard. Celestina chuckled.

"I get to go as well!" Aishe exclaimed, her golden eyes brightening with excitement.

"You'll have to help Vittoria learn about her heritage and teach her what it means to be Benedanti."

"Can't she just stay and learn that from you, Grandmother?" Tsura asked.

"That would be ideal, but something is holding her back from accepting her place here with us," Celestina explained. "I'm not sure why."

"Did she give you a reason for wanting to leave?"

"Not particularly. She mumbled something about her mother wanting her to have a normal life," Celestina said.

"You mean, we're not normal?" Tsura scoffed.

"She needs to take things slow. Can you imagine what would have happened if I had told her she is to be the next Benetrix, mortal mother to all Benedanti? That she holds the responsibility for all the Strega in the clans across Italy? Do you think she would ever accept any of it?"

"Absolutely not!" Tsura exclaimed.

"We'll need to be gentle with her. She's a smart girl, and she is aware of what is at stake, but she is in denial."

"I can be extra gentle," Aishe concurred.

"How long will we be gone?" Tsura asked.

"About three months. Vittoria will turn twenty in February. You will have a lot of work to do."

"There is no way we can train her in three months. It's impossible!"

Celestina quelled Tsura's complaint with the air of authority. "You must. Consider this a challenge, a great important challenge, that if successful will change the course of everything and bring life back to the land and light back into the hearts of men."

Tsura sat up straighter, untucking her legs. "You'd trust *me* with that?"

"There's no one I'd trust more, my child," Celestina said, stroking her eldest granddaughter's smooth cheek.

Aishe smiled at the sister she admired so much.

"When should we leave?" Tsura asked.

"I assume you'd prefer to leave before the wedding."

"You would assume correctly," Tsura acknowledged, a grimace flickering over her face at having to witness Cai's marriage to another in three days' time.

"Take your cart and horse but leave most of your distinctive items. You don't want to draw attention to yourselves. You both have plain clothes, so wear those as you travel. Plague has made ordinaries suspicious of outsiders and even more so of gypsies."

"But we're not gypsies," Aishe said, correcting her grandmother.

"Yes, I realize this, but ordinaries do not. Beware not to draw attention to yourselves."

"Understood," Tsura said.

"Travel north along the Strada Chiantiaga. Enter the Porta Romana, the southern gate of the city, and cross the River Arno. Vittoria's family home is in the wool district in the northwest of the city. Look for the Duomo, you'll be very close then."

Tsura didn't say any more. She'd asked the Lady of Light for an adventure and it had been given her. It wasn't quite what she was expecting, but it was an adventure nonetheless. She would do her best, although the odds were stacked high against her.

"What a long time to be away from Papa. You'll look after him for me, won't you?" Aishe asked Celestina.

"Of course, he's my son *and* your Papa."

"I'll miss him so," Aishe said.

"I'm sure you will, but this is a big job and your sister will need your help to teach Vittoria all she needs to know to help her people. Do you think you can handle that responsibility, Aishe?"

"Yes, Grandmother. If it is your will, I will find a way."

Celestina and Tsura smiled at the child, she was bright, like a shining star in their midst. She'd grow to be a magnificent Strega. They just had to make sure there was a future for her to do so.

"Very well then. It's decided. I'll go inform your father and Vittoria."

The sisters stood and hugged their grandmother, the woman who had raised them, their true north. She wouldn't be with them forever and the strength of the Benedanti must be upheld for the good of all.

Celestina whispered some words in the Old Language before kissing the girls in turn on their foreheads, activating their portals of second sight, then again on the crowns of their heads, expanding their divine connection to Diana, Queen of all Strega.

They had been blessed by the anointed Benetrix. The first step of their journey was complete, the rest was up to them and Vittoria.

CHAPTER 10

Winter 1630

Paolo took his usual path by Vittoria's house as he returned home from his daily rounds. He was relieved not to have to wear his leather suit recently except during occasional lazaretto inspections, where the few remaining plague-ridden were sent for quarantine. Every time he visited, he was thankful he hadn't insisted on sending Vittoria there.

He didn't expect to find anything different than the usual dark windows and sad appearance of Vittoria's home, but he did. Candles had been lit in the upper middle windows. He rubbed his plain brown eyes and looked again, harder than before. There was movement. Shadows flitted across the windows and then other lights appeared in neighboring windows.

Paolo recalled that when he tended to the merchant and his wife their bedchamber had been on the left side of the upper landing at the end of the corridor, not the right. Paolo's memory led him to believe that the lights were indeed near Vittoria's room.

Then one of the curtains was pulled aside in the window and a small child's head appeared. A cute little thing with a heart-shaped face, round plump cheeks, and a small chin. Her auburn hair was loose over her shoulders and she looked toward the west, in the direction of the Tre Sorella Taverna, at the setting sun and seemed to speak something.

She touched her fingers to her mouth and blew a kiss in the direction of the sunset, as if wishing it a good night, and smiled gaily. She appeared to Paolo a little angel. The sight of her recalled his intention to be a doctor to children and he smiled too.

Before moving away from the window, the child looked down over the street below and saw Paolo looking up at her. Out of surprise of getting caught spying the smile fell from his face, but her smile brightened and spread further across her cheeks. Her palm turned outward, and she wriggled her little fingers, waving in his direction. He felt compelled to wave back exposed though he was. She disappeared, the curtain fell back into place, and the shadows disappeared.

Paolo continued smiling as if he had received an unexpected greeting from heaven, a little sign of hope just for him. With that, he moved on to his destination before anyone else saw him skulking about. He was pretty sure Vittoria had returned. He'd have to tell Angelo the news as soon as possible.

He heard rustling on the street behind him and as he turned to look, a female shadow dipped into the alley.

Aishe turned from the window smiling and skipped out of her very own room to find Tsura with Vittoria in her bedchamber.

"I just said goodnight to the sun," she announced. "What a beautiful sunset. There was a little man outside enjoying it as well," she explained.

"What man?" Tsura asked, ever suspicious of the comings and goings of the people nearby.

"I don't know, but he smiled at me," she said, shrugging her tiny shoulders.

"You shouldn't be near the windows, Aishe. We don't want to bring unwanted attention to us."

"I'm sure it's fine," Vittoria offered, defending Aishe. "She's just a small child looking out a window. Nothing suspicious about that."

"Unless they know that your family doesn't have any small children," Tsura argued.

Come here, Aishe," Vittoria said, opening her arms to receive the child. She'd grown to adore her so much. Aishe bounded over and received the love Vittoria had to offer her.

"He seemed like a nice man. He was little, like me, and had lots of shiny curly hair. He was wearing a fancy outfit."

"Do you know anyone by that who looks like that?" Tsura pressed.

Vittoria thought for moment, rocking Aishe in her lap, before answering. She couldn't recall anyone by that description. "I don't think so."

"We'd better be careful. You know the Malandanti can sense our presence in the city, but they don't know *where* we are. That's our greatest advantage and we had better keep it that way," she said, looking at Aishe.

A fog settled over the city obscuring from view the Duomo dome, the beacon of Florence. The rolling hills of the countryside were lost in a winter haze swallowed up in the gloominess of the season. If she didn't know any better, she would have thought that the once joyful, happy season of Christmas had been struck from the calendar altogether.

Vittoria hadn't had a moment alone since her arrival home. Tsura was ever watchful of Vittoria's movements. Aishe was less noticeable in her watchfulness but Vittoria could sense her, every now and then, peeking through the keyhole of her door.

The chill around her bedroom window didn't bother her as she observed people walking up and down the street preparing for Christmastide. To Vittoria, the idea of celebrating the birth of Christ was depressing.

Who could think of celebrating? So much had been lost.

Tears welled in her eyes, but she sniffed hard and straightened her back, willing the tears to disappear. She would not cry again. Tears would not bring back her mother and father, and they wouldn't bring back Marcel. The knot tightening in her stomach when she stepped foot back in her family home was the only reminder of their existence.

From the end of the street, she saw three men approaching carrying bundles under their arms. She couldn't believe her eyes as they were blurry and unfocused from the tears. Pushing her face to the glass she squinted to see their faces. She recognized two of the three men.

Nico and one of the twins!

Pushing away from the window she didn't wish for them to see her. It was good enough to know they were healthy and safe.

She risked another peek out the window. They were coming straight toward her front door.

Dear God! Please keep walking!

They slowed their pace as they approached the yellow stucco building and Nico looked up toward the top window—her window. She pulled back, but surely, he saw the movement in the window. Aishe burst through the door.

"Look Vittoria! It's that little man I saw before. He's with two other men I don't recognize. Do you?" she asked, pointing toward the window.

"I see them too. I know who they are."

"We should tell Tsura. She'll know what to do."

It was too late. There was a gentle pounding on the front door.

"What, in Diana's name, is that?" Tsura whisper-shouted at them from another room.

Aishe started to answer her sister but Vittoria put her finger to her lips to silence the child from answering. The pounding was becoming louder.

"I'll handle it," Vittoria replied.

Dashing to her mirror, she wiped at her eyes and pushed back loose hair from her face. Her face was puffy and her under-eyes dark. She hadn't taken the greatest care of herself and it showed. Straightening her burgundy dress, she lifted her chin high and marched down the stairs toward the door. She would be cordial but send them away. There was nothing between them except that fateful day in September.

As she approached the door she heard murmuring from the other side. Three male voices whispering low, but not low enough.

"Vittoria, please answer the door. It's me, Nico!"

How does he know I am here? How did he find me? Why is he looking for me?

Taking a deep slow breath, she placed her hand on the doorknob and turned. When the door opened, it was as if a warm blanket had been cast over her. Nico, Angelo, and the unknown man stood grinning in the doorway. Though she feared she'd forgotten how to smile, it was impossible for Vittoria not to give one in return. Then the tears fell. She'd never experienced anything like it before—weeping, laughing, sobbing, smiling, all at once.

Shoving his bundle into Angelo's already full arms, Nico bound into the house sweeping Vittoria up into a great bear hug, spinning her round and round, while filling the space with words of gratitude and thanksgiving. With all decorum trampled upon, Angelo and the other man entered too.

Nico put her down, so the others could make their greeting.

"Hello again, Vittoria," Angelo gushed. His face just as Vittoria remembered it, amiable and sweet, though fret marks had settled into his forehead.

"Angelo! It's so good to see you again."

The third man remained silent while the others re-connected. Angelo noticed and pulled him closer to make the introduction between them.

"Vittoria, you may not recognize this man, but he knows you. This is Paolo Salviati, you know him as a Dottore della Peste. He tended your mother and father when they were ill and saw to it that your mother was buried after her passing. He is our friend and told us where we could find you. We hope you don't mind?"

Vittoria looked at the small unassuming man with plain features. The last time she had seen him, it was with his bird mask on. She felt her heart well up with deep gratitude for him.

"I can imagine it was with great effort that you saw to my mother's burial. How can I ever repay you for this kindness?"

Paolo blushed and fidgeted with his bundle. "Your health is all a doctor could wish for," he replied. "There is no debt to repay."

Vittoria bypassed the formality of it all and kissed Paolo on the cheek.

"I've wondered for months what happened to my dear mother and you have brought me the happiest of news."

Paolo grinned. "When the weather clears, it would be my pleasure to take you to her resting place."

"I would appreciate that very much. Thank you," Vittoria replied, now holding Paolo's cold hands in her own. "Where are my manners? Please, come in."

Vittoria ushered her most esteemed guests into the sitting room. The fire was low, so she popped on two more logs and stoked it to get it burning hotter.

"Tsura! Aishe! We have guests!" Vittoria was certain that they had overheard the entire exchange at the door and there was no way she was sending them away. Tsura would just have to live with it.

The sisters made their way into the room. Tsura stood near the entrance, her pretty face frowning. Vittoria ignored it. Aishe bounded straight up to Paolo.

"I know you. We wished the sun a good night together, remember?"

Paolo's cheeked pinked with embarrassment. He remembered very well spying on Vittoria's home, only to be seen by the very child in front of him.

"Yes, I do."

"I love watching the sunset, do you?"

Paolo chuckled. "Absolutely."

"There are so many colors. Pink and purple and yellow. It makes me so happy," Aishe explained, her speech lispy. Since she arrived in Florence she had lost both her front teeth. She also tended to poke her tongue through the gap in her mouth.

Nico laughed. Vittoria never heard him laugh before. It was hearty and deep, and his face lit up brightening his hazel eyes and magnifying the smile lines in his cheeks. Tsura noticed too.

"What's your name, little one?" Nico asked, reaching out his hand to Aishe to make his acquaintance.

"Aishe. I'm seven. I'm Vittoria's cousin."

"Hello, Aishe. I am Nico Apollino. Do you like pretty dresses?"

"Yes! I try to make them for my dolls, but I'm not very good at it," she frowned, looking down at her little feet.

"Well, I am a tailor and I love creating beautiful dresses for dolls. Would you like me to make one for your doll?" Nico crouched down in front of Aishe making himself her size. She looked up into his eyes.

"You're a very good man. I can tell," she informed Nico.

"And how do you know that?" he asked, smiling back at her. His white teeth gleaming in the firelight.

"Your eyes say so," she replied, holding his gaze.

"Well, I try."

"You don't have to try so hard," she said as if she knew he had been bending over backward to get people to see that he was indeed a good man.

"You are quite perceptive, Aishe," Nico admitted. "Why don't you bring your doll to me, so I can have a look and we can talk about the kind of dress to make for her."

Her amber eyes grew big with excitement. "I'll be right back!" Then she hightailed it out of the room up the stairs to find her favorite doll.

"You have quite a way with children, Nico," Tsura complimented. Her demeanor changed since her arrival in the room. Nico rose from his knee and settled himself in the chair by the fire. Angelo and Paolo set their wrapped bundles on a side table and made themselves comfortable as well. Tsura pulled up a seat between Nico and Angelo, leaving Paolo to sit beside Vittoria.

Nervous about making small talk, Vittoria stood abruptly. "I'll bring us some refreshment."

"Thank you, that would be wonderful," Angelo replied. Tsura had already grabbed Nico's attention with conversation.

"Perhaps I can be of assistance. We have brought some sweets from the baker," Paolo said, pointing to the wrapped bundles.

Vittoria invited Paolo to bring the packages into the kitchen. He could unpack them while she made tea. Vittoria felt Nico's eyes follow them out of the room.

An uncomfortable silence filled the kitchen, neither Vittoria nor Paolo knew what to say first. There was so much to say. Vittoria busied with preparation of the tea. Stoking the resting embers to get a flame going, she set the kettle of water over the fire to boil. Pulling out neat bags of dried herbs and flowers she mixed a together a fragrant concoction.

Paolo took a knife from the chopping block and cut the twine from the baker's bundle, unwrapping it to reveal scrumptious almond and honey crisps, buttery fig and walnut cakes, and crunchy pistachio biscotti. The wonderful aroma of Christmas filled the kitchen. They breathed in the scent of the holidays. It brought tears to Vittoria's eyes again.

"I've never been without my parents at Christmas," she admitted. "I miss them so much."

"It must be very painful to be back in this house without them."

Vittoria nodded, her hand over her eyes as she leaned on the trestle table.

"Although it is different from having your parents here, you do have people who care for you very much out there in that room. Even I wondered about your welfare after you left. I'm ashamed to admit, but it was I who often detoured by your home to see if you had come back. It was the most hopeful part of my miserable grind as a plague doctor. You gave me hope every day. You gave Nico and Angelo hope, too. And here you stand, alive! I didn't know your parents, but I do believe they would be happy that you still have the gift of life."

"Sometimes I wish I had my old life back, and it could be simple again," she moaned, her shoulders appeared to slump under an invisible weight.

"What happened to you out there, Vittoria?" he asked. "Did someone hurt you?"

Vittoria jerked her head up, her reddened eyes staring into his. "It was worse than that."

Paolo looked taken aback by her comment.

Vittoria apologized. "Forgive me. Never mind what I've said, it's of no consequence."

She feigned a weak smile, wiped her brow, and returned to the hearth to check the water that wasn't yet hot enough.

"There's a platter on the shelve in the corner, Paolo. Bring it to me, please, so I can arrange the sweets."

While Vittoria arranged the cakes and crisps, Paolo removed the kettle from the hook in the hearth and poured water over the herbal mixture in each cup letting it steep until the water took on a yellow-pink tinge before scooping out the wet herbs.

"There is a tray on the same shelf. You can place the cups on it, so we can take the tea and treats out to the sitting room."

Ever dutiful, Paolo did as he was asked. And Vittoria managed to collect herself well enough to entertain her company.

Vittoria and Paolo returned to the sitting room to find Tsura cozied up to Nico and Aishe sitting on Angelo's lap talking about the Christmas star. Tsura didn't notice their return because she was so caught up in her conversation with Nico. He was explaining his idea about a new style of dress influenced by dreams he had been having. His voice trailed off when he saw Vittoria. Tsura frowned again when she lost Nico's attention.

"Is everything all right?" Nico asked.

"Of course. I have sweets!" Vittoria announced, forcing a bright smile.

"Yay! I love cakes," Aishe exclaimed, sliding off Angelo's lap to fill her little hands with the sweet treats.

Angelo took a cup of tea from the platter Paolo set beside the cakes.

"I'm interested in hearing about how you connected with your cousins, Vittoria. Aishe told me you've recently met."

A thick awkward silence filled the room. Vittoria looked at Tsura, who glared at Aishe. They didn't have an answer other than the truth, so Aishe told it.

"Vittoria's mother is my papa's sister. Our clan was traveling along the Strada Chiantiaga when Grandmother sent Tsura out to collect chestnuts. When she returned, Vittoria was with her."

Tsura cringed.

"Your clan?" Nico asked.

"We're Benedanti!"

"Aishe, hush. You say too much," Tsura scolded through gritted teeth.

"It's all right, Tsura. We can trust them," Aishe assured her sister.

"Trust us with what?" Nico asked puzzled, looking first at Tsura then Aishe.

"What are Benedanti?" Angelo inquired. "I've never heard that word before."

"I will show you," Aishe answered.

"No! Aishe, don't do it," Tsura ordered.

It was too late. Aishe whispered some unintelligible words and up went her cakes into the air. They floated and bobbed in midair for a bit before her favorite dolly joined them. She moved her hands above her head and made it appear as if the doll was juggling the cookies. Aishe laughed at the entertainment she'd provided her guests.

"Incredible!" Angelo exclaimed.

"My God, that's amazing!" Nico shouted standing in awe, he waved his hand between the cakes and Aishe. "No strings!"

"How is she doing that?" Paolo asked.

"I don't know," Vittoria whispered. She'd never seen it before either. She hadn't gotten very far at all in her training with Tsura. She just wasn't that interested in learning her lessons.

Tsura looked over at Nico. Seeing his amazement at the spectacle in front of him, she joined her baby sister in the fun.

"Well, since it seems our secret has been revealed, Tsura said. She too whispered a few words and every cake on the platter levitated and spun around the room above them making patterns of stars and swirls.

The room filled with laughter including Vittoria's. It was a magical sight indeed. Just the thing they all needed to relax and let the good cheer of the season bless them and raise their spirits. It was true that life was different from before the plague, but they had each other in that moment and that was better than having nothing.

Leave it to a child to make everything all right, she thought.

Then in her mind, she heard a voice, not her own.

"They're going to help us, Vittoria, you'll see."

Aishe then lowered one of the dancing cakes into Vittoria's hand and smiled.

She hoped Aishe was right.

The fun carried on into the evening. Aishe and Tsura continued enchanting Nico, Angelo, and Paolo with their magic and telling stories of the Benedanti and the Old Ways. For as much as Tsura chided Vittoria and Aishe to keep quiet and hidden about these things, her lips flapped revealing much, especially when Nico asked questions.

"Are you born with this magic or must you train to earn this knowledge?" Angelo asked.

"Both. Strega, the whole population of Benedanti and Malandanti, are born with innate magical powers. Some of us are more adept at wielding them at a young age, like Aishe, and others manifest their powers as they get older. Our full power is bestowed upon us when we pass an ancient test set down by the Goddess Diana herself, the Five Darts. We must prove that we have mastered five spheres of magical aptitude," she explained.

"And have you passed this test?" Nico asked.

Tsura sat up straight and proud, puffing her chest. "Yes, I passed the test on my fifteenth birthday, six years ago. It was difficult, but I was prepared and overcame the challenges as expected."

"What are the Five Darts?" Paolo inquired. "What kind of acts must you perform?"

"Mastery of defensive magic, protection against dark and evil forces. Sensual magic, utilizing psychic senses for projecting consciousness, manipulating objects by the power of the mind, reading energy of places and people. Natural magic, communing with animals and beings that grow from the earth. Divinatory magic, gleaning impressions of the past, present, and future through various oracles. And finally, healing magic, which requires mastery in the art of harnessing zee, spiritual energy, to balance and harmonize a being requiring healing."

"Absolutely amazing!" Angelo exclaimed. "Are you learning the Five Darts as well, Vittoria?"

Vittoria remained silent while all the conversation was going on. She was still shocked that Tsura was telling so much. But it was refreshing that Nico, Angelo, and Paolo were receptive to the information they were receiving. If it were up to her, she would have gone to her death without breathing a word about her Strega heritage to another.

Tsura answered for her. "Vittoria is on an accelerated learning path. She knew nothing of her heritage when I found her, for her mother abandoned our clan years ago, and she was forbidden to use magic ever again. Besides, a Strega's magic wanes over time the longer she is away from her clan. That is, if she is not with at least two others of her kind. The power of three multiplies anything, including magic."

Vittoria felt like she'd been cut to the quick by Tsura's words.

"My mother followed her heart and left to be with my father. I would not be here if she hadn't done so," Vittoria snapped, glaring at Tsura.

Paolo and Angelo sat back in their chairs, cognizant of the shift in atmosphere.

"Oh, don't be so sensitive, Vittoria," Tsura retorted, waving away the outburst, minimizing its importance. "You know that your mother's abandonment of the Benedanti set in motion a chain of events that left the clan in danger of being without a Benetrix, for the first time ever, and at the mercy of the Malandanti."

Nico came to Vittoria's defense. "Surely, that was not her fault, Tsura." His hazel eyes darkened as he addressed her.

Nico's reproach surprised Tsura and her boastful demeanor fizzled.

"I didn't mean to imply that it was her fault," she huffed, retreating from the attack.

"That's what it sounded like," Nico retorted.

"I'm sorry," Tsura apologized, more to Nico than to Vittoria. "It's not what I meant."

"I don't like this," Aishe expressed. "We were having such a nice time."

Tsura offered a weak explanation for her behavior. "Perhaps, I was getting carried away with my stories."

"Perhaps," Nico said curtly.

"Why don't we all just relax and take a breath, maybe stretch our legs," Angelo chimed in. "Then Vittoria can tell us her story, in her own words."

Tsura slunk back in her seat and folded her arms across her chest, in embarrassment. Aishe came over and rubbed her shoulder.

"You can be nicer," she told her sister. "Vittoria's trying her best."

Turning to Nico, Aishe grabbed his warm hand and tugged him up from his seat. "Come with me, I want to show you my other doll. Can you make her a dress, too?"

Nico found a smile for Aishe. "Sure, I can. Why don't you take me to her? I'll take some measurements and create a stunning dress for her as well."

"Come on, then. Tsura and Vittoria need to talk," she explained, stating the obvious. She tugged his hand again and off Nico went with Aishe up the stairs to her room.

Paolo stood and collected the platter of half-eaten cakes and tray of empty teacups. Angelo was smart enough to head off with Paolo into the kitchen to get out of the way.

Vittoria and Tsura were left alone in the sitting room. The blazing fire crackled.

"Tsura, I don't think you realize how your words can cut like a knife. I know you're still hurting because of Cai, but I'm hurting, too. I didn't want any of this to happen—the plague, losing my parents, finding out that I'm the last hope for the Benedanti to survive. I have no idea what I'm doing, but don't you think I'm giving my best effort under the circumstances? I have my feet in two worlds trying to figure out where and how I fit in. Belittling me, or my mother, isn't helping. If I'm going to learn from you, I must respect you, and I would never respect anyone who treated me in the manner you just did."

Vittoria was standing up for herself, and Tsura's mouth popped open in astonishment.

"I have been tough on you. Pushing you too hard, perhaps. My goal has only been to help you focus on your purpose."

"After everything, a large part of me was left feeling cold and numb, until today, when those three men walked through that door. They came to my rescue in a desperate time of need and they earned my utmost respect. When I think of a world without Nico, Angelo, and Paolo in it, I'm angered. I can't go back and save my mother and father, but I can focus on saving them from the ill will of the Malandanti. If you can help me to learn what I can to protect them, not because my purpose is to be the next Benetrix, I'll move forward with my training. If you can't, I won't."

Tsura smoothed the ends of her loose dark hair, thinking before she replied.

"It's clear you require a more positive form of motivation to help you complete your training. That's why it has gone at a snail's pace thus far. Keeping you cooped up here day after day has done little to raise your spirits. Let's make a deal then? I'll allow you the remainder of the week to celebrate Christmastide, and rest, all with the intention of raising your zee.

Then next week, we will resume focused, purposeful, training. Do we have an agreement?"

Vittoria couldn't believe what she was hearing.

Tsura raised her arched eyebrows as if to say, *"What's your answer?"*

Vittoria smiled. Her heart fluttered in her chest like a bird batting its cage wanting to be set free. "We have an agreement."

"Very well," Tsura concurred. "Enjoy your time. Remember that your twentieth birthday is approaching, and you must pass the test of the Five Darts by then, otherwise, your powers will never be a match for the Malandanti."

"Understood. I will complete my training for the purpose I set forth. You have my word."

"Very good. It's getting late, so I will retire. Enjoy the rest of the evening." Tsura stood, straightening herself out. She walked out of the room calling out goodnight to Angelo and Paolo, then up the stairs calling out the same to Nico and Aishe.

Everyone except Tsura returned to their place in the circle of chairs by the fire. Nico moved to a seat beside Vittoria. Aishe climbed into her lap, and Angelo and Paolo settled into chairs across from them.

"Please excuse our behavior. It's been a tense time for all of us."

"Think nothing of it, Vittoria," said Nico, smiling wide at her. He was as well-dressed as the last time she saw him. Less flamboyant, but fashionable just the same. His tall figure was framed in a finely tailored leather jerkin over an emerald green doublet, the color warmed his hazel eyes and olive skin. His presence beside her was calming. She liked it.

Relaxing into her seat, Vittoria cuddled Aishe, stroking her amber hair, letting the child's essence infuse her with peace. Everyone was silent and waiting for her to speak.

Then she began.

"The day I fled Florence my life changed forever. Everything that was safe and familiar disappeared in an instant. I was at the mercy of God, or the Goddess, maybe both," she explained. "I didn't realize how naive I was. I had everything I wanted—loving parents, dresses, books, and a clear future ahead of me. Then as I came to discover recently, the Malandanti, who thrive off pain and strife, obtained the means to cast a devastating spell over the people of Italy. It was the plague."

Paolo hung his head and shook it mournfully.

"But why would they do that?" Angelo asked. "What was the purpose?"

"We can't be totally sure. Power, control, revenge. It could be anything. One thing I do know is that it was a grand transmutation spell, one that magnified all ill emotion harbored within the people of Italy, mutating it into plague. The affected were those who allowed fear, hatred, guilt, and the like, to reign within. Their inner plague of pain was already draining their life force away a little every day. The Malandanti spell just made it all happen at once. It is why my mother and father both died."

"It is why *I* almost died," Nico admitted.

"Almost? What do you mean?" Vittoria asked.

"I fell ill the day we met. Angelo found me unconscious in my quarters at the tailor shop that night."

"And I didn't want to help him," Paolo admitted.

"Why?" Vittoria exclaimed, shocked and alarmed.

"Because I hated Nico. He tormented me for years. Angelo had to trick me into going to him because I wouldn't otherwise. I am ashamed to say that now, but it is the truth. We've since made our amends."

"It was what I deserved. I was terrible to everyone. My life had been in shambles for as long as I could remember. Drinking, fighting, hating, it was eating me alive from within. I was affected by the spell because I was already sick."

"You're not terrible now," Aishe chimed in. "You've changed. The Lady of Light came to you."

Nico gaped at Aishe who smiled back at him. "She's pretty, isn't she?" she added giggling.

"How do you know that? How does she know that?" Nico sputtered, first at Aishe, then Vittoria.

"Tell me more," Vittoria encouraged Nico.

"When I was dying, I had the strangest sensation of being pulled up and out of my body. Then I found myself in a wooded grove of ancient oak trees with wild animals all around. A young woman, a huntress, fair of skin and dark of hair approached. She had eyes of green and gold, like yours, and she showed me things from my past. Things I had misunderstood and were causing me pain. She spoke of a balance that had been broken. I didn't remember until now, but she called herself the Lady of Light, the Queen of all Strega, the Mother of Witches."

"Are you sure it was her?" Angelo asked, remembering the strange feeling in the air when Nico was unconscious.

"There is no doubt in my mind," Nico responded resolutely.

"The wooded grove you describe sounds very much like where the Benedanti were camped when I first met them. There is great power in that circle of ancient trees," Vittoria explained.

"It was a glorious, peaceful place," Nico said.

"It still is," Aishe replied.

"What happened after you met the Benedanti? Did you know they were your kin?" Paolo asked.

"No, I did not. Tsura had her suspicions, but she wasn't certain either. I supposed if anyone told me the truth I wouldn't have believed them anyway."

"Did you stay with them this entire time?" Angelo queried.

"No, I hid out in an abandoned villa for about two months before they found me," Vittoria lied. She did not want to talk about Marcel, Magda, or Ugo. She felt a wave wash over her of well-being from Aishe and settled once again.

Thank you, she thought, hoping the child could hear.

"I wager you're glad Tsura arrived when she did," Paolo offered.

"You could say that," Vittoria replied, winking at Aishe, and giving her a tight squeeze.

"How did Tsura and Aishe come to be with you here?"

Aishe piped up. "Vittoria wished to return home and Tsura was grumpy because the boy she liked was marrying someone else, so Grandmother sent us on an adventure."

Everyone laughed. Aishe's explanation was adorable, just like she was.

"What about these Malenti's you keep mentioning?" Angelo asked.

Aishe giggled again. "They're called Malandanti, silly!"

Angelo blushed. "Excuse me, Signorina, please tell me about these Mal-an-dan-ti," he repeated, exaggerating the syllables.

"Are they here in Florence?" Paolo asked.

"I've not seen Malandanti face-to-face. Tsura has told me that they tend to live away from nature in places with large populations of people and centers of commerce. Some even serve in houses of rich and powerful citizens."

"So, they could be here?" Nico proposed.

"Yes, they can," Vittoria admitted.

"They *are* here," Aishe corrected her.

"Aishe, we don't want to scare our guests," Vittoria said.

"But it is true. Grandmother told me so."

"How can you tell if one is a Malandanti?" Paolo asked.

"Grandmother says Malandanti mirror us, because we are two halves of the same whole, except they thrive off shadow and us from light."

"I was thinking they looked like scary old hags from what you say about them," Angelo admitted.

"Grandmother says that Vittoria is to be the next Benetrix. You can tell because the Benetrix is marked from birth with eyes of green and gold."

"What's the Benetrix?" Nico asked.

"The Benetrix is the anointed mother luminary of the Benedanti Strega, she is the great mother of our clan. Our grandmother is the Benetrix now, but Vittoria is her heir and that's why she must train and master the Five Darts."

The room went silent and the longer the silence hung in the air the more anxious Vittoria became. She didn't want to be treated differently because they now knew this about her.

"That's quite the responsibility to shoulder. Good thing you get a few days off for fun and play before the real training begins," Paolo said, breaking the silence.

"Sorry, we were eavesdropping," Angelo added, shrugging his shoulders.

Vittoria laughed. "Of course, you were."

"Whatever you need to help with your training, you let me know. Truly."

"Thank you, Nico, I will. For now, let's just enjoy our time together over the coming days."

"Indeed!" said Paolo.

"Great idea," added Angelo.

"Speaking of, where is Emilio?" Vittoria inquired.

"He must have been delayed," Angelo mumbled. He wouldn't meet Vittoria's eye.

"Well, perhaps he'll be able to join us soon," Vittoria replied, ignoring the feeling that he was lying.

"We've kept you too long, Vittoria," Nico said, signaling it was time to leave by standing and stretching his lean legs. "Shall I call on you both tomorrow?"

"That would be very nice," Vittoria replied.

"Can we visit your shop?" Aishe asked. "I want to see where you make the dresses."

"I think that's a fine idea. I'll call on you at eleven o'clock. We can dine together."

Aishe hugged Nico's waist and waved at Paolo and Angelo before dashing off to bed. Angelo and Paolo said their goodbyes and made their way to the front door by themselves.

Nico lingered, taking Vittoria's warm hands in his.

"I knew you were amazing when I met you, Vittoria, and it was the idea of seeing you again, alive, and well, that brought me back from the brink of death. You made me want to be a better man and I have made great strides to be so. It matters not whether you become the next Benetrix, it matters to me that you are in my life again, and I'll do anything to keep it that way."

Nico's sincerity was beyond reproach. Vittoria remembered his tantrum at the bonfire, his wild eyes searching hers for meaning. Now those hazel eyes were aflame with life and purpose. He meant what he said, but so did Marcel, and he left.

Vittoria didn't know what to say in return. She wasn't quite sure how their harrowing hour together could change Nico so much. It must have been the Lady of Light's influence that shifted his outlook on life, not her.

"I'm happy to see you, too," was all she could muster.

Nico nodded. "See you tomorrow," he said and took his leave.

When the door closed behind him, Vittoria exhaled. She'd seen that look before—the look of love. Under no circumstances could she give Nico the impression that she was open to it. Marcel slammed that door shut within her heart. She had to keep her distance and guard up. It was imperative.

CHAPTER 11

Bartholomew, the old monk, entered Marcel's quarters. "Good morning, Brother Barberini." His demeanor had sweetened since Marcel received the Rite of Ordination, and Marcel could tell the monk did not consider it an imposition any longer to bring a fledgling priest of the Holy Office his breakfast.

"Good morning, Brother Bartholomew. You may place the tray over here."

Marcel pushed a pile of books and loose papers away from the edge of the table to make room for his plate of hard-boiled eggs and cheese. He had already been up for two hours studying.

"Early morning again?" the old man asked, nestling the plate so it wouldn't damage any of the surrounding papers.

"Yes," Marcel replied, rubbing his eyes, and stretching. The candle upon the desk had burnt down to a nub, the flame flickered as it clung to life. Bartholomew lit a new candle for Marcel and swapped it out with the other. "Cardinal Moreau is adamant that my waking hours be consumed with an intense examination of the *Sacro Arsenale*."

Bartholomew held out his liver-spotted hand for a look at the book. "May I?"

"Yes. I need a break from it," Marcel replied, handing the hefty book over.

Bartholomew thumbed through the book. He couldn't read well but he could pick out phrases here and there and understand the meaning.

"Why, this book is about witchcraft," he stated, alarm in his deep voice. He crossed himself and handed the book back.

"It's more about how to identify the evil intent of diabolical witches performing acts to satisfy the will of the Devil," Marcel explained.

"Sounds just the same to me," Bartholomew harrumphed.

"Diabolical witches are the most dangerous group of magicians because they commit the two most cardinal crimes against the Catholic faith."

"What? Fornication and devil worship?" Bartholomew guessed.

Marcel cringed. Bartholomew made the word fornication itself sound like a sin the way his old toothless mouth spat it out.

"Close. Submission to the devil, and willful and deliberate abuse of church sacraments and symbols."

"Tell me more?" Bartholomew said, leaning against the simple table, its legs groaning under his weight.

Marcel sat up in his chair and straightened his cassock. His hair, though still short, had grown back and it felt good to run his fingers over soft down again. The act gave him a moment to collect his thoughts before beginning his performance.

"Per Cardinal Moreau, the Holy Father has reason to believe that there is concentrated witch activity near Florence. Not your typical old hedge-witch making herbs and brews for the locals, but truly powerful witches known in Italy as Strega. For that reason, he's intent that I become well versed with the *Sacro Arsenale*, a book written by an Italian Inquisitor expert in rooting out diabolical witches.

"A Strega is a cunning, often beautiful, instrument of the Devil. They are immoral fornicators who practice love magic violating man's free will, and only evil itself would have interest in making an assault on free will. These women are deceivers of imagination and bewitch at will. For that reason alone, they can never be trusted!"

Bartholomew's old grey eyes grew wide.

Marcel continued his rant. "Strega may appear, to the untrained eye, to be normal women. Beware! They will gather with the congregation for mass and recite secret spells with offensive words and abuse the sacraments by reciting vulgar phrases during communion. They may appear to engage in Christian acts kneeling in front of blessed images, praying to saints, and anointing themselves with holy water, but it would be folly not to heed the warning against their use of mirrors, medallions, and small bottles for spells."

Marcel had captivated Bartholomew with his tale of witchery and woe. He hadn't lost an ounce of his ability to sweep people up in his yarns of fairy tale and fear.

"Worse still, they take as offerings into their ritual circles salt and bread, then dance naked with the Devil."

Nervous perspiration sprung from Bartholomew's wrinkled brow. He crossed himself again.

"Well, it's a good thing you are so well prepared to take on these witches. You are much braver than I," he admitted.

Marcel smiled at Bartholomew, his one friend in all of Rome. He was a simple uneducated man with a gruff manner, but his presence was comforting.

"Thank you for my breakfast. I should eat. I'll be off again to the Cardinal's quarters soon."

"Oh, yes. It's probably cold now," a sheepish look appeared on his plain face. He'd kept his charge from eating a warm meal.

"No matter," Marcel replied, remembering he'd eaten much worse when he first arrived in Rome.

"Good day, Brother Barberini," Bartholomew said, shuffling away.

"Good day."

Marcel chucked the *Sacro Arsenale* onto the table. It was nothing but hogwash. Even so, he had to make the Cardinal believe that he had taken it as gospel. With his performance for Bartholomew, it would seem his act was closer to credulous than ever.

His father sent Cardinal Moreau correspondence apprising him of the Pope's desire to move into Florence soon, as increasing reports of treacherous witch activity had been received. One report suggested that the Strega were responsible for the plague that swept the land months before. The whole thing was preposterous. It was just the Church's way to punish the unfaithful and do what they do best, strike fear into the hearts of good people for control and power. Marcel understood everything his father did was motivated by that end.

He picked up an egg and peeled it while he walked to the window. A nativity had been displayed in the courtyard below for Christmas, and it was the first he would spend without his mother. Marcel rarely said prayers, but he chose that moment to say one of his own creation.

"Dear God, have mercy on my mother's soul. She was driven to madness and ruin by the evil in my father's heart. Forgive her for her trespass, she knew not what she did. Amen."

Marcel knew his ordination into the priesthood was a formality, he was never going to tend his own flock in a country parish absolving sin and setting the moral standard. With his university jurisprudence education, he'd be used as a righteous instrument of the Church to hunt down, punish, and exterminate women who threaten men, nothing more. It was all being carried out by his father's design.

A familiar knock came upon the door drawing Marcel away from his disturbing thoughts.

The door opened, and Claudio appeared dressed in black as usual. The silent shadows were not with him.

"The Cardinal will see you now," Claudio said, the same as every day.

"Very well. Let me gather my things."

Without exception, he still traveled everywhere outside his quarters with Claudio. His father would not risk another flight attempt.

Outside the air was brisk. Marcel's new robes kept his lean body warmer than the old, and he had real leather shoes now to keep his feet from freezing. For that kindness, he was grateful. Priests greeted each other as they passed. The holiday season brought cheer to all except Marcel and Claudio who trudged along in silence. Their bondage to Cardinal Antonio

Marcello Barberini and the Church was nothing to celebrate.

Aishe bolted through Vittoria's bedroom door the next morning, excited to visit her new friend.

"Wake up, sleepyhead!" Aishe announced in singsong. "Nico will be here soon!"

Vittoria rolled over to face the wall, pulling the covers up higher over her head. "It's too early, Aishe. Go back to bed."

"No, it's not. We've already had breakfast."

Vittoria pushed the covers away from her face to peek toward the window. It was true. The big, bright sun was warming the winter sky. It was quite a change from the days of fog and rain that had come before. Sitting up in bed, she stretched and yawned. Her body felt relaxed and rested. She had slept well.

"My dolls can't wait to try on their new dresses. They were talking about them all night and they wouldn't let me sleep," Aishe complained, climbing into Vittoria's warm bed.

Vittoria chuckled. "If the dolls are that excited, I'm sure Nico will have something wonderful waiting for you at his shop. We should get dressed then, what do you think?"

Aishe lay quiet under the covers.

"What's the matter Aishe?" Vittoria asked, squeezing the child into her arms.

"I don't want you and Tsura to argue anymore. I love you both and it upsets me to see you fight."

Vittoria kissed Aishe's auburn head consoling her. "No one likes to argue, Aishe. Especially me, though sometimes one must stand their ground. Are you worried that I don't love Tsura, or that she doesn't love me?"

Aishe nodded.

"Well, I do love Tsura, very much. She has a willful character and oversteps boundaries sometimes, but we all do that on occasion. It's nothing to fret about."

There was no response.

"Is there something else you wish to say, Aishe?"

Aishe plucked up the courage to reveal her true concern. "I'm afraid that Tsura is going to get hurt again."

"What makes you think that?"

"Her zee was all over Nico last night, practically swallowing him up. I don't think he liked it though."

"You saw that?"

"Yes, didn't you?" she questioned.

"I think she was excited to have the company," Vittoria replied, making up an excuse for her cousin's behavior. For Vittoria, love was out of the question, so what did it matter if Tsura sought Nico's affections?

Aishe didn't seem sold on her justification for Tsura's behavior.

"The Lady of Light told me he is special and would help us, but if Tsura makes him angry he might go away. I don't want Nico to go away. If he can help the Benedanti keep the balance, he has to stay."

"I'm sure all will turn out well," Vittoria replied.

"I do hope so."

"I know what will make you feel better, Aishe."

"What?"

"Tickles and kisses!" Vittoria proceeded to tickle Aishe on her belly, under her arms, and on her feet until they were both laughing with delight.

Tsura heard the ruckus and came to the door. "You two had better get moving. Don't you have some-where to be soon?"

"Yes, Nico is taking us to his shop. Why don't you join us, Tsura?"

"I don't think so. Not after last night."

"Don't worry about that. Get dressed. You need to get out of the house too."

Tsura was hesitant. "If you think it's a good idea."

"It'll be fine! Go on. We don't have much time."

Tsura smiled a dreamy sort of sideways grin and walked away to her quarters.

Vittoria swung herself out of bed and marched to-ward her large cassone. Opening the lid, she pulled from it a brown velvet dress with full sleeves. It would be toasty warm on a sunny cold day. Stripping her nightgown, she stepped into the dress pulling the bodice up and over her waist and shoulders. It was tighter around the belly than she remembered.

"That color suits you," Aishe complimented, pinching a piece of the fuzzy fabric between her fingers and rubbing. "It feels nice too."

"I haven't worn it in a long time. It feels a little snug. I may have to ask Nico if he can let it out a bit."

"I want a dress like this too," Aishe gushed.

"Well, if Nico can't fix it, then I'll have him remake it into one that fits you. How does that sound?"

Aishe giggled and did a little jig of excitement.

"All right then. Go get dressed!"

Aishe dashed out of the room.

Vittoria stood in front of her mirror, turning from side to side, looking at herself. There was something different. She hadn't been out of doors recently so that must have something to do with it. She caressed the contours of her face, the dark circles under her eyes had disappeared, but she looked paler than normal.

"Oh, never mind," she chided herself aloud.

She sat down and proceeded to brush and braid her hair. She hadn't bothered to do much about her appearance in weeks. It felt good to tend to herself. She pinched her cheeks to draw color into them and nibbled her lips to do the same.

"That will do," she said, approving of her transformation. Upon standing, a dizzy spell and a sick feeling in her stomach manifested. Vittoria grabbed the bed post and steadied herself with slow deep breaths until the feelings passed.

Aishe skipped back into the room.

"Are you well, Vittoria?"

Vittoria took another deep breath.

"I'm fine. I'm past due for breakfast."

Aishe eyed her suspiciously.

"Are you certain?"

"Yes, some bread and jam would do nicely. Come on," Vittoria said, sweeping past Aishe toward the door. "We cannot keep Nico waiting, now can we?"

Aishe smiled eagerly followed. It would seem her dolls couldn't wait any longer either.

At the stroke of eleven on the clock, a firm knock thundered upon the door. Vittoria suspected that Nico had been waiting to make his presence known. Tsura answered the door, but Aishe knocked her out of the way pushing herself forward to greet Nico.

"Well, hello again, Aishe!" Nico addressed her cheerily. "How are you this fine morning?" he asked, gazing up at the sky toward the bright sun.

"I'm well, thank you," she gushed.

"Good morning, Nico," Tsura said, standing aside to welcome him into the foyer.

Nico stepping inside he looked around the space. His brow furrowed slightly. "Good Morning."

"Did you all enjoy your evening?" Tsura asked, trying to make small talk.

He seemed distracted and answered her simply.

"Yes, we had a very nice time."

Vittoria appeared and the furrow in his brow vanished. His face lit up at the sight of her.

"You look wonderful! That color is stunning," Nico announced.

"That's what I said!" Aishe concurred. Tsura said nothing. Her plain white blouse and blue dress paled in comparison to Vittoria's ensemble.

"Well, aren't I lucky to have two delightful young ladies to escort about town today," Nico expressed, grinning at Aishe.

"I invited Tsura to come along if you don't mind," Vittoria informed him.

A shadow of disappointment crossed his face, but he replaced it with a perfunctory smile.

"Certainly."

"Thank you, Nico. It'll be good for all of us to get out for a while," Vittoria explained, wrapping her cloak around her shoulders. Tsura and Aishe did the same.

Nico retreated out the door. Standing on the threshold he swept his arm out toward the street.

"Florence awaits, my ladies."

Nico was quite the insightful guide. He pointed out buildings, fountains, storefronts, and people. Though the air was brisk, the company was warm. Vittoria felt like she was discovering anew the city she had lived in her entire life.

"Over there is the Fountain of Neptune, it's a representation of Neptune, God of the Sea. It's said his face is that of Cosimo de'Medici," he explained, as they strolled through the Piazza della Signorina.

"It looks like a big white giant to me," Tsura commented.

Nico chuckled. "You wouldn't be the only one to think that."

"What about that over there?" Aishe asked pointing to the massive cubical stone building with a crenelated battlement.

"That is the Palazzo Vecchio, it was once the magnificent palace residence of Duke Cosimo de' Medici and his wife Eleonora of Toledo. It is adorned with works by great masters such as Michelangelo, Vasari, and Donatello."

"I mean *that*," Aishe clarified, pointing high above the building at the clock tower standing sentry above the city.

"They call that the Torre di Arnolfo, and it contains two jail cells used to hold prisoners."

"I don't like that tower, there's something dark about it," Aishe expressed, grabbing Nico's hand for comfort.

"Don't worry little one, you'll never find yourself up there," he promised. He'd taken the long way around from Vittoria's home to show them the sights of his city. "We're not too far now."

Vittoria was glad of it. The sun's heat was beating down on them in the open piazza and she was sweating, it was making her dizzy again.

Above a quaint unassuming entryway hung a sign with golden shears upon it.

"Here we are, Amore's Tailor Shop, the finest bespoke creations in all Florence," Nico announced.

The business was situated at the corner of a busy intersection of streets.

"It's quite a good location, Nico," Vittoria observed, looking around at the neighboring businesses which included linen drapers, cloth vendors, and weavers.

"It is! Eventually, I plan to take over the shop and it will be called Apollino's Tailoring."

"How wonderful!" Tsura exclaimed, clasping her hands together.

"Shall we go in?" Nico asked, opening the door for them to file through.

Movement caught Vittoria's eye and drew her attention across the road to the mouth of an alleyway. A figure stood in the shadow lurking. Squinting she saw the profile of a familiar face, one forever burned into memory.

It cannot be!

Fear clawed at Vittoria's insides and her heart pounded. Her knees buckled then she felt herself falling. Deft hands found themselves under her arms before she hit the ground. She swore she heard a female cackle.

"Vittoria! Vittoria! Are you, all right? Vittoria!"

Multiple voices shouted at her, it seemed, from far away. Somebody slapped her cheek trying to bring her around.

"Something frightened her," Aishe said. "Her zee is black around the edges."

"Dear God in Heaven! Vittoria come back," Nico coaxed, he held her tight in his arms. "What could she have seen that could have frightened her so?"

"What's she saying? She's murmuring something," Tsura observed, leaning closer to hear.

Vittoria's mouth was having difficulty saying the word, but her body was trying to get it out.

"Mmm-ma-ma."

"Come on Vittoria, what is it?" Nico urged, rocking her.

"Maag-da! Mag-da!"

"Magda?" Tsura repeated. Everyone looked around at each other confused.

Vittoria's eyes shot open, she found herself on the floor inside the shop.

"She found me!" she shrieked, pointing toward the door.

"She's going to pass out again. We've got to calm her down," Tsura said, her face hovering in front of Vittoria's.

"Follow me," Nico instructed, lifting her up into his arms. He walked behind the counter, through a set of worn yellow curtains and into private living quarters. A small daybed set against the back wall of the room. There he lay Vittoria.

"Easy now," he whispered, stroking her cheek. "You're safe now, here with me. Nothing is going to hurt you. Try to slow your breathing. That's right, nice and slow."

His tenor voice did the trick, Vittoria blinked several times, her awareness focusing in the room and on the worried people around her.

Vittoria was licking her lips.

"She needs something to drink," Aishe said.

"There's a pitcher of spiced cider over there on the table," he directed.

Tsura dashed over and splashed some into a mug. She held the cup up to Vittoria's mouth allowing her to smell the beverage first before taking a sip.

"Go on, drink it."

It was still warm, the spicy taste of clove, cinnamon, and apple filled her mouth before rolling down her parched throat. She was afraid to say anything yet, so instead, she sipped more of the drink.

Nico crouched beside the bed on his heels. Tsura stood beside him with a hand on both her forehead and hip. Aishe sat next to Vittoria on the daybed. They all waited for an explanation.

If Vittoria revealed who Magda was, she'd have to reveal she murdered a man—a trifling despicable man—but a man nonetheless. She was just starting to put the pieces of her life back together and divulging that information would ruin everything. She couldn't risk it.

"Vittoria, look at me," Tsura commanded. Vittoria met Tsura's inquisitorial gaze. "Who is Magda?"

"I don't know what you mean," she lied. "I think I was overheated from the walk. I was feeling a little dizzy this morning. Perhaps that's why I fainted."

"What did you see outside that spooked you so?" Tsura pressed.

"I just saw a shadowy figure near the alley, is all."

"And that sent you into a fit?" Tsura questioned. She was having none of it.

"I don't know."

"Fine. Perhaps we should go home then?" Tsura threatened.

"No one is going anywhere. Vittoria needs rest and I still have an order to complete for some doll dresses. Besides, I'm hungry and you must be too," Nico said, pinching Aishe's cheek.

"I am!" Aishe exclaimed.

"Very well. Make yourselves at home. I'll be right back." Nico disappeared through another set of curtains and reappeared minutes later with a platter of cold meat, cheeses, fruit, and bread. He vanished again and returned with a steaming pot of minestrone.

"Nico, did you prepare all this for us?" Tsura asked astonished.

He organized the dishes around a smallish table in the front of the room.

"I gave it my best, for such fine ladies!"

Aishe scooped up her dolls and made her way to the table.

"It smells good," she said, holding her face over the pot inhaling the aroma.

"Signora Amore used to make this soup often."

"Used to?" Tsura queried.

"The plague killed Signor Amore's wife and daughter. He harbors guilt that they died, and he did not. He spends most of his days praying at the church."

"That's very sad," Vittoria said.

"It is, they were good people. Anyway, we have the place to ourselves, so feel free to do as you please."

Tsura sat down at the table next to Aishe and Nico, and a chair was left open for Vittoria. Nico looked expectantly over at Vittoria.

"I don't think I'm quite ready to eat. I'll just rest right here," she said. Letting her head drop back against the pillow she closed her eyes. Her stomach was still tied up in knots and she feared that if she ate it might come back up.

Vittoria listened to their conversation while she pretended to rest. Tsura chattered away asking Nico questions about his work and the business, which he answered politely in full sentences. When she asked more personal questions pertaining to romantic interests and the like his answered petered out to one or two-word responses. Finally, he'd had enough.

"Aishe, I have a surprise for you!" he announced, standing, and removing his dishes from the table.

"What is it?" she exclaimed.

"I worked on it all night. I hope you like it, otherwise, my reputation as the best tailor in all of Florence will be ruined," he explained, feigning a sad face.

"I bet I will love it," she replied.

"Please give me your dolls," he directed, opening his hands to receive them. Aishe jammed the dolls into his palms and he whisked them away through the curtain out to the fitting area of the shop.

"I'm so excited!" she bounced in her chair, nibbling her fingertips in anticipation. They heard the banging of drawers opening and closing, then silence.

"You may come out now, Aishe!"

She leaped out of the chair, knocking it sideways, and darted through the curtains. Standing upright upon the counter were her two dolls, decked out in silk and lace, ribbons in their hair, and shoes upon their feet. She squealed with delight. They looked like magnificent princesses in miniature.

"Nico! You have made me so happy," she hugged him as tight as she could. He lifted her up, so she could sit on the counter with her dolls.

His deep smooth laugh filled the shop. "Thank goodness. My reputation was on the line. I cannot have unhappy customers."

She hugged the dolls to her chest then held them up to her ear as if they were whispering to her. "They are happy, too."

Tsura appeared at the counter's edge. She looked over the stitching, hemming, embellishment of the dolls clothing.

"Absolutely wonderful! Your work is masterful."

"Can you fix Vittoria's dress? The one she's wearing. She said it's gotten too tight around the middle," Aishe explained.

The comment caught Tsura's attention, and she looked back through the curtain at Vittoria.

"If she wishes me to, I'd be more than happy to let it out for her," Nico replied.

"She says that if you can't fix it, you can remake it into a dress for me."

"Is that what she said?" Nico teased.

"Yes, but after seeing these dresses, I think you can fix anything," she admitted.

"Perhaps we should see if Vittoria is ready to go home yet," Tsura said to Aishe.

"Can't I stay with Nico?" Aishe grumbled. "I want him to teach me how to sew like this."

"We have plenty of time for that, little one," he explained.

"All right," she said and slid down off the counter.

"I'll walk you home," Nico said, keeping his distance from Tsura.

"That would be much appreciated. I couldn't lift her myself if she had another spell."

"Perhaps I should have Paolo call on Vittoria to check on her," Nico offered.

"I think she'll be fine. Thank you."

"She's awake!" Aishe called from beyond the curtains. Vittoria took her time walking into the shop space.

"Are you sure you're well enough? You can stay as long as you like," Nico insisted.

"I'll be fine, still a little tired."

"But you slept so much last night," Aishe reminded her.

"I know. I suppose that fainting spell did me in."

"Let's get going then," Tsura said, pushing Aishe and Vittoria toward the door.

They took a direct route home. Everyone was quiet, lost in their own thoughts. Upon arrival at their destination, Nico spoke.

"I'd like to invite you all to the Grano D'oro Inn tomorrow. Bianca, the innkeeper, is throwing a party to celebrate the return of health to the city."

"Oh, can we go?" Aishe piped up. "Please!"

"Only if Vittoria is well enough" Tsura decided.

"I'll be fine. A little rest and I'll be good as new."

"Very good! I'll come by at five o'clock," Nico said, stepping back from the door so they could make their entry. "We'll have a nice time."

"I sure hope so," Tsura mumbled under her breath.

Vittoria heard her and shot her a look.

"I know we will," Vittoria promised, then stepped inside with her cousins, closing the door behind them.

Angelo stood outside the Tre Sorella Taverna. Merry people marched along the street, heading this way and that, calling out greetings to friends and neighbors. He had seen his brother but a handful of times since September.

He recognized someone walking toward him who knew Emilio.

"Cesare!" he called.

The young man, around his own age of twenty-two, paused just outside the entrance.

"Hey, Angelo! Where have you been? I thought you were dead."

"I've been around. Are you heading into the Tre Sorella Taverna?

Cesare nodded. "Yes."

"Will you please do me a favor?"

"What do you need?"

"Deliver this letter to my brother, Emilio," he said, handing the folded note to the wiry young gambler.

Cesare's hooded eyes narrowed as he considered the request. "Why can't you deliver it?"

Angelo shuffled his feet. "I've been banned from entering," he replied.

Cesare flashed a lopsided smile and punched Angelo's arm. "Crazy night, huh?"

"I suppose you could say that. It's a letter from my mother. She's sick and Emilio needs to know."

Cesare tensed and inched away from Angelo. Fear of the plague still fresh in mind.

"It's her heart," Angelo explained.

"I'm sorry to hear that," Cesare replied, relaxing.

"Will you do it?"

"Sure! Why not?" he replied, opening his hand to receive the letter. "It's nearly Christmas, after all."

"Thank you, Cesare! Tell Emilio, I'm waiting."

He gave the messenger the letter and a few coins for his trouble. Cesare smiled again. Kindness did have its rewards.

"I will. Good to see you, Angelo," he replied, before disappearing into the Tre Sorella Taverna.

Angelo walked away from the entry, perched himself on an old stone block jutting from the ancient wall abutting the Taverna, and waited for his twin to appear. It took a half-hour for Emilio to come out.

"What's this?" Emilio demanded, waving the letter brusquely in the air.

"Hello, Emilio," Angelo replied stiffly.

Emilio stopped short. He hadn't seen his twin brother in the light of day in a long time.

"Mother wants you to come home now. Why are you still here, Emilio? I don't understand."

Emilio hadn't thought about his mother, just soothing the vexing anger he harbored inside. He couldn't sleep, eat, or relax while at home. He always felt unwell there. Only in the company of the three sisters did he feel more himself.

"I feel better when I'm here," he said.

"How can that be? We haven't spoken in months!" Angelo argued. "Help me understand why you need to stay here?"

Emilio's upper lip stiffened. He couldn't explain to Angelo the hold Nerezza had upon him or the sorcery that he'd witnessed. He'd never be believed. Even his own brother would think him mad.

"Is it true about Mother? Is she unwell?"

"She's worried about you, as are we all. It's Christmas and you should be at home, with us."

"What do you mean, *we all*?"

"Paolo and Nico," Angelo answered. Emilio's face went dark at the mention of his cousin's name. "Vittoria."

Emilio flinched. "Vittoria? Is she returned? How do you know this?"

"We called on her just two days ago." Angelo explained.

"She's dangerous! You stay away from her. Do you hear me?" Emilio warned.

"What's come over you?" he said, taken aback by his outburst.

"I've seen things."

"Oh, I bet you have."

"I'm serious."

"So am I. You need to get yourself together, Emilio. Your behavior is getting worse than Nico's ever was.

Do you want to be known as a motley-minded buffoon? Keep talking like that and you will."

Passersby turned to stare at the twins.

"Keep your voice down," Emilio commanded. "I am *not* Nico. I can't believe you still hang about with him!"

"He's turned his life around. He's not the same man you remember."

"I will never forget who Nico really is, though it seems he's deceived you into thinking differently. Don't be a fool, Angelo. Nico is, and always will be, a degenerate."

Angelo's round cheeks flushed with indignation.

"I don't give a damn about what you think about our cousin, I'm not here to argue that point with you. I am here to inform you that Mother has had enough of your foolish rebellion. You better come home for Christmas or you will have hell to pay," he threatened, shoving his brother into the stone wall before storming away.

Emilio shrugged off the offense. Angelo always had a soft spot for their cousin. He was naïve and blamed Nico's antics on tough childhood circumstances. He tapped the letter against the inside of his palm and watched Angelo as he trekked away. Then he returned inside find Nerezza.

"I know you're there," Nerezza said, her eyes still closed. "Where have you been?"

"My brother, Angelo, was here. He says our mother isn't well."

"Is that so?" Nerezza replied, blinking her green eyes open. "Whatever is the matter?" she asked, gazing upon Emilio, waiting for the lie. Medea had already reported that Cesare delivered Emilio a note.

"Angelo says her heart is overburdened and she bids me home for Christmas?"

"And what did you tell him?" she asked, propping herself up on the elbow. The covers fell revealing her ripe breasts. He averted his eyes to concentrate.

"I didn't answer. I wanted to discuss it with you first. What shall I do?"

"My darling, don't fret," she cooed, patting the bed calling him to lay beside her.

"You know when I stray too far away from you I get terrible headaches and feel ill. I cannot go home, even if I wanted to," he replied, crawling into the bed beside her.

"True."

Nerezza had bewitched Emilio's shoes to make him feel ill whenever he roamed out of range of the Taverna.

"What else did he say?"

"He said that Vittoria had returned to Florence. I told him to beware. She is dangerous."

"No, she is viperous," Nerezza said, correcting Emilio. "This confirms what Magda reported yesterday, that Vittoria has indeed returned."

"Magda saw her?"

"Yes. Vittoria was gallivanting around town with your cousin Nico and two other girls. Vittoria saw Magda and fainted at the shock of it." Nerezza laughed. "I suppose she didn't expect to see a ghost from her past."

Emilio was shocked. Nico had reunited with Vittoria who, as it turned out, was cut from the same troublesome cloth.

"Vittoria saw Magda, so surely she will try to kill her. We can't risk injury to Magda, the one witness alive who can place her at the scene of a vicious crime. Vittoria won't want anybody to know that she killed that man. You, on the other hand, know nothing of Vittoria's savageness as far as she is concerned. You can collect information from Angelo, and even play nice with Nico, to find out where Vittoria lives and who these two girls are with her. I believe they're just as wily."

Emilio bolted upright in disbelief. "You wish me to risk my life to collect this information?"

Nerezza stroked Emilio's cheek and chin easing his panic at the suggestion.

"Darling, do you not want this murderer to be brought to justice? Your brother and mother are at risk," she explained, plucking Emilio's heartstrings.

"Of course, I do," he blustered.

"Then you must go tonight and talk to your brother. Find out all you can about this Vittoria, for she is aligned with the terrible clan of Strega that killed my own mother. They must pay for what they've done."

"Are you certain they are one in the same?" Emilio dare ask.

"Do you doubt me?" Nerezza challenged. Pointing her forefinger into Emilio's chest. "You will go home tonight and obtain the information I desire, or you will regret ever stepping foot into the Tre Sorella Taverna. Do you understand?" Her green eyes flashed like lightning, her voice like thunder.

Emilio blinked a lot while comprehending the threat she'd laid down upon him. He was terrified of both options—putting himself in harm's way to collect information and angering Nerezza further. But the former seemed a less frightening option.

"I'll do as you say, Nerezza. I'm sorry for doubting you. It will never happen again," he apologized.

Nerezza's eyes softened. "That's what I like to hear," she replied, clutching the front of Emilio's shirt pulling him forward and laying a deep passionate kiss upon his lips. His hands clasped her bare shoulders and she pressed into him.

"Show me how sorry you are," she whispered, and her wish was Emilio's command.

Emilio performed well under pressure and Nerezza was pleased. "I think you've earned yourself a gift, Emilio," she said.

"How so?"

"When you please me, you are rewarded."

Rising from the bed, Nerezza collected Emilio's clothes and laid them out over the end of the bed. She uttered an incantation and waved her hands above the clothes. The air cracked and sparkled, and his old outfit disappeared and a new one appeared. A dark green velvet vest and breeches with a matching coat. A decorative scene of stags in a grove of oak trees was stitched on it in a golden thread of the finest sheen. His old shoes transformed into polished brown leather with bright buckles. A ring of gold with a stone of black appeared upon his little finger, the image of the huntress embossed in it.

"This ring has protective power. So long as you wear it Benedanti cannot harm you, and you will look so fine in this outfit that your mother will forget everything that's happened since you last saw one another."

Emilio smiled, he would err on the side of pleasing the glorious woman before him at all costs, whatever may come.

"Thank you, it's magnificent. I will wear it with pride," he said and beckoned her back to bed.

There was loud knocking upon the shop window. Nico looked up. It was Angelo. His face was tense, and lips pursed. Nico waved and skirted the shop counter coming around to unlock the door for him.

"I wasn't expecting you for another hour," he said, stepping aside to let his cousin in along with a cold blast of December air. It was already getting dark outside.

"I just didn't know what to do with myself at home. I feel anxious," Angelo admitted, pacing the shop floor.

"Why is that?" Nico asked, closing, and locking the door before moving back to lean against the counter.

"I saw Emilio today."

"You did? Where?"

"Mother's had enough of the servants gossiping about her wayward son taking up in the Tre Sorella Taverna, so she wrote a note to Emilio demanding he come home for Christmas. I delivered it to him."

"You talked to him?"

"We argued with each other."

"About what?"

"Vittoria."

Nico paused before answering.

"What could Emilio have against Vittoria?"

"He tried convincing me that she's dangerous, that I need to stay away from her."

"What in God's name would give him that impression? Did he tell you why?"

"No, just that he had seen things. He didn't give me any specific details. I think he's just found himself at the bottom of a bottle much too often."

"Perhaps, or he's being influenced by the sisters. But what would they have against Vittoria?"

"I don't know, but something is off. He's acting suspicious. Just for a moment, I could see in his eyes that he was scared about something, but he wouldn't tell me."

"It doesn't make sense."

Nico's thoughts trailed off thinking about Vittoria. *She is a good, respectable, young woman. What would give anyone the impression that she was dangerous? Unless...*

"Angelo, do you remember the other night at Vittoria's she told us the story of those witches who thrive off pain and strife. What were they called?"

"Malandanti?" Angelo replied.

"Yeah! Do you think that maybe the Malandanti are controlling Emilio in some way? His whole demeanor changed the last night we were at the Tre Sorella Taverna together, remember? He punched me in the eye! I mean, didn't Vittoria say that Strega must live in groups of three or more to retain their powers. The Taverna is run by three sisters."

Angelo's soft brown eyes widened.

"Perhaps they've caused his affliction by enhancing his sense of anger and irritation with you," he replied. "He didn't seem that annoyed with you prior to that night of the incident with Pitti's men. Besides, I can't remember it ending, do you?"

"Could be. That was strange because although I was quite drunk, I do remember experiencing a vague sense of confusion like none of us knew why we were scuffling to begin with.

"Emilio had a bloody cut on his neck too. He never told me how it happened."

"Well, if the Malandanti have done something to Emilio, the question we need to answer is, why? Why would they want him? What do they need him for? If they are as powerful as Vittoria claims, then what's the purpose of keeping him around?"

Angelo thought for a moment, tapping his fingers on the countertop. "Well, maybe it's simple. They know he knows Vittoria. So, they know that *we* know Vittoria. That means they'll know how to find her."

Nico's gut tensed with the niggling of danger. The wheels in his mind churned. He recalled the previous day's events again—Vittoria fainting, talking in frightened tones, the name Magda, denial of it all.

Nico recapped the story for Angelo. "Do you think it's related?" he asked his cousin.

"It's certainly suspicious."

"Do you know a Magda?"

"No, can't say I do."

"There's something strange going on here, Angelo. I feel it. Vittoria, Tsura, and Aishe aren't safe. I think that whoever this Magda is, she's working with the Malandanti, if she isn't one herself."

"Wait, hold on. You think that these Strega are using my brother, and this Magda, to spy? But I've not seen Emilio in weeks, so how could he be spying on us?"

"I don't know," Nico admitted. "But they have him for some reason and, you know as well as I, that it's not in Emilio's character to leave his family and take up in a brothel. Something, or someone, has control over his mind. You said it yourself, he seemed scared. What if he's afraid of the Malandanti and their powers? What if they've threatened him, or you?"

Angelo leaned over the counter, head in his hands.

"None of it makes sense."

"I know. If I hadn't seen what I saw the other night, I wouldn't believe it either. Magic is real."

"I believe it, too," Angelo concurred.

"Then we must trust Vittoria, and if she believes the Malandanti are capable enough to cast a horrid plague spell to draw power, then we must tread very lightly. It's clear they would stop at nothing to get what they want."

"How can we fight them and get Emilio back? Vittoria doesn't even have her powers yet!"

Nico shook his head, his angular face tight with worry. "We've got to tell her our suspicions. She needs to know about potential threats. I don't think it's a good idea for them to be alone and unprotected."

"And you think you can protect them from the Malandanti?"

Nico knew he could do nothing to protect them from magic, but he'd feel better if he could keep his eyes on them all the same. "They shouldn't be alone."

"Are you suggesting we take shifts standing watch?"

"It couldn't hurt, and we could help out with other things too."

"Like what?"

"Seriously, Angelo? Whatever they need!"

"All right! I get it. When do you think we should talk to them?"

"Immediately!" Nico exclaimed. "Well, at least tonight, when we return them home from the party."

"It should be safe then. We don't want to risk being overheard by anyone," Angelo added.

They shook their heads in agreement.

"What about Paolo? We've got to inform him too."

"We will," Nico agreed, looking over at the corner clock. It was a half past four. "We best get going. Vittoria will be waiting for us."

CHAPTER 12

The festivities at the Grano D'oro Inn were in full swing. Many families in the neighborhood made the effort to come to the party. The inn's courtyard was full of men, women, and children who had suffered much but were content to set aside their sad memories to enjoy a few hours of happiness with remaining friends and family.

"Isn't this wonderful?" Nico asked Vittoria. She sat on a stool near the stacked wine casks. He stood beside her sipping from his cup.

Hmm?" she mumbled, pulling her faraway gaze back to the courtyard. A deep furrow had appeared in her brow.

Perhaps she was thinking of the Malandanti. Nico couldn't stomach knowing that they were in his city, harming and killing at will. They almost killed him, but he wouldn't let them harm Vittoria.

"Vittoria, where are you?"

She forced a limp smile. "I'm right here."

"You don't seem to be enjoying the party at all. Look at all the happy faces," he said, waving his hand out in the general direction of the activity. "Though the one face I wish to see smiling is yours."

Vittoria pushed up her body from the slouch it had settled into and stretched her back. "It's strange how tragedy brings people together, isn't it?" she asked Nico, inclining her head toward Angelo and Tsura who were chatting, and Aishe who was playing with some children her age. "I suppose we have the plague to thank for it."

The innkeeper Bianca and her husband Ciro were heading in their direction.

"Hello there, Nico! Very good to see you again," Ciro greeted him. "And..." He seemed to search his mind for Vittoria's name, but it wouldn't find it there because he had yet to meet her.

"Vittoria," Nico interjected.

She stood up and greeted Ciro. "It's a pleasure to meet you."

Angelo and Tsura joined the conversation.

"I understand you are responsible for this delicious Chianti, Ciro," Angelo complimented. "It's much better than that swill they serve at the Tre Sorella Taverna."

"I should hope so!" Ciro exclaimed.

"It is a treat," Nico concurred. He hadn't taken a sip of wine in months, but he was drinking to celebrate now, not drown his sorrows. He took another swig from his cup. Vittoria wasn't drinking hers.

Benches and tables were moved, and people shuffled around in the courtyard. The musicians were setting up their stools and instruments.

"It's time for the music!" Bianca announced for all to hear. All eyes in the courtyard turned to look at her. "We even have a special guest who I've been told is an excellent lute player," she said, before walking away to greet the other guests, dragging Ciro along with her.

"What have I missed?" a familiar voice asked. Everyone turned to find that both Paolo and Emilio had just arrived.

"Emilio!" Angelo exclaimed. "What are you doing here?" he asked, suspicious of his brother's sudden appearance.

"I ran into Emilio on the way over and I asked if he'd like to join us tonight," Paolo explained. "It is a party after all."

Nico looked sideways at Angelo. They hadn't spoken to Vittoria and Tsura about their suspicions yet. They had hoped to do so after the party.

"So glad you could join us, Emilio," Nico said politely.

"Hello, Nico. Is it true that you've taken over management of old man Amore's tailor shop? I've heard that you've even joined a guild."

"Signor Amore's wife and daughter died of plague. He's old and tired and cannot concentrate on the work, so I stepped up to run the business."

"Is he planning on handing it over to you since he now has no living family?"

Nico knew the answer, but he didn't want to share it with Emilio. "That remains to be seen."

"It's good to hear that you've settled down and are engaged in a respectable trade in which you can make a name for yourself, Nico."

"Hello Emilio, it is wonderful to see you again," said Vittoria, offering her hand in greeting.

Emilio grasped her hand, and even went as far as to place a soft kiss on it.

"Welcome back to Florence, Vittoria," he replied.

"This is Vittoria's cousin, Tsura. Her other cousin, Aishe, is over there. The one playing with the dolls," Paolo explained pointing to the group of girls admiring Aishe's finely dressed dolls.

"How wonderful!" Emilio smiled. He struck up conversation with Tsura. "It's a surprise to meet you, Tsura. What brings you to Florence?"

Nico stared hard at Tsura, subtly shaking his head back and forth, encouraging her to remain mum on that subject. She didn't notice his attempt to catch her eye. She was receiving attention from another.

"I thought Angelo may have told you already why we're here."

"Why no, enlighten me. I'd love to hear about your adventures."

Angelo interjected, his tone was stern with a warning. "I haven't gotten around to it yet, Tsura. I haven't seen my brother in some time."

"It's true, we haven't seen much of each other lately. I've been away working on a very important undertaking assigned by the Pope himself!" he boasted, loudly for all to hear. Everyone's attention turned in his direction, even that of other guests.

"And what would that be?" Tsura asked, against better judgment. There were too many ears around to hear the answer.

Emilio raised his voice even louder. "There have been rumors of witches prowling in the area. The Pope believes that they were responsible for casting a spell that incited the plague that caused so many deaths," he explained.

"My goodness, Emilio! I had no idea you were working on behalf of the Pope. How did this come to be?" Paolo asked.

No wonder he had been so secretive, Nico thought.

It explained the clothes and his polished appearance. He was dressed in fine apparel, gold ring upon his little finger, and golden thread upon his coat. He looked closer at the design and noticed it depicted a scene of stags in a grove of oak trees.

"I was approached by agents of the Holy Father and shown evidence that these evildoers are at work in our very city. I took up the yolk of responsibility and have been working to identify them ever since."

"Why are you staying at the Tre Sorella Taverna then?" Nico asked, realizing the conversation was heading in a dangerous direction. There were too many people present.

Emilio had a quick answer for him.

"Well, of course, that is where I'm able to interact with shady sorts and uncover information that may lead to the arrest and trial of these witches."

"You don't believe in witches do you, Emilio?" Nico asked, delivering his question in a joking manner.

"Of course, I do! If the Holy Father believes they are doing the work of the devil, I do as well."

More people had gathered around to listen.

"Indeed!" concurred a woman to her husband.

Nico recognized her as a devout woman who followed scripture to the letter.

"What else do you know about these witches?" the same woman asked Emilio.

Emilio looked Vittoria in the eye and replied. "They crave power, they trick people into believing they are who they are not, they hex and curse, and they kill the innocent. They are the worst kind of beings on the earth and they must be stopped at all costs!"

"All this talk of witches is frightening the little ones," Nico said, pointing at the children.

Aishe sat looking wide-eyed at the adults who were looking back at her. "I'm not afraid of witches," she reported.

"You should be," Emilio replied. "They could be right under your nose and you wouldn't even know it."

"Emilio!" Angelo scolded. "Don't frighten the child."

"I said, I'm not afraid," Aishe repeated, standing up and approaching Emilio. She stood her ground in front of Nico and looked up at Emilio. "Evil will never overcome the light. It never has, and it never will. I know this to be true."

"Well said, Aishe," Nico agreed.

It seemed to Nico that Emilio was unwilling to argue with a child, whom he likely believed had no concept of the real world and the evil in it, so he did not pursue the matter.

"Luckily, I haven't met a real witch yet," he chuckled, turning his eyes away from the child and out toward the group of adults that had gathered around to hear his words.

Angelo, ever the light-hearted chap, was first to speak. "Thank goodness for that!"

"Thank goodness," Tsura and Vittoria replied in unison.

"But if anyone here has, the Holy Father calls on you to do your duty, and report what you've seen. These witches cannot go unpunished. I can be found at the Tre Sorella Taverna awaiting your reports of witch activity. They must be stopped. Be not afraid."

"Emilio, that's quite enough now," Angelo ordered.

"I must be going anyway," he responded. "Enjoy the party."

He made a polite bow of the head to his company and exited. Several of the people from the crowd followed him out of the courtyard to ask more questions. The rest disbursed themselves to rejoin the festivities.

Emilio had planted the seed of fear in their minds. It wouldn't be long before fingers pointed, and accusations flew, at Vittoria.

The musicians in the ensemble tuned their instruments. One ran a bow over the strings of his viola da gamba while another warmed up his wooden flute with a flutter of breath. The third musician plucked at his well-worn fiddle.

"I'm not feeling very well," Vittoria muttered to Nico. "I'm going to go home."

"Oh, no you don't! If you leave now, it'll look suspicious. We must stay and appear to enjoy ourselves."

Nico's jaw set, and his hazel eyes narrowed. He took another swig of his wine and urged Vittoria to do the same.

"Why didn't you say that your brother was working for the Pope?" Tsura queried Angelo.

"I didn't know. I think he's been put up to this. We were going to talk to you about it after the party."

"It's a little too late now," Tsura quipped.

Aishe whispered. "Are we in danger?"

Nico answered. "Not if I can help it, little one. Come on, let's have a dance." He held his hand out to Aishe and she entwined her fingers in his.

Giggles and gasps escaped from a few of the young women in the crowd as Nico led her out to dance.

"Who is that?"

"My goodness, he's handsome."

Vittoria smiled. Tsura did too.

The band played some upbeat songs to get the crowd moving. Tsura danced with Angelo and Paolo pulled Vittoria out for a spin around the courtyard. Paolo wasn't a very coordinated dancer, he bounced frenetically, but it elicited some laughter from Vittoria and she made the best of it. After a while, Nico came to the rescue when he saw Vittoria was ready to call it quits with Paolo.

The music slowed and there were some groans from the audience. Some folks found a place to sit and rest. Ciro refilled cups and Bianca brought out the crescent cakes she'd made for the guests. With food and drink in hand, the guests were content.

The lute player found his place in the center of the ensemble. He strummed his borrowed lute, tweaking the knobs here and there. Then spoke to each of the musicians and they nodded their heads at him. There was a stool for him to sit on, but he stood, putting his foot on it instead, and rested the instrument against his thigh. He swept his long fingers over the strings with little effort and a series of melodic chords filled the courtyard.

Nico held Vittoria around the waist with his left hand and her other hand with his right. The last time they were that close was on the edge of the bridge after he had rescued her. She swayed in time with him. Aishe danced nearby with her dolls and Paolo. Angelo was sitting and talking to Tsura, but she was busy watching Nico and Vittoria, a frown had settled upon her face.

The lutenist told a tale of a love, danger, and bravery in the face of adversity. Nico held Vittoria tighter, but instead of warming she became ice cold and shivered. Nico rubbed Vittoria's back and offered to get her cloak, but she declined.

The performer received a thunderous applause at the culmination of his song. He smiled, bowing to the crowd. He handed his instrument to one of the musicians and shook hands with the others before taking his leave. He was bombarded with compliments and pats on the back as he made his way through the crowd.

"Brava!" Nico shouted and clapped.

Vittoria didn't move. Nico pulled back and saw the serious look on her face.

"I must go," she said, then she ran off.

"Wait! Don't leave," Nico called out to her.

Tsura stood and followed, sweeping Aishe out with her. Nico, Angelo, and Paolo were left on their own in the center of the courtyard with nothing but questions and worry.

Vittoria stood weeping in her bedchamber. She had returned her parents' portrait diptych to its place upon her desk. Their faces still peaceful and unchanged. Not only had she remembered her most precious possession when she wandered from the villa, she also found she had the bejeweled Book of Hours.

The devotional book was a gift from Marcel and, had she been in her right mind, she would have left it behind. She did not want to remember him, but he was going to be difficult to forget because she had determined, without question, she was with child. The clues could no longer be ignored. She was an unwed pregnant murderer, and deeply ashamed of herself. Her parents would be too. She'd made a mess of everything.

Tears rolled down her cheeks. She picked up the Book of Hours and opened it. Her eyes rested upon Psalm 51. She read the words aloud.

"Have mercy on me, O God, according to thy great mercy. Blot out my transgressions. Wash me thoroughly from my iniquity and cleanse me from my sin."

The door creaked open. There stood Tsura.

"What are you doing? Why are you crying?"

Vittoria fell to her knees. She had to confess her sins. She sought release from her mental prison.

"I have done terrible things, Tsura. I have done things that have put you, and Aishe, in danger."

Tsura came to Vittoria and kneeled beside her.

"What have you done that is so terrible?"

"I'm with child."

Tsura's face remained calm. "How do you know?"

"My monthly cycle has eluded me twice, my stomach is swelling, and I'm tired all the time."

A knowing look came over Tsura's face, agreeing these were true symptoms of pregnancy. "Whose child is it?"

Vittoria did not want to answer because she could never take it back if she did.

"Come now, you can tell me," Tsura coaxed.

"His name is Marcel Barberini. It was his villa where I found shelter. We had a love affair and then he abandoned me without warning, leaving behind a letter with a vague explanation for his departure."

"What was the explanation?"

"That his father is a very powerful man and a threat to all that we could build together."

"And he just left you all alone?"

"Yes."

Tsura sighed. "I know it's difficult, but you aren't alone. Aishe and I are here. We'll help you care for the child."

"That's not all."

"There's more?"

"Remember when I fainted outside the tailor shop the other day?"

"Yes."

"I saw a ghost from the past."

"What do you mean?"

"When I arrived at Marcel's villa it was empty, so I decided to stay for a couple days before moving on. But two thieves set upon robbing the house while I was there. I hid in an armoire but was found by a woman called Magda."

"Magda! That's the name you were saying over and over."

"Yes, I lied and told her I was a servant. Her partner Ugo was awful. He groped and threatened to do things of an obscene nature to me. They wanted to kill Marcel when he returned home and steal all his valuables and coin, including this Book of Hours," she explained, handing it to Tsura for a look. She opened the book and gasped at the beauty of the illustrations within and jewels without. "I had a vision, while we were waiting for Marcel to return. I knew he was coming, I could see his horse in my mind and hear the thundering of hooves."

"Your powers helped you to see!"

"I didn't know they were powers. I had been praying a lot before that happened."

"The Lady of Light heard you," Tsura replied, smiling.

Vittoria shrugged. "All I know is that I had to find a way to warn him of danger. I managed to get away with a meat cleaver. Magda and Ugo chased him down the lane and cut down his beloved horse, Lunetta."

Tears welled in Tsura's eyes.

"Marcel went flying from his horse and laid injured on the ground. Ugo was going to stab Marcel with the cleaver. I took action and..." She could hardly bring herself to say the words.

"What happened?" Tsura pressed.

"I killed him. I hacked Ugo's neck with a cleaver until he died."

Tsura's hand flew up to cover her mouth.

"I overexerted myself and fell unconscious. Marcel took care of me until I was well again. It was just the two of us together for over a month."

"So, that's how you bonded."

"I suppose you could call it that."

"What happened to Magda?"

"She ran off to save herself after I killed Ugo. I think she's been following me. How else could she have ended up in Florence?"

"That's a good question. She could have killed you before I found you."

"True, I was alone at the villa after Marcel left."

"How long were you there alone?"

"I don't remember exactly. I drowned my sorrows in wine. I don't even remember leaving. I was still under the influence of drink when you found me."

"That would explain a few things."

"What am I going to do, Tsura? I'm going to have a baby. Magda is after me. Emilio is involved with the Church hunting witches, and the Malandanti are still a threat."

A small wise voice answered. Tsura and Vittoria looked up to see Aishe standing in the doorway holding Nico's hand. Nico's face was pained. He knew that another man's baby grew in her belly.

"You're going to forgive yourself," Aishe said, coming closer to Vittoria. "The Lady of Light reveals all. You must trust her."

"I had no idea you were suffering so, Vittoria," Nico said.

"There is always a balance that must be upheld. Death is a part of life and when one life is taken another is given," Tsura explained, pointing toward Vittoria's stomach. "The Lady of Light gave you the courage to take action when others would have turned tail, and you defended a man from evil. It is courage and selflessness that the Benetrix embodies, and it is in you to be a great Benetrix."

Aishe nodded her head in agreement.

"And we'll teach you all you'll need to know to receive Diana's blessings. We still have plenty of time."

"I will help any way I can," Nico promised, holding her gaze.

"Thank you," Vittoria expressed to them all. "I am very grateful."

Moving deeper into the room, Nico sat down with the three of them on the floor. "There is one thing I wanted to discuss with all of you. Angelo and I don't believe you're safe here alone. Emilio has made some serious claims and you need protection. I suggest that one of us stays with you at all times."

"We can't ask that of you, Nico," Vittoria replied.

"I know. I'm offering. We'll escort you wherever you need or want to go. We'll keep watch at night, so you can rest. And whatever needs doing, we'll do it."

Tsura nodded at Vittoria. It was a good idea.

Vittoria looked at Aishe who smiled. Nico was her knight in shining armor.

"Very well," she agreed.

"Besides, Christmastide begins tomorrow," he reminded her.

"What is that?" Aishe asked.

"It's twelve days of feasting and merrymaking celebrating the birth of Jesus Christ."

Aishe's eyes grew wide. "We're celebrating a baby? How wonderful!"

Nico laughed. "Yes, a very important baby."

Aishe rubbed Vittoria's tummy and said, "I like that kind of celebration."

Nerezza sulked in her den. It was Christmas and her patrons were celebrating the birth of their Messiah. She could hear the merrymaking happening in the Taverna above. She was certain that the Pope was celebrating too, and it annoyed her.

Since joining in union with the Holy Father, the Malandanti benefited from the pain and suffering of the people. He enjoyed a great purge of sinners, the return of his flock, and money pouring into his coffers. She'd acquired a lover in Emilio and a spy in Magda, but she did not have what she desired most—revenge on the Benedanti.

Though her powers doubled during the height of the plague, she was not able to draw the Benedanti to her as she had hoped. It had been six months since they set the Scourge loose, but the spell's magic had diminished and with it her patience. She toyed with the gilt edge of the parchment before unrolling the Scourge Scroll revealing an ancient script, written in the blood of a sacrificed bull.

Another sacrifice needed to be made. The Pope was in no hurry to do away with the Benedanti, but she was. She had Magda following Paolo since the night he came into the Taverna asking after Emilio. She also followed his brother Angelo, which led her to Nico, and then to finding Vittoria. Medea had been retrieving Magda's investigation memories and showing them to her, so she could see for herself what was going on.

Nerezza was certain that Vittoria was in the company of two Benedanti because the efficacy of her magic had waned since their arrival. A trio of lightworking Strega balanced the magic of a trio of shadow workers in the same vicinity. She found that projecting herself over great distances had become much more difficult. She was afraid she'd have to resort to other methods of contacting the Holy Father with progress updates. Ulyssa also struggled to inflict the torturous level of dream visions she so enjoyed, and Medea was unable to hold sway over another's mind as usual. It made her weary to do so. But it seemed no one had noticed yet.

A roar of laughter and singing could be heard from above and an idea struck Nerezza. She'd take advantage of this period of Christmastide to spread rumors of witches in Florence. People would be visiting each other all over the city and sharing news and tidings. Emilio did a good job stirring up the crowd at the Grano D'oro Inn, but more had to be done. If she was going to have her revenge, she'd have to move things along at her own pace. The Benedanti would take the blame for setting the scourge of plague upon the city. She had the perfect plan.

"Ulyssa! Medea!" Nerezza called in her mind to her sisters. Even though they were in the upstairs brothel they could hear.

Moments later her younger sisters entered the room. "What is it, Sister?" Medea asked.

"We must take further action to bring the Benedanti to heel. It is Christmastide and the perfect time to share gossip and news with our patrons, who will then share it with others."

Ulyssa twirled a lock of her black hair. "What would you have us do?"

"I want you to tell all the serving girls and whores that witches have been discovered in Florence. It was they who set the plague upon the city and cast it into chaos, so they could move in unnoticed. It was these evil minions of Satan who killed their fathers, mothers, and children. They are dangerous and must be rooted out and put on trial."

Medea rubbed her hands together. "I will implant images into their minds of Vittoria killing that man and some of her companions. The girls will be able to describe their appearances to whomever they tell the rumor."

"People love to gossip," Nerezza explained.

"Yes, they will embellish the tales and the fear will grow. People will accuse each other of witchcraft and worse."

"Medea, for good measure, implant Nico's likeness into their memory as well. He is known to be a hell-raiser and it won't take much for people to believe that he's in league with the accused."

Medea clapped her hands with glee. "Before the year is over all of Florence will believe they are under siege by witches."

"Go now and handle this business. When you are finished come back, for I will have further instructions. I will reach out to the Pope. The time has come to send the Inquisition."

Medea and Ulyssa whispered and tittered as they exited. Nerezza sat back in her chair and exhaled. She savored the prospect of seeing justice meted out. She knew that Vittoria was Celestina's heir because she had seen the color of her eyes in Magda's visions. Vittoria was to be the next Benetrix, though she had not yet developed her powers, and Nerezza would see to it that she never would.

Pope Urban VIII was removing his ceremonial regalia in his quarters when he saw, from the corner of his eye, the familiar sparkling of light hailing Nerezza's presence. He sat down and took a sip from a wine goblet and waited for her to materialize. It seemed to be taking longer than usual.

"Nice of you to visit," he said snidely.

"Your Eminence," she replied. "I have the news you've been waiting for."

"And what is that, pray tell?"

"The Benedanti have made themselves known. Rumors are flying all over the city. People are fearful that these Strega are going to cause more injury and death. It's all my patrons are talking about."

"And how did this become known?"

"People have grown suspicious of others in the wake of the plague. New arrivals and unfamiliar people are prone to suspicion. The girl, a Benedanti, who Magda saw murder a man returned to Florence with two others. Her name is Vittoria and she takes up with an infamous troublemaker called Nico Apollino. Everyone knows he's mad and she carries on with him. They are up to no good."

"You are certain?" He was skeptical but had no reason to disbelieve her.

"Yes, and there's more."

"Go on," he said.

"There have been suspicious deaths in Florence. Murders."

"And you believe they are related?"

"Yes, Your Holiness. I do."

"What was the nature of these murders?"

"One of my very own serving girls and the local tailor have been found with their throats cut and strange markings upon their foreheads. It must be the work of the Benedanti. They are warning us of their presence and I fear who will be next."

The Holy Father gasped. He took another long draught from his cup. He'd gotten all he desired from the Scourge—more parishioners than he'd seen in years packed in to attend his masses and the offerings were immense. He didn't need to make an example out of these Benedanti for he'd already gotten what he wanted. The only thing he desired now was immortality, so he could forever benefit from the power of his position and the money in his coffers. Killing Benedanti wouldn't serve him at all. However, his nephew needed to prove his commitment to the Church. It was a good opportunity for him to solidify his place in the Inquisition and please his father for once.

"I will instruct my brother, Cardinal Barberini, to come to Florence at the turn of the new year to investigate these claims of witchcraft and murder. He will have with him, my nephew, who is a new Inquisitor. As I mentioned before, he must have success."

"And I assured you he would have it, did I not?"

"Very well."

Nerezza smiled. "Thank you, Your Eminence. I will assist your nephew in any way I can," she promised.

The Pope nodded. He waved dismissively in her direction and her presence diminished.

CHAPTER 13

The city of Florence was abuzz with talk of witches and two people had indeed been found murdered—Constanza, the Tre Sorella Taverna serving girl, and Signor Amore, the tailor.

Paolo was shocked to hear from the coroner that both bodies were found in public locations. No effort had been given to hide the bodies. It was as if the perpetrator had wished them to be found. Both victims had sustained the same horrendous injuries.

Paolo couldn't believe such a terrible fate would come to two good people. He always enjoyed chatting with Constanza when they had played cards at the Taverna. Constanza was good at her job but she did not seem to fit in with the other more severe personalities who worked there. It always seemed to him that she would find herself a good man, get married, and have lots of children. And Signor Amore, in his opinion, was a saint. Anyone who would take Nico in and put up with his bad behavior all those years had to be.

He knew that Angelo and Nico were taking turns keeping watch over Vittoria and her cousins, so he headed over to her house to deliver the bad news. Paolo knocked on the door and waited. He heard shuffling and voices. The door opened, and it was Angelo. He had just arrived to relieve Nico from his overnight watch, so he could open the shop for business.

"Paolo, come in! I didn't expect to see you today."

"Nor did I. Is Nico still here?"

"He is, you just caught him."

Nico appeared in the foyer looking tired, but cheerful. "Hello Paolo, what brings you here this morning?"

"I have some terrible news, Nico," he admitted.

Vittoria arrived in the sitting room where the trio had gathered.

"I think you should sit down to hear this," Paolo said.

Nico's grin fell from his face and his eyes narrowed. "You're worrying me, Paolo."

Tsura and Aishe entered in time to hear the grim report.

"I'm sorry to tell you this, Nico, but Signor Amore has been murdered."

"What? That cannot be!" he exclaimed. "I saw him yesterday evening before I closed up the shop to come here."

Angelo shook his head. It was indeed terrible news. Tsura moved to Nico's side and placed her hand on his shoulder. He flinched. Vittoria pulled Aishe closer to comfort the child.

"He was found at the end of an alley, just a block away from the church."

"That's where he was going when he left the shop." Nico slumped in his chair and dropped his dark head into his hands. "What was the manner of death?"

Paolo looked at Vittoria and then Aishe. He was uncomfortable speaking of it in front of a child. Vittoria understood and led Aishe out of the room.

"His throat was cut, and his tongue pulled through."

"Oh, my goodness," Tsura said, covering her mouth at the horror of it.

Nico ran his hands through his hair and stood up. "What else?" he demanded.

"His forehead was branded with the sign of an inverted cross."

"For God's sake!" Angelo exclaimed.

Nico leaned onto the mantle of the fireplace to steady himself.

"I'm so sorry, Nico. I heard the news from the coroner. I came straight over to tell you."

"Thank you, Paolo," he said, his voice cracked. He was struggling to hold back tears.

"This must be the work of that Magda, Vittoria told us about. You can be sure of it," Tsura claimed.

"Magda, you say?" Paolo asked.

"Yes, do you know a Magda?"

"When I went to the Tre Sorella Taverna a few weeks ago looking for Emilio. The serving girl Constanza was tending our table that night. When I started asking after Emilio, a strange woman I never met delivered my drink instead of Constanza. She tried to make small talk with me but was rude to the other men at the table. It felt very awkward. She said her name was Magda and that she was new in town."

He paused and looked around the room.

"What else?" Nico asked.

"Signor Amore was not the only one found dead. Constanza, whom I just spoke of, was killed in the same manner."

Angelo looked at Nico, then spoke for them.

"We believe that Malandanti are at the Tre Sorella Taverna. Tsura said three Strega must remain together for their power to stay strong. Three sisters own that establishment."

Paolo gulped hard.

"I also made eye contact with Nerezza, the eldest sister. She was up in the brothel balcony looking down at me. She didn't appear very happy when I was asking about Emilio. It spooked me, so I left."

"Why didn't you tell us these details?" Angelo asked.

"I don't know," he admitted. "I didn't think they mattered. At least not then. We didn't even know the Malandanti existed."

"True," Angelo agreed.

"Magda must be mixed up with the Malandanti. She was following Vittoria and perhaps she's been following you too, Paolo."

Paolo blanched. He did think he was being followed when he was watching Vittoria's home.

Nico noticed his unnatural pallor. "You think you've been followed?"

"Maybe, the day Aishe saw me from the window," he confessed.

"Then Magda knows we keep Nico's company because Vittoria saw her in the alley near the shop. And if she followed you, she knows where we live," Tsura explained.

"This is all too suspicious. Emilio raving about witches a few days ago, my own mother mentioned she'd heard rumors from the servants about the presence of witches in Florence, and now two murders of people we know," Angelo explained. "It's like they're setting a trap, but for whom?"

"What could they want with Vittoria," Paolo asked. Nobody in the room had an answer.

Overhearing the question from the kitchen Vittoria returned. "I know why."

Nico rubbed wearily at his eyes and waited.

"Tsura, do you remember in the circle when Celestina addressed the clan? She told us she had a vision of her niece. The one who obtained the Scourge Scroll to set loose a plague over the land. She was working with the Church. Wasn't her name Nerezza?"

Tsura's mouth fell open and recognition dawned on her face. "She knows you're Celestina's heir and the next Benetrix."

"What does that mean?" Paolo asked.

"It means that if Vittoria dies or never takes up her mantle as the anointed Benetrix after Celestina, the Benedanti way of life will die out. The Malandanti will be stronger than ever and shadow will reign."

"I thought it was imperative that the balance of shadow and light be upheld," Angelo said.

"It is," Tsura replied. "At all costs."

"Then she must have some other issue with the Benedanti. We need to find out what," Nico insisted.

"We can contact Grandmother, she can tell us," Aishe said, peeping her head into the room. Vittoria had told her to stay put while the adults talked.

Tsura responded. "She's right. We need to know why she's after Vittoria."

"Yeah. No one in their right mind sets out to destroy the world unless they have been hurt or angered by something. Trust me, I know," Nico explained, shaking his head.

"In the meantime, we must be very careful," Angelo warned. "I don't have a good feeling about any of it."

Heads nodded in agreement around the room.

"Paolo, take me to Signor Amore, please. I must make arrangements for his burial," Nico said.

"Of course."

Upon exiting, Nico turned to Angelo. "Don't open that door for anyone until I return."

Marcel had made the trip across the Vatican courtyard, with his shadows, several dozen times. It was always the same. He would arrive at Cardinal Moreau's quarters to find him stuffing his fat face with boiled eggs. Marcel would greet him and sit down. Then Moreau would quiz him on his studies while he gobbled his breakfast. The shadows would stand outside the door and wait. But this morning was different. He barely stepped foot into the room before the Cardinal launched into his news.

"Sit down, sit down," he said, motioning toward the empty seat at his work table. Marcel sat down. His shadows were standing by the door. "You too, Claudio, come in. This concerns you as well."

Claudio approached the Cardinal's desk.

"We're going to Florence. There have been credible reports of dangerous witch activity in the city. The

Holy Father has authorized our travel on the morrow. There is little time to waste. There have already been two murders related to the arrival of suspected witches."

Marcel had never seen the cardinal in such a state. He was out of breath with excitement and his forehead glistened with perspiration.

"Will Cardinal Barberini be accompanying us?" Marcel asked. He had not seen his father since his arrival in Rome. He was Moreau's problem for the time being.

"He will," the Cardinal replied. "Normally, he would remain here, and I would go out to investigate. However, as you know, Florence is his home. It pains him to know there are witches terrorizing his city of birth."

"Of course," Marcel replied. He knew his father could give a fig about Florence. He was after something else. He never did anything out of the kindness of his heart.

"It is unusual to travel during Christmastide to investigate claims of witchcraft, but the Pope is adamant that we arrive by the turn of the new year to deal with this mess."

"Do we have any suspects?"

"We have quite a few witnesses. They will be brought in to give their testimony at a place called...," he looked down over the letter he had received with instructions from Cardinal Barberini. "Ahh, yes. Here it is. We are to convene at the Tre Sorella Taverna, on the western side of Florence. We will be greeted by the Taverna's mistress Nerezza Ascerbi. She will provide us lodging and assist in any way we may need. Arrangements are being made in secret as we must not bring attention to our presence. Strict privacy is required so that we do not risk alerting the accused of their impending arrest."

Claudio nodded but remained silent.

"You will ride ahead of us, Claudio, and secure our lodgings and speak to the head of police at the Bargello. We will arrive in plain clothes so not to draw attention. Cardinal Barberini will join us after we have spoken to all the witnesses."

"Yes, your Eminence." Claudio looked over at Marcel. "Does the young Inquisitor no longer require my assistance?"

"If he's learned anything, Claudio, it's that the Church is always watching," he said looking at Marcel.

Marcel nodded. He wasn't about to make a move to escape, yet.

"There is no need to worry. I'm looking forward to putting all my new knowledge into practice," he said, hefting his constant companion, the *Sacro Arsenale*, in his hand.

"I am interested to see it done as well," the Cardinal agreed.

Claudio bowed before the Cardinal and took his leave with the shadows.

"Don't make me regret my decision," the Cardinal said to Marcel.

"I won't, Your Eminence."

"Go prepare yourself. We ride at first light."

Marcel rose and, for the first time ever, walked alone to his quarters.

An unexpected sight awaited Cardinal Barberini at his villa. The residence of his mistress and bastard was in total disarray. It had been a very long time, years even, since he had stepped foot inside, and it was a shell of the gem it once was.

There used to be lavish carpets and tapestries, fine furniture, decorative paintings, glass vases, metal candelabras, and clocks. They all were gone. What little remained had been destroyed. Wine bottles had been thrown against the mural walls and glass littered the tile floor.

As he moved about the villa to take stock of the damage he found that unwelcome guests had taken up residence in the kitchen. Rummaging around in the larder was an animal with an elongated body, reddish-brown fur, and a long bushy tail. The cardinal shouted at the animal and it pulled itself out of the bag of dried lentils. Its flattened head appeared, and its black eyes stared up at the Cardinal as if it was annoyed to be interrupted from foraging his dinner.

"Out!" shouted the Cardinal. He stamped his feet and clapped his hands at the animal to scare it. The polecat, with its short legs and hopping gait, dashed away along with several dormice that were hiding in other areas. The Cardinal kicked at the animals as they scurried by.

"That damned boy!" he shouted out. "He did this to spite me."

Storming out of the kitchen into the garden he pushed through the door hidden behind the withered bougainvillea to survey his property. The stables were empty except for some tack and a bale of hay. As he walked up the lane away from the stable he stumbled upon the remains of a horse and something else. He inched closer. Just yards from the horse appeared to be the bones of a man who died face down from an attack of some sort. The body was picked clean of skin and muscle. On the vertebrae of the neck, he could see hack marks.

"Dear God!" he exclaimed in disgust. "What in Heaven's name has happened here?"

He could accept that Marcel had everything to do with the destruction of the villa. It was the act of a petulant child. But he could not believe that Marcel had the nerve to kill a man. This had to be the work of someone else. The Cardinal stepped away from the body and carried himself with haste back to the villa.

Inside the library, he scoured his old office. The desk had been razed of its contents. Books and papers were strewn over the floor. Marcel's prized lute was smashed to bits in the corner.

Marcel did not do this, he realized. He would never destroy his own instrument. He continued to inspect the damage and noticed that the Book of Hours he had given as a gift to his mistress was missing. He had planned to take it back with him to Rome. He dropped to his knees and rifled through the mess on the floor but did not find it.

He rushed to Veronique's bedchamber. Except for the writing desk and the bed, it was empty.

This is where it happened, he thought.

A year ago, when he'd been elevated to Secretary of the Holy Office, the severity of his attitude toward Veronique and Marcel increased. As the man who was tasked with wiping out all sin in Christendom, the Cardinal's first task was to erase any evidence that he himself had sinned. He ceased all contact with them. Squelching the ample allowance which had taken care of his offspring and kept the villa running. Veronique begged for the allowance to be fully restored but he did not acquiesce. Consequently, Marcel, he knew, sold off all but two of the horses and many expensive pieces of furniture.

The Cardinal wouldn't allow himself to believe that it was his neglect that took its toll on his son's mother. Veronique was weak and allowed herself to be possessed by evil diabolical witches. Their magic made her take her own life. He was angry at Veronique for allowing that to happen. She would never find her way to Heaven. Because of her suicide, she would remain forever in Purgatory. Her weakness made Marcel weak and he had every intention of rectifying that.

As he exited the room he noticed a letter on the desk addressed to Veronique's maid. He picked it up and read the words on the page.

Dearest Therese,

The meeting went as expected. Although I prayed for mercy, it was not God's will to receive it from Cardinal Barberini. Mama was laid to rest in the pauper's cemetery outside of Rome. Prepare the villa for closure, as I will not linger. As we discussed, I am moving forward with my plans. As soon as the work is done, please take your leave.

With deepest regret,
Marcel

The Cardinal balled the letter up in his fist. He was angrier than ever, and someone had to pay. He was eager to get to Florence and begin the trial.

Marcel and Cardinal Moreau arrived at the Tre Sorella Taverna on a soggy Monday afternoon. The trip had been long and arduous in the frigid winter weather and Marcel's rear was numb from riding all morning. Cardinal Moreau complained about the conditions of their journey the entire way. Marcel was happy to get inside, away from the Cardinal's griping, and into some dry clothing.

They were greeted by a stable boy who settled their horses and their baggage for them. Upon entering the Taverna, all three sisters, and Claudio awaited. They approached and bowed in welcome to the Cardinal and Marcel.

"Welcome to the Tre Sorella Taverna. I am Nerezza Ascerbi, mistress of this establishment. These are my sisters, Medea and Ulyssa."

"Your Eminence, Inquisitor Barberini, welcome to Florence," Claudio said, bowing.

Cardinal Moreau grumbled about the weather and how hungry he was. He hadn't eaten anything in an hour. Marcel eyed the roaring fire in the large shadowy room and rubbed his hands together.

"Where are my manners?" Nerezza apologized. "Please do come in. You must be tired and cold."

"Thank you," Marcel replied. The place seemed nice enough and empty in expectation of their arrival and subsequent investigation. He removed his damp traveling cloak and took a seat close to the fire. The warmth of the flames thawed his fingers and toes and relaxed his tight muscles. The Cardinal sat too. Claudio stood by.

Nerezza snapped her fingers and a woman appeared with a jug of wine and two goblets for their guests. She poured the wine while another woman delivered a terrine of hot soup and warm bread to the table. She ladled it out into bowls and set it before Marcel and the Cardinal. Marcel thanked the women for their kindness. The Cardinal wasted no time diving into his meal, he grunted his thanks between bites.

"When you are finished with your dinner, Magda will show you to your quarters," Nerezza explained, pointing toward the older woman who had just served them their food.

Marcel looked up at the older woman standing beside the table. Something about her appearance was familiar to him. Her bottom lip trembled. She seemed nervous. His eyes lingered upon her haggard face. She kept her eyes cast downward avoiding his gaze. He was tired from the long ride and couldn't quite place her in his memory. He shrugged and gave her a wry smile instead.

"Claudio, give me your report," Cardinal Moreau ordered.

"Your Eminence, I visited the Bargello this morning and advised the police that the Holy Inquisition was in Florence investigating claims of witchcraft. Your request to utilize the jail cells in the Torre di Arnolfo for the accused has been obliged. And since we traveled without a notary to record the trial proceedings one has been made available to us."

"Very good," he responded. "There is no time to waste. We will interview the witnesses first thing."

"Also, I've been informed that the coroner has kept the bodies of the murder victims for you to confirm evidence of foul play by these witches. They are beginning to putrefy so one must be quick about it."

A sour look appeared upon the Cardinal's face. "Inquisitor Barberini, I suggest you go now and speak to the coroner. Find out what happened to these poor souls. I need rest."

There was no point in arguing. Marcel put down his spoon. The idea of eating turned out not to be a good one.

"Very well."

He excused himself and put his damp cloak back on and, accompanied by his shadow once again, he headed out to investigate.

Marcel walked with Claudio to the offices of the coroner. He couldn't bear to ride another step on his horse. His body couldn't take it. They were greeted by Dottore Blanco, a grumpy bear of a man, and brought down a flight of steps into the cold stone cellar. A chill went over Marcel's body. It smelled of decay and excrement and he gagged. He was glad he decided to pass on eating beforehand.

"I've never seen anything like it," Dottore Blanco admitted. "It's got to be the work of the devil."

He led them into an alcove where two bodies were laid out on trestle tables and covered by sheets.

"This city has experienced tremendous suffering over the past six months. First the plague, now witches."

"What brings you to believe there are witches in Florence?" Marcel asked, trying not to breathe through his nose. He was quite certain that witches did not exist.

"There's been talk about strange women arriving in Florence during the plague. They look like gypsies."

"Just because they look like gypsies, doesn't mean they're witches."

"Well, they've taken up with that damned hellion, Nico Apollino. Everyone knows he's a wolf in sheep's clothing. And one of the victims was his very own maestro, the tailor, Signor Amore!"

"Maestro?"

"Yes, Nico apprenticed for Signor Amore for many years. It's my opinion that Nico killed him, so he could take over the business for himself. He's even joined a guild! How standards have crumbled if they would allow filth like Nico into their ranks."

"What has he done to receive such notoriety?"

"What hasn't he done? He's a drunkard and rabble-rouser. And he tormented one of my own students, Paolo Salviati, for years," he explained. Then he leaned over and whispered to Marcel. "Some even say he's a sodomite."

Claudio cringed.

Marcel did his best to keep a straight face.

"He came here after the murder to arrange for Signor Amore's burial, but I would not allow it. He is not family."

"Does Signor Amore have any living relatives?"

"Not anymore, his wife and daughter succumbed to plague. It's my opinion that Nico saw an opportunity to profit and he took it, no matter the cost."

Marcel was curious about this Nico Apollino. He was linked to a murder victim. "Do you know where Signor Apollino resides?"

"He can be found near the corner of Via Calimala and Via Orsanmichele. Look for the shop with the sign of the golden shears."

Marcel looked to Claudio to confirm he would remember the address.

"Thank you. Why don't we look at the bodies now?"

As much as he did not want to do it, he knew he it had to be done.

"Very well. Brace yourself," Dottore Blanco advised, as he walked over to the first body and pulled down the sheet.

Marcel held his breath and squinted his eyes in anticipation of the ghastly sight. Long blond hair spilled out from under the cover first, then a pale forehead appeared marked with an inverted cross. Even Dottore Blanco averted his eyes as he unveiled the worst of it all.

The young woman's throat was slit wide open and the tongue had been pulled through the opening. Rigor mortis had set in and the tongue no longer dangled but stuck out like a sore thumb. It was awful. Marcel coughed and gagged. Claudio exited the alcove and vomited in the corridor. One thing was for sure, evil was responsible for this desecration, he just wasn't sure it was witches.

Upon returning with Claudio, who still looked sick, to the Tre Sorella Taverna, Marcel was given yet another shock. Speaking to Cardinal Moreau was none other than his father. His appearance stopped Marcel dead in his tracks. He didn't expect to see Cardinal Barberini until much later in the investigation.

"Your Eminence," he said, bowing as expected.

Cardinal Barberini still had his traveling cloak on and his face was red with rage.

"I have just come from *my* villa and I found it in shambles when I arrived. It is not fit for a pig!"

He glared at Marcel who had no idea what he was talking about. He left the villa in fine shape when he departed.

"What happened?" he dared ask.

"It was torn to shreds. Wine bottles smashed upon the walls, furniture broken, books and papers strewn about, and on the road a horse carcass and the remains of a dead man."

Cardinal Moreau crossed himself. "How terrible!"

"Indeed." Marcel played dumb, but he knew how the horse died. It was his horse. And he also knew how the man was cut down. But he dared not say a thing. What he didn't know was how the villa came to be destroyed. Then the answer came to him.

Vittoria.

She must have gone into a rage after he left her.

"I cannot abide in such a state of disarray. Besides, there is no staff."

Marcel knew the true reason for that as well.

"Surely, a room can be made up for you here, Your Eminence," he said. "Take my quarters."

Cardinal Barberini stared down his nose at his son. "That is most kind," he said as if there were any other options.

Magda eavesdropped on Moreau and Barberini's conversation just as she did on every other she heard.

Cardinal Moreau was surprised by Cardinal Barberini's unexpected arrival. He hefted his body up to greet his superior.

"We weren't expecting you for a few more days."

"I wasn't expecting to arrive so soon either," Barberini blustered. "My villa has been ransacked and a very valuable item has been stolen."

"What was stolen?"

"An illuminated Book of Hours given me as a gift from the Holy Father."

"That *is* of great value," Cardinal Moreau agreed, shaking his thick head in pity. "Do you know who could have done such a thing?"

"I believe it was the work of the diabolical witches plaguing Florence. Why else would they target the villa of a servant of God? They took a bejeweled Book of Hours inscribed by the hand of the Pope. They can use that book in their magic to harm the Church."

Magda's body tightened. She had held that very book in her own hands. It was precious indeed, with jewels encrusted on the cover and gold upon the pages. She couldn't read and didn't recognize the inscription, but she knew how dangerous witches, especially the Malandanti variety, could inflict pain and punishment.

Since she stepped foot into the Tre Sorella Taverna she had been nothing but Nerezza's slave. She waited on the sisters' hand and foot, then ran around town at all hours following Paolo, Nico, and Vittoria, all before subjecting herself to Medea's brain-bending retrieval of her memories. Not to mention, her life had been threatened on multiple occasions, and she'd been made to perform acts she wouldn't have even expected of Ugo.

Her station in life had worsened since meeting Vittoria. Initially, she desired revenge but had come to find she desired freedom from the Malandanti more. Now she had her chance.

CHAPTER 14

Two days later, before dawn, Magda knocked lightly upon Cardinal Barberini's bedchamber door. Her hands were trembling with fear at what was to unfold. She'd spent the entire night playing out scenarios of possible repercussions for the confession she was going to make.

The previous day, when she was called as a witness against Vittoria and her companion Nico, she lied, as she'd been told to do. It wasn't Vittoria who killed those poor souls, but something much worse. And she hoped the Inquisition would rid the world of it.

There was already the faint hint of candlelight emanating from the crack at the bottom of the door. Cardinal Barberini was awake. The door opened a crack and the Cardinal peeked out.

"What do you want?" he asked.

"It's urgent, Your Eminence. I would like to confess."

"I don't take confession."

"It's about the witch trial," she whispered.

"What about it?" His voice was too loud. Magda looked back over her shoulder through the dark hall and hoped no one heard them.

"May I come in?"

"No!" He closed the door in her face.

Leaning her head into the crack of the door frame she whispered again in a desperate manner.

"Your Eminence, please. I want to retract my witness testimony and confess my guilt. I killed Constanza and Signor Amore."

The door was yanked open and the Cardinal stood there in his nightshirt and cap.

"You?"

Magda nodded.

The Cardinal stepped aside allowing Magda to enter his small quarters. He looked out into the hall, to make sure no one saw, before closing the door.

He motioned for her to sit in the chair in the corner of the room. She took her seat and looked up at the Cardinal.

"Speak," he commanded.

"My life was threatened if I didn't take their lives. The witches you are looking for are right under your nose."

The Cardinal rubbed the divot between his eyebrows. It was too early for such nonsense. The whole thing was preposterous.

"What in God's name are you suggesting?"

"It's not the wool merchant's daughter, Vittoria, that is the real danger, although she has killed a man. But she did it to save your son. It's the three sisters Nerezza, Medea, and Ulyssa. They have powers. They can control people's will by casting enchantments on them."

"Wait! Wait one moment. What did you say? This Vittoria killed a man?"

"I was there. At the height of the plague, I left San Gimignano with a plan to make a fortune of my own by any means necessary. I had an accomplice called Ugo. We were going to steal from your villa. When we entered, we found Vittoria hiding in an armoire and we took her hostage and lay in wait for your son to return. When he arrived on horseback, Ugo cut down his horse and almost killed your son too. Vittoria had gotten away from us. She saved your son from certain death by killing Ugo with a cleaver."

The Cardinal's face was aghast. What she divulged fell in line with the clues he likely found at his villa.

Magda continued babbling her confession.

"I was going to take your Book of Hours, but after Ugo was killed I ran off to save myself. I don't know what happened to it. Then I came here. I've been in the service of the sisters ever since."

She kept going, wringing her fingers. Her nervousness had taken control.

"At first, I hoped to take revenge on Vittoria for spoiling my chance of gaining riches. But then the sisters looked through my memories and they saw Vittoria killing Ugo. They took great interest in her because they saw she was wearing a witch's talisman around her neck. They identified her as a Benedanti witch, a sworn enemy of their own clan. Nerezza has some bone to pick with them, I'm not quite sure why."

"So, Vittoria *is* a witch! She could have the Book of Hours."

"Perhaps. I don't know. I didn't see the talisman with my own eyes. It looked to me like she was wearing a silver cross, but they claimed to see something I did not."

"You still haven't told me why you are confessing to killing two people. You could be put to death for such a claim, and at the very least thrown in jail for attempting to steal from me."

"They forced me, *us*, to kill those people."

"Us? You and who else?"

"Emilio Apollino."

"How? How did they force you?"

"The sisters commended us for spying on and providing information about Vittoria and her company and spreading the rumors that she was a witch and cause of the plague. Ulyssa gave us each a goblet of wine and encouraged us both to drink. When we did, Medea cast a spell to lock open our jaws, so they could not be closed. Wine poured in great abundance with no end from the cups. We couldn't move or breathe. We felt like we were drowning. It was then that Nerezza told us the Inquisition would not come if there wasn't a murder pointing to Vittoria. She demanded that we slit the throats and brand the heads of Constanza and Signor Amore. They said if we didn't they would curse us to feel like we were eternally drowning. We believed them."

"Obviously. What was so special about these two victims? How would they point to Vittoria?"

"Perhaps Nerezza wanted it to look like Vittoria was threatening her safety by killing one of her best serving girls. Nobody would believe that Nerezza would kill one of her own. She did after all make the report about witchcraft in Florence to the Church."

"What about the tailor?"

"Nico worked for him and is a close companion of Vittoria's. From what I understand, he has quite the reputation as a troublemaker in town. Maybe she wanted it to look as if the two were in league."

"What do you want? Undoubtedly, you didn't come here to confess all this to me out of the goodness of your heart."

"I'm giving you the truth. All of it."

"And what do you want?" his voice raised.

"I want your leniency and protection. Please," she begged. "I've given you your witches. Put them on trial, in jail, or burn them. Whatever it is you do. They are guilty of murder, not I."

The Cardinal sneered. "Leniency? As far as I'm concerned, you're all guilty, and you will pay for your crimes."

Magda's face fell, and her shoulders slumped. He opened the door with a flourish signaling it was time for her to leave. She rose from her chair and walked to the door. As she exited, the Cardinal leaned over and whispered.

"I wouldn't go far if I were you."

"You've been betrayed!" Emilio exclaimed, shaking Nerezza from her slumber. "I just overheard Magda confess everything to Cardinal Barberini."

Nerezza shot up from the bed and rubbed her tired eyes.

"Are you certain?" she asked.

"Yes, your suspicions were confirmed."

"That snake! She was acting strange, with all that fiddling and fidgeting, as she gave witness against Vittoria yesterday. She would not make eye contact with me afterward. I knew she was up to something."

"They will come for us next. She gave them my name. What are we going to do?"

"We?" Nerezza questioned, rising from the bed she shared with Emilio.

"Yes, of course," Emilio replied.

Nerezza walked toward her glamour glass. She wished to see the face of her betrayer. She waved her hand over the surface of the mirror and thought of Magda. The mirror shimmered, and Magda's long face came into view. She was still in the Tre Sorella Taverna. There was nowhere for her to go. Tears streaked her guilty face and she rocked back and forth trying to console herself. She'd taken a huge gamble with her life by going to the Cardinal and she had lost. Nerezza snickered. She waved her hand again over the mirror and thought of Cardinal Barberini. He had dressed in his finest scarlet silk vestments with a broad sash around the waist. A large golden cross hung from his neck. It looked to Nerezza like he was drenched in blood and out for more.

"What do you see?" Emilio asked, his voice quavering. Nerezza still hadn't answered his previous question.

"I see that Cardinal Barberini is going to make his arrests. He's dressed and waking the others. He thinks he's got the element of surprise on his side. You are going to go upstairs and tell him you will take him to Vittoria, so I have time to contact the Pope. I will report that I have been betrayed and now the Inquisition is hunting me as well. He will make this problem go away."

"But, I'll be arrested if I go to the Cardinal," Emilio argued, moving to Nerezza's side.

Her answer was cold. "Perhaps."

Emilio stood still in stunned silence.

"Do you need to be motivated?" Nerezza asked, glaring at him. Her eyes sparkling with malice.

Emilio backed away. "Do I mean nothing to you?"

"Darling, my life is at stake and naturally you must risk yours to save mine. I would trust no other to protect me."

Confusion appeared on Emilio's face.

"You have served me very well," she complimented. It was her final farewell to him.

Tears welled in Emilio's eyes. He walked away from Nerezza, pushed aside the tapestry hiding the secret stairway to give himself over to the Inquisition. He did not look back.

The unfamiliar feeling of fear flooded Nerezza's guts. She never expected for the tables to be turned and she to become the object of the Inquisition's wrath. Surely, the Holy Father would take care of the issue.

"Your Eminence," Nerezza said, as she materialized into the Pope's familiar quarters. He had not yet woken. "Please, Your Eminence, wake up. It is urgent."

Pope Urban VIII rolled over in his bed and shouted at her. "Go away!"

"It's the Inquisition. Your brother, he's coming for me. I've been betrayed," she sputtered. "I need your help."

He sat up in bed and adjusted his nightcap. "It seems to me that you've been careless in your dealings."

"That is not true! One of my spies, Magda, confessed to killing two people and blamed me, claiming I made her do it."

"And did you?" he asked outright.

"It was the Benedanti who murdered those people. I had nothing to do with it," she stammered, looking away as she answered his question.

"That is hard to believe, Nerezza. I know you would stop at nothing to get your revenge," he countered.

"My mother deserves to be avenged!" she argued. "The Benedanti took her from me."

"Well, I have nothing to gain from intervening on your behalf. You took a risk and because of your impatience you have made yourself vulnerable to arrest and possible death."

"You must help me!" she pleaded.

"I must do no such thing," he replied.

"Did I not give you a tremendous gift? You benefited greatly from the scourge of plague. The faithful have returned to your flock, money pours into your coffers, and your power grows. I have yet to benefit."

"I will not put myself at risk of losing all I have gained."

"What if I tell the Inquisition the truth? That you and I performed magic together to bring a plague upon the people."

"No one would believe you, Nerezza. You are a depraved harlot. There is not a soul on earth that would believe a word you say about me."

Nerezza knew he spoke the truth. "There must be something you want. I will give it to you." She was desperate.

The Cardinal stroked his goatee, thinking before answering. "Immortality."

"I cannot give that to you. There must be something else."

"I desire immortality. If you won't give it to me, we have nothing more to discuss."

"Resurrection and immortality magic is forbidden. I will be punished by the Goddess if I perform it."

"I don't care about your Goddess. You swore on the one true God when we met. You swore to *me*!"

"But I will be put to death, as my mother was if I give you what you ask," she cried.

"Then I suppose you should call on your Goddess to save you then, shouldn't you?" he retorted and laughed.

Nerezza could hear stomping and shouting coming from the upstairs levels. The Inquisition was looking for her and her sisters. Emilio and Magda had been arrested, she was sure of it. They would not find the entrance to her subterranean den. Medea and Ulyssa rushed in from their rooms, panic upon their faces.

"What's happening?" Medea cried out. Ulyssa clung to her sister's arm.

Nerezza considered her options. If she gave immortal life to the Pope, she would be punished by death, and her dear sisters would perish as well. She couldn't risk their safety.

"I will not do it," she declared. "I will not give you immortality. I'll risk torture before I give *you* eternal life," she spat at the Pope. "I'll find another way to overcome this problem."

"Have it your way," he responded, his eyes cold.

"I plan to."

Emilio was arrested as soon as he appeared in the Taverna's main hall. Magda was already shackled and guarded by Claudio. Cardinal Barberini's men searched the building from top to bottom looking for evidence to use against the accused. Emilio was tempted to reveal to his captors where the entrance to the subterranean level could be found so the sisters could be apprehended, but he feared Nerezza's magic more than being arrested. He gave up the location of Vittoria Giordano's home instead.

Cardinal Barberini led the expedition to the wool district. To his right, was Cardinal Moreau, who forced his heavy body to move at a much faster pace than normal and was sweating even on the frosty January morn. The young Inquisitor Barberini walked at the Cardinal's left. Behind them, Emilio and Magda were marched through the streets of Florence in restraints.

Magda cried the entire time and begged for the Cardinal's mercy. Emilio imagined his own mother would wail, too, when she learned of his incredible fall from grace that was bound to reach her ears forthwith. Claudio pulled up the rear along with the captain of police and a few the men he brought along for muscle.

The procession was a spectacle and people poured out into the street to watch. They jeered and threw rotten food at Emilio and Magda as they passed by. They arrived at their destination, and the police captain approached the front door and banged hard.

"Open up this door! The Holy Roman Inquisition is here to take Vittoria Giordano and her gypsy companion into custody, under charges of witchcraft and heresy."

"And theft!" Barberini added.

"Under charges of witchcraft, heresy, *and* theft!" the captain clarified.

Inquisitor Barberini looked up at the top windows of the building. Emilio followed his gaze. There he saw a young girl with auburn hair and Vittoria looking down at them. An expression of angry recognition appeared on Vittoria's face. Emilio's body burned with shame for what he had done, even though he had been shown Vittoria killing a man in cold blood.

Bystanders gathered in the street and shouted for Vittoria to come out. They wanted justice for their loved ones who had been taken from them by plague, and the innocents who had been murdered.

Emilio noticed that the young Inquisitor was still staring up at Vittoria's window and that his face had paled. Vittoria and the girl disappeared from view. Then a voice boomed from the crowd and all turned to look.

"Vittoria is innocent! You have no grounds with which to arrest her!" Nico shouted, pushing his way through the mob. He glared at Emilio. "What have you done? The sisters put you up to this, didn't they?" he blustered, shoving Emilio in the chest.

Emilio didn't answer, part of him was satisfied to see Nico incensed. Magda cried louder.

The police captain continued banging on the door. "Come out now or we will have no choice but to break down the door and extract you by force!"

"You will do no such thing!" Nico challenged. Someone threw a half-eaten apple at him.

"And who do you think you are to stop us?" Cardinal Barberini asked, his tone icy.

"Nico Apollino, I presume?" said Inquisitor Barberini.

"And who are you?" Nico demanded.

"He is Inquisitor Marcel Barberini," Claudio informed him. "And it would serve you well to hold your tongue."

Nico went quiet. Emilio watched as a familiar look appeared on Nico's face. His hazel eyes darkened, and his brow furrowed. The muscles in his square face tensed. With great anticipation, Emilio braced himself expecting Nico to attack him. Instead, he grabbed for Marcel.

"You'd do this to the mother of your child?" Nico charged. "You piece of shit."

"You dare slander an officer of God?" said Cardinal Moreau, his jowls quivering in disbelief.

As all watched the attack on Marcel, the door swung open.

"Nico! Please let him go!" Vittoria pleaded. "He's not worth the trouble." She stepped out into the street. The crowd jeered.

Nico glared hard at Marcel and shoved him into Emilio before unhanding him. Nico spat on the ground in disgust.

"Are you Vittoria Giordano?" asked the police captain. Vittoria looked at Marcel and nodded. "You will come with us." The police captain motioned to one of his men to secure Vittoria in bonds. She did not put up a fight.

Angelo and Tsura appeared at the door. Cardinal Barberini pointed at Tsura. "This must be her fiendish companion," he said.

Emilio nodded at Cardinal Barberini.

"Put her in chains as well. Blindfold them both. They must not be able to see, for they may cast the evil eye or curses upon us," the Cardinal ordered.

Rough woolen sacks were thrown over Vittoria and Tsura's heads. Marcel winced as he watched them manhandle Vittoria.

Nico pushed forward to reach Vittoria but was shoved back by police muscle. Angelo grabbed Nico's arm and pulled him away, so he wouldn't be arrested too. Cardinal Barberini ordered his men to search the premises.

Angelo caught Emilio's attention before they were all hauled away. "Mother will never forgive you, and I don't think I can ever either," he informed his twin.

Emilio was yanked away to jail. As he was pushed through the throng of bystanders he glanced over his shoulder to see Angelo wrap an arm around Nico's shoulders.

That bastard has won again, he thought.

Aishe clung to Nico's neck and cried. Though he comforted her in his strong arms, Aishe was terrified for both her sister and cousin. The Inquisition ripped through the house for over an hour before they left. They sought incriminating evidence linking the girls to witchcraft.

Cardinal Barberini dug through Vittoria's belongings himself and when he discovered the Book of Hours, he said aloud, "I've got you now, witch!"

They needed help. When Angelo, Nico, and Aishe were left alone, she said, "We need to get word to Grandmother about Tsura and Vittoria. She can help us."

"Where is your Grandmother?" Nico asked.

"In the country with the clan," she replied.

"But how are we to get word to her?" Angelo questioned. "We can't send a messenger. It's too dangerous to try. We'd be putting your people in harm's way."

"We'll use magic," she explained.

Angelo and Nico looked at each other. It was the only option.

"Let's go upstairs away from prying eyes," Nico said. "Angelo, lock the door."

Angelo bolted the entry door and they all ran up the stairs to Aishe's bedroom.

Nico closed the curtains and took a seat by the window, so he could peek out to keep watch. "I wonder where those damned Malandanti are now? They're responsible for this whole mess," Nico muttered to himself.

"What do we do now?" Angelo asked Aishe. He paced back and forth.

"We must all join hands to raise power," she instructed. "We're going to fly on the wings of a bird."

Angelo's eyebrows raised in surprise.

"Whatever it takes," Nico replied.

They all joined their hands together.

"Close your eyes and take three deep breaths," Aishe instructed. She could sense the tenseness and worry inside Nico and the disappointment in Angelo. As they breathed in unison, their zee relaxed, and she knew they were ready.

"Upon wings of a bird, we take flight. By the grace of the Goddess, guided by light," she chanted.

Their zee was soft and malleable. It was time to bind the three of them together. She could sense Nico wanted to open his eyes to see what was happening, so she sent out a pulsing wave of calm around the circle to quell any worry or fear of the process and then returned to her work. She wove their zee together to form a great majestic hawk at the center of their circle. All their consciousness was connected inside this great bird. She could hear them thinking, and they could hear her. The hawk flapped its wings.

"Are we inside a bird?" Nico asked.

"We *are* the bird," Aishe replied.

"This is amazing!" Angelo exclaimed.

"Our minds are in the bird, but our bodies will remain in this room. We will see through the bird's eyes and feel what the bird feels as it flies. When we arrive in the camp, we will be able to speak to Grandmother to tell her we need help."

"Does Vittoria know she can do this?"

"A question for another time, Angelo," Nico said. "Let's get going."

"Hold on tight!" Aishe said. The hawk flapped its wings and lifted off the ground. She felt the others tense. "Easy now," she encouraged.

The bird headed straight for the wall and Nico and Angelo both winced. Aishe smiled to herself because she knew they were going to pass right through. They sighed with relief and opened their eyes to see they were sailing out the window and up and over the rooftops of the buildings below. The hawk pumped its wings and they could all feel the cold air move over them. Angelo shivered.

Nico said to the others. "I've done this before. When the Lady of Light came to me. She lifted me up and out of my body and I could see the land below."

The hawk changed course and headed in a southern direction and flew until a grove of oak trees appeared by a creek. It dived toward the center of the grove. They felt their stomachs lurch as they plummeted toward the ground. They landed outside a deerskin tent and announced their arrival with a shrill scream. The tent door swung open and Celestina appeared wrapped in a woolen blanket.

The hawk opened its beak and spoke. "Hello, Grandmother. It's me, Aishe!"

Following the hawk's departure, Celestina hurried to the meadow. On the stump, in the center of the grove, she unfolded a leather bundle containing the crystal keys to summon together, from across the land, The Eight.

Celestina said the invocation. "One by one I unlock the gates of time and space summoning The Eight."

Her aging hands worked deftly, placing a polished diamond point at the center of the stump. It represented herself, the Benetrix and Mother of the Toscana Clan. Clockwise around the diamond, in a hub and spoke fashion, she placed polished crystal keys pointing toward the center.

"Through the Garnet Gate, I call forth Vela of the Liguria Clan!" She set down a red key.

"Through the Amber Gate, I call forth Arazia of the Romagna Clan!" She positioned an orange key.

"Through the Citrine Gate, I call forth Thana of the Marche Clan!" She lay a yellow key.

"Through the Emerald Gate, I call forth Zola of the Umbria Clan!" She positioned a green key.

"Through the Aquamarine Gate, I call forth Vivina of the Abruzzi Clan!" She arranged a blue key.

"Through the Lapis Gate, I call forth Tetia of the Lazio Clan!" She fixed an indigo key.

"Through the Amethyst Gate, I call forth Floria of the Campania Clan!" She situated a violet key.

"The way is clear, the gates are open, I bid you forth!"

As the gates opened streams of light shot out through the keys towards the diamond point in the wheel's center. A rainbow of light exploded into the sky and showered around Celestina and The Eight materialized in the grove around her.

Celestina opened her arms wide to welcome the governing members of the Strega High Council comprised equally of four Benedanti and Malandanti.

"I bid you all welcome! It is with a heavy heart and great urgency that I have summoned you."

The Eight murmured polite greeting, then Celestina launched into her petition with great fervency.

"As you all know, the eight seats of the High Council represent the balance of power between shadow and light. And for centuries we, Malandanti and Benedanti, have worked together. Through contrast of shadow and clarity of light, our magic has supported the spiritual growth and enlightenment of man. We are two halves of the same whole and, though it is a constant push and pull, we abide because we have a greater purpose. That purpose was bestowed upon us by the great Lady of Light. We cannot fulfill our purpose if we ourselves are out of balance. Our daughters are in great danger. And if we do not pull together to restore the balance we all will perish."

The murmuring turned to squawking as The Eight clamored to be heard over one another.

"Please one at a time! I'll answer everyone's question in order," she said turning to Vela of the Liguria Clan.

"What's happened?" asked the Malandanti from the northern clan.

"Nerezza obtained the Scourge Scroll over the summer and with the aid of the Pope drew down the power required to unleash a plague upon the people of our fair land."

"Why would she do such a thing?" Vela challenged. "She's the Malatrix, she knows that would not serve the greater good."

"It's my belief that she is avenging her mother's death. It is no secret that she holds The Eight responsible for meting out justice upon her for performing unlawful magic."

Benedanti Tetia interjected. "Let's be clear. Vadoma broke the ultimate rule as laid down by the Goddess. She used her knowledge and great power as Malatrix to wield magic to raise the dead, and she did so knowing that the consequence for it was death. She could not be allowed to set a precedent."

"Yes, she did break a great covenant and we all upheld that ruling. However, she is holding the Benedanti particularly responsible. Because it was I, Vadoma's sister, who cast the final vote sealing her fate."

"So, are you suggesting that she's trying to punish the Benedanti for carrying out the will of the Lady of Light by setting pestilence upon us?" Thana asked.

"Yes, because the negative emotion generated by that level of fear strengthens and emboldens the power of shadow. As you are Malandanti, had you not yourself noticed an increase of your own power as the scourge of plague spread from north to south?" she asked Thana.

"Yes, I did notice," Thana replied.

"I noticed as well," admitted Floria.

"But I would never have believed Nerezza capable of such a thing," Malandanti Vivina replied. "To collude and conspire with the Holy Father of all Christendom requires great forethought. She must have been planning this for a long time."

"She's had several years to think about nothing but her revenge and ways to weaken the Benedanti, following her mother's death," said Zola, a Benedanti from Umbria.

"How have you come to know all this?" asked Vela.

"My granddaughter Aishe came to me, by the wings of the hawk, just before I called you all to order."

"What of your granddaughter, Aishe? Where is she?"

"Aishe and Tsura are in Florence with Orabella's daughter, Vittoria," Celestina explained.

There was a collective intake of breath from The Eight.

"But Orabella renounced us. Why in Diana's name would you allow your granddaughters to go to her?" Arazia, Benedanti from Romagna, queried.

"Because Orabella reached out to me from her deathbed as she was succumbing to the plague that Nerezza unleashed. She was sending her daughter to find safety in the country and used the last of her zee to entreat us to find her. Vittoria is my heir."

"You mean to say she is to be the next Benetrix?" Zola asked.

"Yes, and there is no time to spare. The girl knows very little about our ways and she's nearing twenty."

"She has to receive the blessings!" Zola exclaimed.

"In addition, because of Nerezza's plotting, the Inquisition is now in Florence investigating allegations of witchcraft and murder. Vittoria and Tsura have been arrested by the Inquisition."

"Inquisition? They could be killed!" Vivina exclaimed.

"Yes, and if Vittoria perishes, the lineage of the Benetrix will die with me. We are in between a rock and a hard place because, if she lives, we have mere weeks to train her to receive the blessings from the Lady of Light."

"Impossible!" Arazia proclaimed. "It takes years even for the most talented of Strega to master the Five Darts. It cannot be done in a month."

"If she lives there is still a chance she can receive her blessings and the Benedanti can prosper. If she dies there is no chance at all," Tetia pointed out. "We must do what we can to uphold the balance. It is our duty."

"What about Nerezza? She must be punished. Her actions have put all Strega at risk," Vivina pointed out.

"After we deal with the Inquisition, we will call her to answer for her crimes before the Lady of Light," Celestina answered. "In the meantime, we must protect her life as well."

There was some grumbling amongst The Eight.

"So how are we to, as you say, deal with the Inquisition?" Thana asked.

"We must think of the Inquisition as the Church's dog," Celestina said.

"And all dogs have a master!" Arazia chimed in.

"Exactly! And who is the master of the Church?" Celestina asked.

"The Pope," Vivina answered.

"Yes. This started with the Pope and Nerezza, but together we must direct our power to influence him to call his dog off the hunt," Celestina concluded.

"We don't have much time," Tetia said.

"We may not have much of it, but we do have time," replied the Benetrix.

"Then let's get to work," concluded Floria, Malandanti of the Campania. "We have miracles to manifest."

CHAPTER 15

Tsura's screaming sickened Marcel. Over the course of twenty-four hours, his father had poked, prodded, and punished the poor girl in the interrogation chamber. He had never witnessed such malice in all his life. He stood as far back in the dank chamber as he could, away from the violent activity.

Tsura's fingers had been put through the screws and several of them were broken. The Heretics Fork, a bi-pronged fork, had been placed under her neck overnight disallowing her sleep. It impaled the tender skin of her chin and chest if her head bobbed forward. And she was just placed upon the painful Judas Chair, a seat covered with hundreds of painful spikes, to elicit a confession.

Nothing had gone as planned since Marcel arrived in Florence. His father's appearance had thrown everything into disarray. He was not, as he expected, leading the inquiry during the trial. His father had taken over and was on his own witch hunt.

Cardinal Moreau even objected, once, to his father for ignoring the procedural methods of the *Sacro Arsenale.* But he was harshly rebuked and, since he was not the Grand Inquisitor, did not speak up again. It seemed his father sought to avoid proper trial altogether and achieve his means by torture and terror.

Vittoria was, in fact, determined to be in a family way by a local physician and by law she could not be tortured. So, she sat in the dismal jail cell in the top of the Torre di Arnolfo awaiting her punishment. Tsura was bearing the burden for them both.

Marcel could not handle the screaming anymore and ran out of the room. Behind him, he heard his father shout at the girl.

"Tell me where to find that filthy diabolical witch, Nerezza!"

Up the stairs, to the topmost floor, Marcel tread with haste. There, Vittoria was being held in one cell, and Magda and Emilio in the other. A guard stood outside picking his teeth. Marcel approached, and, to the surprise of his appearance, the guard fumbled to attention.

"Unlock the door. I must speak to this prisoner," he ordered the guard.

"But sir, I've been ordered not to allow anyone access to these prisoners," he replied.

"I am an Inquisitor of the Supreme Sacred Congregation of the Roman and Universal Inquisition, and I order you to unlock this door now," Marcel commanded, utilizing the formal title of his position to scare the guard.

The guard fumbled with his keys until he found the right one and unlocked the door. Marcel entered.

"Lock the door behind me and leave us. I will call out for you when I'm ready."

The guard looked worried. "She's a witch! You should not go in there alone."

"I said leave us!" Marcel shouted.

The guard locked Marcel inside with Vittoria and took his leave, shaking his head at the stupidity of Marcel's actions.

Vittoria was blindfolded. She sat on the floor leaning into the corner of the stone cell. Her hands and legs were shackled. Marcel's stomach heaved. It disgusted him to see the woman he loved in such a crisis. It was all his fault. He believed running away was the answer. If he hadn't been such a coward, none of this would have happened.

"Vittoria," he whispered, removing the blindfold from her head. Her face was dirty, and her dark hair matted with sweat and grime. "Oh, Vittoria, I am so sorry." Tears filled his blue eyes.

Vittoria squinted and blinked. What are you doing here, Marcel?"

"I had to come and see you."

"Why? You left me like a thief in the night. You never cared about me." She turned her head away to look at the slick stone wall instead of him.

"That's not true! I love you, that's *why* I left."

Her green eyes glared at him. Anger filled them, and the gold burned like flames.

"You lied to me! You led me to believe we could have a future together. I am going to bear your child!" she shouted.

He reached for her hand and she ripped it away from him.

"When I awoke cold and alone and read your letter, I wanted to die. I tried to drink myself to death. But alas, I am destined to suffer," she concluded.

Tears spilled from his eyes. "No, I will not allow it," he argued.

"You are a coward, Marcel. Plain and simple. You stand by while innocent women are terrorized. We have done nothing!"

"I'm being held captive myself," he explained. "The day I met you I was finalizing plans to escape my father's iron grip forever. My mother had committed suicide and I had no other reason to stay. But then you came along, and I had the best time of my life. I fell in love with you, Vittoria, knowing all the while my father expected me to join him in the church to increase my family's power. My uncle is Pope Urban VIII," he revealed. "I knew my father was going to bring me to Rome, by force, if I didn't return of my own accord. I feared they may hurt you too. So, I left."

"Your uncle, the Pope, is in league with Nerezza, a Malandanti witch. The two of them drew down plague upon the land using an ancient spell. Your uncle is as bad as the Strega he has sent your father to hunt."

"How do you know this?"

"Because I, too, am Strega. I'm Benedanti and I would never have known if you hadn't left. My people found me wandering in the countryside."

Marcel felt an expression of shock come over his face. "You didn't know?"

"No, and I suppose I never will. My mother left her clan for the love of an ordinary Florentine merchant. She was forbidden to speak of her past or teach me the ways of her people."

"There truly are witches?"

"Yes, and most of them are working for the greater good. It is not right what your father is doing to Tsura. She would never hurt anyone. She is Benedanti too. You must find a way to stop this madness, Marcel. Your father will kill the three of us to make an example. He will kill your child."

Marcel hung his head in shame, and tears fell in great abundance from his eyes. "I never meant for any of this to happen. I'm so sorry, Vittoria."

"You can make this right, Marcel. You can make this right for your child," Vittoria implored him. Her shackled hands lifting his chin the way he used to lift hers. "You can find a way."

"I promise you, I will," he swore, taking her cold hands in his. He steeled his resolve to confront his father and beg for Vittoria's life and the life of his child. She nodded and leaned back into the corner.

Marcel picked up the blindfold. It was not going back on her head. He marched to the door and called out for the guard. He would not fail Vittoria again.

Marcel marched back down to the chamber to find Tsura passed out from the pain of her interrogation.

"Father, I must speak with you," Marcel demanded.

Never was he to address his father as anything other than 'Cardinal' in public.

Cardinal Barberini turned to meet Marcel with a lethal gaze. Marcel did not pretend to flinch from it this time.

"It's about Vittoria, the mother of my child."

"Leave us!" roared the Cardinal. Everyone in attendance, including Cardinal Moreau, the police captain, and the notary documenting the interrogation, fled the room. He stalked forward toward Marcel.

"I've come to plead for the life of Vittoria Giordano. She is no threat to you, or anyone else."

The Cardinal laughed. "You are such a stupid boy, and weak just like your mother."

"My mother was not weak. It was *you* who crushed her spirit. She was left to wither and die while you were out plotting for power with your brother," he accused.

"Your mother was possessed and driven to madness by witches," he argued, pointing to Tsura who slumped in the Judas Chair.

"You're trying to exorcise your own demons by punishing that innocent girl. And you'd seek to punish me by hurting Vittoria."

"Vittoria stole the Book of Hours that I gave to your mother. She also broke into my home and killed a man on my property."

"She did not steal it. I gave her the book as a gift."

"It was not yours to give."

"Vittoria saved my life. If it weren't for her I would have been killed by a bandit in my own home."

"It is a pity," the Cardinal replied, looking down his nose at his son.

"I know that you have despised me since the moment of my birth, but I know you once loved my mother. I'm asking you, please, to spare Vittoria. Not because you harbor any love for me, but because she is carrying Veronique's grandchild."

"Even if I once cared for your mother, she committed the ultimate sin. Her memory does not deserve to live on in another."

Marcel felt nauseated, like he'd been kicked in the groin. It was unconscionable to him that such malicious conduct could be carried out in the name of the Holy Mother Church. By his very own blood no less. It was not hard to believe Vittoria's claim that his uncle was party to unleashing a plague either. He would have had much to gain from it. This damnable behavior had to be put in check.

"What if I vow to remain a servant of the Church? I will not seek to abandon it or run away, ever."

"You already swore that vow."

"But I didn't plan to keep it. If you do this one thing for me, I will be forever in your debt."

"I cannot leave Florence full of witches. I am head of the Inquisition and it's my duty to set the precedent for eradicating evil."

Marcel looked pitifully upon Tsura. The girl was close to death already. He fell to his knees in petition.

"I'm begging for Vittoria's life. Please."

The Cardinal looked down upon his son for a long time, there on the floor, begging for the life of a witch. "You will never speak of her again, and you will forget about the child. Your position will be by my side in Rome as an unrelenting servant of God."

Marcel was screaming on the inside. He hated the man in front of him with every fiber of his being, but he loved Vittoria more. If this is what it took to see her and the child safe and free, he would do it.

"I agree to your terms. I will never speak of her again." To stop himself from crying, Marcel bit the inside of his cheek so hard it drew blood.

"Stand up and stop sniveling," the Cardinal commanded. Marcel obeyed.

"Tell the guards that Magda and Emilio are to be hanged in the courtyard at once. They are guilty of murder and will suffer the consequence, as must this witch," he ordered.

"What of Vittoria?" Marcel asked, tasting the metallic tinge of blood on his tongue.

"Vittoria may go free."

"Thank you, Father," he replied.

"You will never again call me Father, nor will you ask another favor of me. Do you understand?"

"Yes, Your Eminence," Marcel answered.

"Now leave me."

The Cardinal returned to Tsura's side and slapped her face hard. "Wake up!"

Marcel carried out his orders.

The clip-clop of horse hooves sounded outside. Aishe peeped through the closed curtains down upon the street below.

"They've come!" she cheered.

Nico and Angelo, who had not left her side for a moment, rushed to the window, and tore open the curtains. Two cloaked figures—one male, and one female—dismounted their horses and approached. Aishe tore down the stairs and wrenched open the door before Nico and Angelo even reached the landing.

"Papa! Grandmother!" she exclaimed, hugging both in turn. "Come in."

Pushing back their hoods, Celestina and Lucio made entry into the house. They looked around observing their loved ones' dwelling. Nico charged down the stairs followed by Angelo.

Lucio held Aishe in his arms while she kissed his weathered face.

"I've missed you so much, Papa."

"I've missed you too, butterfly," he replied.

Celestina approached Nico and Angelo and addressed them both.

"The Lady of Light placed you here to protect my granddaughters, and I thank you for heeding her call." Her green-gold eyes appraised Nico first, then Angelo. "I know you have done all you can. Though I fear we are too late in arriving."

"Vittoria and Tsura were taken to the Torre di Arnolfo and imprisoned. They're certainly being interrogated by the Inquisition," Nico reported.

"The Malandanti are still running free, and no one knows where to find them," Angelo explained.

"I do," Celestina said.

"What is your plan, Mother?" Lucio asked.

"I will take care of Nerezza. You go with Nico and Angelo."

"What about me, Grandmother?" Aishe asked.

"You stay here and hold on to this," Celestina said, withdrawing a leather bundle from under her cloak and tucking it into Aishe's hand. "Give it to Vittoria when the time is right. Will you do that for me?"

"Yes, but how will I know when it is time?"

"You'll feel it in your heart, my dear," Celestina replied, before kissing Aishe upon the top of her auburn head. "We must go, there is much to be done."

"We can't leave her unprotected," Nico argued.

Celestina smiled at Nico. "We won't."

Lucio put Aishe down and kissed her cheek. "Run along back upstairs," he said. She obeyed without question.

As everyone filed toward the door, Celestina placed her hands upon the walls and chanted a short incantation. "Infusing light into these walls I banish darkness from whence it crawls."

Protective blue light emerged from her hands until a shield of light surrounded the entire building.

"She'll be well protected now. Only Benedanti and bearers of good will can enter," Lucio explained.

"Let us go," Celestina ordered.

Lucio and Angelo stepped out into the street. As Nico stopped to close the door behind him Celestina turned to him and spoke.

"Look after my granddaughter. Only you can love her the way she's meant to be loved."

"I will. Always," Nico promised the Benetrix.

Celestina, satisfied with the answer, nodded. She squeezed her son's hand then headed in the opposite direction to confront Nerezza.

Lucio, Nico, and Angelo raced down to the Piazza della Signoria to find that a crowd had gathered in the Bargello courtyard. It was hard to see over the many heads, but it appeared that two prisoners were being marched up to the makeshift gallows. Their hands were bound behind them.

Cardinal Barberini stood at the platform's edge, alongside Cardinal Moreau and Marcel. He signaled the guards to have Magda and Emilio step up onto stools. Nooses were tightened around their necks. Angelo cried out and slumped against Nico when he saw his brother.

Cardinal Barberini stepped forward and addressed the mob. "Magda Marino and Emilio Apollino have been found guilty of the brutal murders of Constanza Gatto and Ernesto Amore, and for their crimes, they will be hung by the neck until dead."

Emilio's eyes scoured the crowd. Magda was still crying.

"Do you have any last words?" the Cardinal asked.

"Forgive me, Lord. Please forgive me," Magda sobbed.

Emilio's voice cracked. "Mother, I'm sorry to have disappointed you. Lord, please forgive me."

The Cardinal nodded at the guards who then kicked the stools out from under Magda and Emilio. They jerked and wiggled like fish on a hook. Their faces reddened as they efforted to breathe. At last, they both fell silent and still. Death had come.

"No, no, no!" Angelo cried beating his fist against Nico's chest. He struggled to keep upright.

Lucio murmured prayers for the dead and for Angelo. Magda and Emilio were cut down from the ropes and dragged away.

"Tsura and Vittoria," Nico said. "They'll be next."

No sooner had he spoken the words did Tsura appear. She was carried out by two guards as she could not stand. Her hands appeared mangled and her neck and chest raw and red. Lucio gasped at the sight of his eldest daughter. She had suffered greatly.

Then a messenger on horseback came racing up into the courtyard. He wore the livery of the Pontifical Swiss Guard. Jumping down from his horse he pulled from inside a saddle bag a folded letter affixed with silken cord of red and yellow thread, the leaden mark of Pope Urban VIII.

"Your Eminence, Grand Inquisitor Barberini. I have an urgent message from Pope Urban VII," he announced, bowing deeply to the Cardinal.

The guards were binding Tsura's arms and legs to a post set up in front of the gallows. She couldn't stand, and a guard had to hold her up, so she wouldn't slide down.

"They're going to burn her!" Nico exclaimed.

The Cardinal snatched the letter from the messenger's hand and tore it open to read. While he did so the guards placed kindling around Tsura's feet.

Lucio pushed through the crowd, but the going was difficult. Nico followed, dragging Angelo behind him. Guards lit torches and stood by ready to light the pyre at the Cardinal's direction. The three pushed and shoved with all their might to reach Tsura. Her head hung forward. Just as they reached the front of the mob the Cardinal folded up the letter and a look of abject disgust twisted his features.

"The Pope has declared mercy upon this pitiful soul. She will not be purified by fire. Her punishment has been sufficient," he announced. "She is to be released."

He shoved the letter back at the messenger and stalked away, leaving a trail of expletives in his wake.

Marcel moved quickly to Tsura's side and loosed her bindings. Lucio ran forward and caught his daughter before she fell to the ground. Angelo ran off to recover his brother's body.

"Where is she? Where is Vittoria?" Nico demanded of Marcel.

"She is safe. I will take you to her," he replied. "Follow me."

Nico looked to Lucio and Tsura.

"Go find her," Lucio ordered. "We'll meet you back at the house."

Marcel led Nico to Vittoria's cell and unlocked it. Nico rushed in and cradled Vittoria. Lifting her face into his hands he kissed it all over.

"Thank God, you're all right."

Vittoria fell forward into his arms and he held her.

"Everything is going to be fine now," he said, rocking her back and forth.

Marcel stood in the corner. "You're free to go, Vittoria," he said, his voice small. He handed Nico an iron key to unlock her bonds.

"You found a way," Vittoria replied, an infinitesimal smile flickered in her weary eyes.

"Yes. I begged for the lives of you and the child."

Nico unlocked the shackles and helped Vittoria to her feet. "You stay away from her now," he warned Marcel.

"I must, as part of Vittoria's release agreement."

"What agreement?"

"That I will never seek a life with you and the child in the future."

Vittoria's lip quivered. "It could never be anyway."

"Yes, I know. But, I will do whatever I can within the Church to keep you safe from harm. And I know Nico will give you all that you deserve. I will always love you, Vittoria," he concluded, tears again clouding his vision.

"Thank you, Marcel," she replied.

Nico moved her toward the cell door and freedom. He nodded curtly at Marcel. As Vittoria departed from Marcel's presence with him, Nico recognized Marcel realized his dream of a life with Vittoria now belonged to another man.

"I've been waiting for you, Auntie," said Nerezza, rising to meet her great enemy. She knew it was a matter of time before the Benetrix arrived. She had often fantasized about the very moment she would step out of the shadow of light. Now she had the chance to banish her mother's judge into darkness forever.

"Niece, you have shamed yourself," Celestina scolded, her face stern, as she appeared in the underground den.

"No, I have not! I have in fact done the opposite. I have brought honor upon myself, and my mother, for avenging her death. You should be ashamed of yourself for sending your own sister to be mauled to death by a pack of dogs!" she bellowed.

Celestina remained calm. "I loved your mother. I still love her. But she knew the consequence of performing resurrection magic. I warned her of it myself, yet she declined my counsel. Out of the deep love she had for your father she risked everything. She risked her own life. *She* chose to do so. It was never my will to harm your mother. Yet it is my duty as anointed Benetrix, and Mistress of The Eight, to mete out justice as dictated by the Laws put forth by the Lady of Light, even if it is upon my own sister."

"You are righteous as ever, Auntie," she mocked. "Even now at the hour of your own death."

Medea and Ulyssa appeared in the room and jeered at Celestina. They glowered at her and a deep rumbling sound filled the room.

"Your misguided anger has set us all upon the edge of a great precipice, and because of it, death and destruction have nearly destroyed our way of life. Our purpose is to support mankind, and you have a major role still to play, as the blood of the Malatrix flows through your veins. There is still light in you, Nerezza."

"Enough! Stop your babbling. You will not sway me from my course," Nerezza shouted, stalking toward Celestina.

"I do not wish to hurt you, Nerezza."

"Then don't!" she shot back, waving her hands toward Celestina a powerful zee wave knocked the Benetrix sideways onto the floor. The rumbling got louder. Medea and Ulyssa were causing a quake with their magic. The stone walls shook, and the floor cracked. Rubble tumbled from the ceiling.

"This will be your tomb, Auntie. Forever," Nerezza taunted. "And I will hunt down the rest of your clan and kill them all myself. Though the Inquisition did save me the trouble of dealing with your granddaughters."

Medea and Ulyssa giggled. The quake grew even stronger. They were going to destroy the Tre Sorella Taverna leaving no evidence they were ever there.

Pushing her aged body up from the quaking floor, Celestina argued. "You are mistaken, Nerezza. They live and, so long as they do, you will never succeed. They will make sure you are called to answer for your crimes, as will The Eight."

The ceiling buckled and Celestina's confidence infuriated Nerezza.

"No! I will prevail. And you will feel the same pain my mother felt as she died."

Unleashing all her anger, Nerezza shape-shifted into a snarling black wolf. Medea and Ulyssa dashed for the hidden passage to the outdoors, but Celestina was quick enough to throw the dagger she had hidden in her hand the entire time. It lodged in Medea's spine and she crumpled to the floor. Ulyssa did not look back. She ran into the passage to save herself.

Nerezza howled then attacked Celestina locking her jaws around her throat, squeezing and gnashing until she gurgled blood and lay dead. The ceiling caved in and furniture from the upper levels tumbled down around them. She growled at Celestina once more then darted toward the passage, after Ulyssa to safety, leaving Celestina in her promised tomb.

Lucio, Vittoria, Tsura, and Aishe were waiting for Nico to return. Though he hated to leave Vittoria's side, Tsura was in terrible shape and needed a doctor. He called on Paolo, who hurried back to the house with him. On the way, Nico informed Paolo of all that had transpired.

"I was called on to examine Vittoria. I know she's with child," Paolo told him.

"Yes, but I will still stand by her side."

"You're a good man, Nico," Paolo said.

Nico was surprised to hear Paolo, of all people, offer those kind words. He was becoming the man he wanted to be, but he knew that there was much he had to do to keep Vittoria and the others safe.

They arrived to find Tsura had been carried up to bed to rest. Aishe had not left her side. Lucio guided Paolo upstairs to tend to Tsura's wounds. Vittoria remained with Nico.

"I've never been so glad to see your face, Nico," she said, reaching for his hand to hold.

"And I've never been so glad to see yours," he replied. Pulling her close, he wrapped his arms around her slight shoulders. "I thought I had lost you, again."

"Even after learning all the things I've done, things I'm not proud of, you still feel that way?"

"Have you forgotten how we met?" he asked.

"No, I have a very clear memory of that," she replied. "I could never forget."

"I could have kicked myself for my behavior. But there is nothing you could ever do that would keep me from wanting to be the man by your side. I've loved you Vittoria since the moment we met, and I will love you always."

He gazed into Vittoria's ever-mesmerizing eyes, but pity wasn't stirring there as it was the day of the bonfire. It was something else, something that called him closer. A memory of a dream came to mind. A vision of when he stood in the ancient oak grove and the Lady of Light approached. How glorious she was to behold, and how she reminded him so much of Vittoria.

He leaned in and placed his lips upon hers, as the Lady of Light did to his. She returned his gentle kiss with great tenderness. They lingered awhile before he pulled away to lean his forehead against hers. He placed a hand upon her stomach.

"You are *my* family now and I will go to the ends of the world to protect you both."

Tears filled Vittoria's eyes. "I know you will," she said, hugging him again.

A strange rumbling occurred, shaking the ground beneath them, then a shrieking cry came from above. It was Aishe. Nico grabbed Vittoria's hand and together they dashed up the stairs to see what happened.

They arrived at the threshold of Tsura's room to find Aishe wailing in agony. Lucio was also crying. Paolo seemed not to know what to do.

"What's happened?" Vittoria rushed in to check on Tsura. She was still alive although tears slipped from the corners of her closed eyes.

"Dear God, what happened?" Nico pressed Paolo.

"I don't know. Everything was fine, then the room quaked and they all went into a fit," he replied.

"Where is Celestina?" Nico asked. "She hasn't returned."

"Celestina was *here*?" asked Vittoria.

"Yes, she went to confront Nerezza. She should have been back by now."

"She's not coming back," Lucio cried. "She's fallen."

"No! How do you know?" Vittoria exclaimed.

"We're all connected to the Benetrix. And when the Lady of Light reclaims her zee we all feel her loss within us," Lucio explained. The crags in his face sagged deeper with sorrow.

"What's going to become of the Benedanti now? Nerezza must still be out there," Vittoria cried, and Nico held her close.

Tsura spoke with great effort. "You must take up your place, Vittoria."

"I can't. I don't know how!"

"You must, you are Celestina's heir," Lucio said. "Her death must not be in vain."

Aishe was clutching a worn leather pouch. She brought it over to Vittoria and placed it in her hands.

"Grandmother told me to hold on to this for her," she sniffed. "It is yours now."

"What is it, Aishe?"

Lucio answered for her. "As part of your divine duty as Benetrix, you will serve as Mistress of the High Council of Strega. These are the crystal keys to unlock the gates of The Eight." Vittoria still looked puzzled. "It will all be made clear during your training. You must receive the blessings of the Five Darts."

Vittoria remembered. She had very little time left before her twentieth birthday. And it seemed an impossibility that she'd be able to achieve that level of knowledge in so little time.

"The clan is in danger and we must return to them as soon as we can move Tsura," Lucio warned them.

"That will be several days, at least," Paolo said.

"We don't have that kind of time," Tsura groaned, rolling over on her side. She tried to sit up, but it hurt her too much.

"Don't move, Tsura," Lucio ordered.

"There's no need to stay in Florence any longer, Vittoria," Nico said. "Wherever you go, I go too."

They all heard the front door open down below and footsteps trudged up the stairs. Angelo appeared at the threshold. Nico moved to embrace his cousin.

"I'm so sorry, Angelo," Paolo said, his face glum.

Several moments passed, then Angelo spoke in a strained voice. "After I bury Emilio, I must leave the forsaken city. It's too painful to remain here."

"Our minds are as one, Angelo," Tsura said.

Angelo broke away from Nico and rushed over to her. He kneeled beside Tsura at the bed's edge.

"You are meant to come with us," she told him.

Nico and Vittoria gazed at Tsura, who nodded to them in recognition of their merging paths.

"Where to?" Angelo asked Tsura.

"To the center of the Strega's circle," she replied.

ACKNOWLEDGEMENTS

I owe a great debt to the family and friends who read this book and listened—or convincingly pretended to listen—as I worked out the details, and who offered insight, guidance, and moral support during the process of bringing this work to fruition: Sean, Rowan, Mom, Dad, and Cheryl. While on about family, I also must thank my dog, Jonah, for keeping me company during the long hours of writing and for knowing just when to take me out for a long walk to save my sanity.

I am appreciative of the editorial work provided by Kristen Hamilton of Kristen Corrects, Inc. for constructive suggestions for improvement during the substantive editing process and Patience Grey for her attention to detail in the final proofreading stage.

I must also thank Sean Causley for his cover design, Catrin Welz-Stein for her cover artwork, Fionnghuala Mauritzen with Blush Away Makeup, and Jeff Mauritzen with InPhotograph for their professional author styling and photography.

Finally, and most importantly, I would like to thank you, the reader, for taking a chance on this book. There are millions of novels you could have chosen to read but you picked this one in which to invest your time and energy. For that, I am humbled and grateful.

For several years of my childhood, I lived in Germany because my father was serving in the United States Army. At the age of eight, together with my parents and brother, I had the opportunity to visit Italy and experience the beauty and culture of this ancient land for the first time.

From the hallowed corridors of the Vatican, crumbling ruins of Rome and Pompeii, rolling Tuscan countryside, to the magnificent city of Florence. I was intrigued and enchanted by it all.

Ever since, Italy, particularly Florence, has held a very special place in my heart. Looking back at my life I can see how that one life-changing experience has shaped me.

I became a little history geek, digesting every piece of information about Italy and Europe I could, watching hours of travel documentaries. I even went as far as to toss aside my preferred —at the time—

ghost stories for perusing the encyclopedia on distant places and exotic cultures.

Later, I went on to study ancient Mediterranean art and archaeology obtaining a Master of Fine Arts degree in Art History with the intention of working as a museum curator. Though I loved that field of study, my life took another direction.

Like Vittoria, who believed her life had a straight and certain trajectory, I found myself traveling a different path. There was something missing, but I couldn't quite put my finger on it at the time. Perhaps I was searching for deeper meaning in my life, a connection to something greater than me, or just figuring out who I really was.

During that time, I worked as a real estate agent, a travel director, almost joined the Air Force, became a mother, did my time in a call center, and eventually opened a holistic center establishing myself as a spiritual life coach, Reiki practitioner, and teacher.

Through all the twists and turns, I learned a lot about myself and the deep silent power I hold within that I can call on anytime when I'm afraid or resistant to change or personal growth.

All the while I read lots of historical fiction, taking note of the trials and tribulations women have endured throughout history, especially when standing in their power or making waves. Stories of independent, wise women and witch trials caught my attention, and I often wondered if I had lived in the distant past would I have been subjected to scrutiny or persecution in this way.

Soon after my daughter was born in 2008, the image of Vittoria Giordano appeared in my mind. When I would go out for my daily walk to burn off the baby weight, Vittoria's essence and her story grew in my heart. Later Nico appeared, then Tsura, and the twins. So many ideas came as we walked that I had to keep a notepad and pen stashed in the stroller, so I could stop and take notes.

Over the years of developing the story, there have been lots of changes, but one aspect has been set in stone from the beginning—the city of Florence, because of the renaissance that's to take place for these characters over the course of this book series.

It is here that I've married my love for Italy and interest in the supernatural. And it is my sincerest hope that you find yourself falling in love with Florence and the characters you find in this work of fiction.

Vittoria's journey is only just beginning. Although the road ahead for her will be difficult, I am confident that she will find her footing on the path leading to her destiny. Thank you for staying the course with her.

CPSIA information can be obtained
at www.ICGtesting.com
Printed in the USA
LVHW050129050719
623232LV00008B/161/P